STONE MAGIC
THEA ATKINSON

Have you got your free ebook yet?

Be sure to visit http://theaatkinson.com to get your freebie.

AUTHOR THANKS

Several loyal readers have special places in my writer's heart. Some of them, like Caroline Jenkins and Denise Sherman always take the time to find my little oopsies and sometimes my big ones. An author needs readers like that.

Then there's readers like Crystal Amason, who isn't just a reader, she's a sponsor, and you don't get more loyal than that. She is the first reader to make me feel like my tales were worth reading. Thank you, Crystal. I hope I can continue to write stories you enjoy.

To my other patrons who prefer to remain anonymous, I thank you. You know who you are.

I really appreciate you all.

-thea-

CHAPTER ONE

TODAY, I PULLED OUT the drugs. It's not something I do all the time, and it wasn't hardcore ones like crack or meth. Just a light blend of all-natural psychedelics that can be ground into coffee or tea and served up warm and comforting to an eager customer who has a healthy dose of skepticism to go along with their desire to believe in magic.

Because now and then, I get a true skeptic, someone who books a séance just to prove I'm a fraud. And to be honest, that's exactly what I am. It's what every psychic I know is, so I don't feel too guilty over it. I just do my best to feel my way around those who want to point at me and cry liar and leave them feeling as though they'd got their money's worth at the end of the session. The others, I already know I'm helping.

So it's all good, really. I make a living and I help people believe in something greater than they are. Not a bad gig.

Except today, I got a new client straight off the street. Someone who I knew by looking at her would need an extra push to help her see what she came to see, believe what she wanted to believe. She carried a Dolce Gabana purse, so she was a good mark. Affluent. Clean. Her pretty pink nails sported tiny moons and stars. Her complexion was creamy and smooth.

"Sherry," she said, sticking her hand at me through the handles of her purse.

"Nice to meet you Sherry," I said with a smile that I knew made folks feel at ease. I always made sure to put just the right amount of teeth in it, just the right amount of curve to my lip. I was already mining her posture, the flick of her gaze as she roamed the shop without taking a step. I needed to bring her attention back to me. Reel her in and seal the deal.

"You say you want a reading?"

She pointed at the menu style services list I had sitting on a podium at the front of the shop where she stood. "Your menu says you contact the dead."

"I do."

She edged closer to a shelf at the front of the shop, a squat little thing that held candles and sachets of herbs. I had to force myself to stay where I was. She reminded me of one of the alley cats I fed, skittish enough to bolt if I moved to fast. One by one, she picked up candles from the shelf and then set them down without really looking at them.

To encourage her, I took one from a shelf nearby and lit it, letting the warm scent of vanilla and sandalwood waft through the air, hoping it would put an end to the way her fancy shoes kept tapping on the floorboards.

The shop always smelled a little like incense and herbs, a mix of calming and mysterious that put people in the right headspace to believe. It's much easier to convince someone their dead relative is speaking through you when they're relaxed. As if on cue, her shoulders dropped. I took that as a sign to wave her closer.

"Let's go into my back room and see what we can do," I said.

Head down, she followed. I spun on my heel and shouldered past the my apothecary galley toward the back, listening for her footsteps as she came. Once inside, I set the candle on a glass shelf and paused to adjust a few of the crystal balls beside it, making sure they caught just enough of the low light.

As I pulled my arm back, the flame did something... weird.

It flickered higher than usual, stretching tall like it was suddenly fed by some invisible fuel. Then, for a split second, the flame split—two separate tongues of fire danced side by side, as if the candle had sprouted a second wick. I froze, watching the strange movement, too keenly aware that Sherry was beside me. I glanced sideways to see her twisting her purse handles. With a swallow, I told myself the strange effect was nothing but a draft.

Certainly, this old building had more than its fair share of them. I shook my head and flicked the candle-holder once, half-expecting the flame to pull another trick. It didn't. The twin flames merged back into one, flickering innocently, as if nothing had happened.

Weird.

"Would you like some tea?" I asked her. I had an all-natural blend of 'mocha' tea or coffee that I prepared, depending on the client, and I'd usually chat about the stray cats I feed as I got it ready. Sometimes I offered them a chance to chip in on some kibble. I did everything I could to make that moment authentic and normal and casual.

This time, I carefully ground the blend of mushrooms into the coffee, stirring with a slow, deliberate rhythm trying to keep my mind focused on the task. There wa always a moment before I handed over the cup when familiar, unwelcome memory flickered at the edges o

my consciousness. The faint smell of damp earth, the way the basement air used to cling to my skin, heavy with something I didn't understand back then.

I pushed the thought away, shoving it back into the dark corner where it belonged. I had learned to avoid thinking about those nights, to stay focused on the here and now. But today, with the sharp scent of mushrooms rising from the brew, I felt an uneasy tremor run through me. A scent like damp stone, like something buried too deep.

It was nothing. I swallowed the unease, turned back to Sherry, and smiled as though my pulse wasn't thundering in my throat. "A little magic in every cup," I said, the same line I'd blithely spoken a hundred times. But this time, as I set the mug down, I could almost hear my mother's whispered chants—just beneath my own words.

I tilted the cup in her direction, steam curling up from the mug like a beckoning finger, and gave her the chance to decline, because I might be a cheat and a con, but I'm not a monster.

She wrapped her hands around it, blowing gently over the surface before taking a tentative sip. I leaned back, ready to guide her through the session once the herbs took effect.

Suddenly, a sharp hiss pierced the quiet.

I glanced down to see one of the tabby that sometimes got brave enough to stiff-leg his way inside the shop, standing in the doorway of the back room, fur bristling along his spine. His pupils were blown wide, two black pools nearly swallowing the yellow, and his tail flicked back and forth like an agitated metronome. He stared into the corner behind Sherry—right where that gauzy curtain hung over the badly painted wall.

I shot Sherry a comforting smile, my nerves up as I prayed the little thing hadn't just queered the deal before it got started.

"What's up, buddy?" I asked it, glancing from him to the corner he was glaring at. Nothing there but shadows.

The hiss turned into a low growl, and he bolted out of sight back into the shop proper something had spooked him. The hair on my arms rose, the prickling sensation crawling up my neck.

"Cats," I muttered with a forced laugh, hoping to ease the sudden tension. "They're always seeing things that aren't there."

Sherry didn't seem to notice the cat at all, her focus entirely on her drink. Good. The last thing I needed was her thinking I was setting the scene for some supernatural freak show. Still, I couldn't help but keep one eye on Felix as I waited for her to finish the cup.

But he wouldn't relax. His tail lashed again, and without another sound, he bolted into the back room, disappearing under the table where I kept my stock of herbs and candles. I didn't follow. Whatever had spooked him, I didn't have time to deal with it right now. I had a client to charm.

And that was when all hell broke lose.

She grabbed the decorative knife I used to open mail from my wicker IN basket on the buffet style table that functioned as a desk and aimed it at me with an intent that made me jump out of my chair. I dodged out of the way just in time to avoid having my hand skewered.

Then, the rabid looking thing pressed herself into the corner of my back room, all wild-eyed and panting.

Because I'd leapt out of the way, I stood behind the table I used for the sessions, safe for the moment, but growing more anxious by the second.

I knew the knife wasn't sharp, but even dull knives can be bad news if thrust just the right way.

Like she was doing right then.

I circled the table warily, wondering what she might have in her system that could have reacted so badly to the mushrooms. I paused long enough to blow out the nearest candles so she wouldn't decide to tip the table and catch my shop on fire.

Hidden in a basket beneath, I had a nest of mourning dove eggs I'd saved from an obese rat behind my shop. I certainly didn't want any too-quick movements to break them.

"It's alright," I crooned. "There's no need to panic. You're safe."

I edged out from behind the table because I hated the feeling of being trapped there. I needed room to duck and run if things amped up to bat-shit crazy.

She laughed with a high-pitched sound that could have cut the air as effectively as the knife she used to slice away at the space in front of her. I feinted left just in time to avoid a jab to the side.

I nearly stumbled over the chair she'd upended earlier but caught myself on the corner of the table. It was large, made of pure oak with wrought iron drawer pulls that I'd purchased at great expense so I could nail little compartments to the underneath on my side.

Again, not a monster, just a shrewd practitioner.

The thick, solid oak steadied me. I was no athlete, but I managed to put the furniture between us again.

"You're going to be alright," I said with my hands in front of me where she could see them. "Your father just wants the best for you."

"I wanted you to exorcise him," she said, stressing each word more than the last, "not bring him back. Fuck."

Sherry's ample chest heaved on each of the words. She sounded too tight, her voice rheumy.

She laughed again, and it ended in a little burble that made her fold inward over the knife. I thought maybe she was going to calm down and give up her weapon.

Some movement behind me caught her attention. She stabbed at the air in front of her.

Yup. Definitely a bad trip. There was nothing in those shadows except a bit of gauzy curtain disguising a poor paint job on the wall.

I didn't think she'd die from the reaction to the mushrooms, but maybe she was allergic. Maybe I needed to call an ambulance.

I groaned inwardly at the thought of all the questions that would bring down on my head. The thought of explaining away my use of a controlled substance wouldn't go over well, even if I only used it occasionally to help my clients believe I could call to their dead loved ones.

In some parts of the world, the mushrooms were used as a sort of therapy, but here, I'd get charged as the fraud I was.

"Just breathe," I said, trying again to calm her without losing all the emotional real estate I'd laid ground to. I really didn't want to call an ambulance, and the drink didn't have a lot of psilocybin. She'd be fine in about twenty minutes if I could keep her from killing me. "He doesn't want to hurt you."

She snorted. "Then you don't know my dad."

She canted her head at me a little too astutely. I read the suspicion in her face.

"He's a spirit, Sherry," I whispered, pressing on with the charade despite her paranoid expression. "He can't hurt you."

"What about my dreams? Touching me, hurting me, all over again. He's dead!" she yelled at me as though I was to blame for her pain. My heart ached for her.

"He shouldn't be able to keep doing this to me," she said. "I want him gone. Really and truly gone."

She let slip a sob and then bit down on it with her bleached and beautiful teeth. She brandished the knife at the darkness of the space behind me.

Her desperation and panic shouted from every muscle showing in her peek-a-boo shoulder blouse. Just the sight of the tension in her did something to me, made me ache to hug her, and without thinking, I took a step toward her.

She flinched. Stared into the corner.

"You called him here." She stabbed downward with the knife point. "While I was in the room. I didn't ask you to do that. You can't just take advantage of people like that."

She sobbed, and a bubble of snot bloomed in her nostril. It caught the red light from the beaded lamp on the shelf across the room. When she wiped it away with the back of her wrist, her hand trembled. The knife quaked in her grip.

She didn't pull her gaze from the dark corner for one second.

I understood now what the problem was. I'd mistaken her request to find her dead father too literally. The suggestion I'd made earlier that he was in the room with us had triggered some pretty nasty memories. Now we were both facing that spiraling descent of her bad trip.

All was not lost. I could pivot. So long as she didn't leap from the corner at me and stab me in the eye, I could adjust.

"I shouldn't have done that," I murmured. "I shouldn't have called him forth."

I edged around the table, my hands at my sides but ready to grab for the knife if I had to.

"Just put the knife down," I said. "He won't hurt you. I promise."

"I can't sleep," she said. "I can't eat. I've lost three pounds since he died last week. He's tormenting me from the grave, for Christ's sake. How can he even do that?"

Her eyes were owlish in the light.

"You want him gone?" I said. "Really gone?"

I inched a bit closer, my gaze on the knife and the way her grip seemed to be loosening.

"Damn straight," she said, her gaze flicking to mine before being drawn straight back to the corner. "Dead as a rat in a trap—mind, body, and spirit." She yelled at the shadows as though it was a taunt to a man who stood there.

"I can do that for you," I said. "There is a spell...."

I let the words trail off, putting my finger to my lips thoughtfully, just enough to make it look like I was thinking. I hesitated just enough for effect and then shook my head, indicating it might be too hard, this exorcising.

Part of me wanted to ease her pain, but the other part, the one with a hefty overdue mortgage payment on the building, knew that help had to come at a price.

"What?" she said in an even shriller voice. "What kind of spell?"

I spun around to face the corner instead of her, holding my breath that she wouldn't jump out at me while my back was turned.

It was a risk, but I hadn't come this far in my career without having some sense of human nature. She'd wait for me to throw out the life preserver before she thrashed around anymore.

I glanced back at her over my shoulder. She was leaning forward attentively. The knife had dropped in her grip to hip level. Progress, thank God.

"It's a tough one," I said to her in a conspiratorial voice as I cocked my head toward the corner, a slight enough movement that it might appear someone was talking to me.

She saw the movement, as I'd hoped she would, and she reacted pretty much how I expected.

Her whole face screwed up in fury. "Fuck you, Dad. Fuck you. Straight. To. Hell."

She came out of her corner a foot when she yelled. I turned my attention back to her with the reluctance of someone trying to get away from a bad guest at a dinner party. I held my hand up to the side, a gesture that might be politely asking someone in the shadows to wait.

"He doesn't want me to exorcise him," I said. "That always makes the spell trickier."

She snarled, and the prettiness in her face disappeared. "Not exorcise. I want him gone. Fucking Hellbound." She pointed at the floor. "You do it. I don't care what it takes."

"It might take more than one session," I said.

"Fat fucker." She spat on my oiled wood floor.

Inwardly, I cringed.

"I can bind him for today," I said, letting a doubtful expression slide over my face. "Keep him tied to my shop until I get the things I need. Just so he won't bother you."

Her face lit up with hope in disbelief at my generosity, and my stomach clenched at the lie. "You'd do that for me?"

"Sure," I said. "I hate to see you suffer."

At least that was true. I had my own demons from my past. I understood childhood trauma. In part, it was why I did what I did. I had no real magic. I couldn't conjure a spell to save my soul or draw out a spirit from the ether if a necromancer stood at my side.

That kind of stuff just wasn't actually possible anyway. But my customers either believed it was or wanted to believe it was, and that was what mattered.

Placebo of the most powerful kind, rooted in anger and grief and trauma. If they were going to throw good money in desperation at a fraud, they might as well give me the money.

Despite me being a charlatan, I fancied I'd helped as many people as a therapist, and I did it a lot faster. It was hard to feel guilty about duping them when I saw the shadows that clung to the hollows of their cheeks let go when it was over.

"I can bind him here, but it won't last long," I said, eying the knife and the way it was drooping in her grip. "It's a temporary measure at best, but it will give you a few nights' rest. Looks like you could use it."

"But what about the spell? The first one?" Her eyes darted to the corner again, and she narrowed her eyes to slits. "I want him gone."

I sighed heavily. "I wouldn't feel right selling you that. It's really expensive."

It was a risk, that tactic. I would benefit if she coughed up the cash, sure, but it also needed to be steep. She wouldn't believe truly damning someone to hell would be cheap.

I had to charge more for her to believe it was real, and she needed to believe it was real to be freed from this mental prison she was in. She had to feel the shift deep in her marrow.

"I'll pay," she said in a rush. She took a step out of the corner, but she didn't drop the knife. "I don't care what it costs."

Her eyes darted to her purse where she'd left it on the table. Then she looked into the shadows again.

"Hear that, you pig? I'm going to be rid of your ass."

She laughed, and the discordant sound of it partnered with the twisted expression chilled my spine.

She swiveled her head in my direction. "Do it."

"I will. I promise." Everything in me sagged in relief at her words. "But you'll have to give me the knife."

I held my breath and waited. It seemed to take an eternity for her to hold it out to me, and when I finally had it in my grip, I tossed it toward my table so that it clattered beneath. She'd have to crawl under to get it.

I all but sighed in relief, then schooled my face into the careful practitioner again. "Consider it done," I said.

"Just like that?"

"Well," I said as I pulled the chair out for her, "not just like that. More like I'll take care of it for you. I don't need you here to bind him to my shop or to work on the spell."

Her shoulders sagged. "Oh. I can go?"

I nodded. "And come back in a few days. I'll have the things I need to perform the severing spell. Like I said, it's tricky—"

"I don't care. It's worth a shot, right? Anything is worth trying if it'll get rid of the bastard for good."

I gave her a reassuring smile, and she settled onto the edge of the chair. Her shoulders sagged as she reached for her purse and dug around inside.

My tone was the softest, warmest caramel when I said, "It will be fine."

"Right," she said.

She lifted out her wallet and folded through several twenty-dollar bills as she inhaled deeply. "I feel better already," she said. "Not perfect, but hopeful."

She swiped a shaking hand across her face, and the manic look went with the motion. I believed her. Some part of me warmed at the thought she might get a good night's sleep.

"That's a good start," I said as I eased the bills from her grip and shoved them into my bra like any good cliché. "And so is the down payment. Thank you."

I took a step toward the door to send the message it was time to go.

She nodded. "Yes, it's a good start."

She rose from the chair and headed to the back door of the shop that I used for these types of appointments. She looked back over her shoulder toward the corner where she'd hallucinated her father, but she didn't look afraid. The "magic" was wearing off, thank God.

I followed her so I could close the door behind her.

Clutching the frame, I watched her retreating back head down the alleyway, right past a large dog sitting next to the dumpster at the mouth of the alley. She passed it by without so much as glancing down at it and turned onto the street that led to the pier.

The dog stared at me, its tongue lolling out the side of its mouth. I'd never seen a stray that big before, and certainly not this close to the tourist block of the piers. No one would tolerate that kind of scruff and mange. Bad for business.

My shoulders sagged against the door as I eased it closed. A sound from the front of the store caught my attention, and I peered through the beaded curtain that separated the shop proper from the back room to see if a customer had come in unannounced.

But I knew right away the two men weren't customers. They were police officers. Soul's Harbor's brightest and ruggedest, apparently.

How long they'd been there, staring at me from the other end of the apothecary galley, I couldn't say.

But I did know their drawn weapons were pointed straight at me.

CHAPTER TWO

I WAS ABOUT TO spend a few hours in jail. It wouldn't be the first time I'd been arrested. I knew the drill. I even knew how many hours I'd be hanging around a holding cell after they rummaged through my psyche to pull out every dirty little secret. They'd make me feel like a loser. Like I belonged to the ranks of the lost.

My heart sped at the thought of sleeping on a bench, sitting up next to prostitutes and female thugs.

And if they found contraband on me, I wouldn't just land a hefty fine but also earn a month or two in prison. The officer nearest me ordered me to drop to the floor. Through the beads in the curtain ticking together against the air currents he made as he approached, I recognized the charcoal colored suit he wore as Hugo Boss.

A scene from the movie *Legend*, where Tom Hardy meets Frances, flashed through my mind. The sensation of the image and the way it crept over my skin as I caught sight of the officer made me both clammy and heated. It was enough to stop me in my tracks.

I envisioned this Reggie look-alike with his scruff of beard, planting his broad hands on the small of my back. It was such a powerful impression that I didn't realize he'd taken another step toward the curtain until his leveled pistol poked through the beading.

I had to shake myself loose from the odd sensation that wormed through me, an impression of falling that was more mental than physical but enough to make me dizzy.

"On the floor," he barked. "Now."

My gaze flicked past him to the other officer. Neither of them had a clean shot. There was too much on display in the shop, interfering with their line of sight.

My statue of Napoleon at the side of the door faced the full sized King Tut sarcophagus that held small paperbacks and journals. Gauzy material draped from hooks in the ceiling. The shelves that lined the space between my reading table and the beaded curtain swelled with stones and pottery bowls that effectively cut off from view anyone in the front shop seeing what I might be doing in the back.

There, in that knot of space set aside specifically for the sessions, I kept items that veiled the industrial appearance of the area. The customer could sit in that small space, ensconced and safe. Two things they all wanted when they booked time with me and needed as much as they did closure.

The girl who'd just left had upended a shit-load of things in her attack, things that still lay cluttered about. The officers would have to fight through it all to get to me.

I was already so close to the exit. My hand was right there on the knob. I imagined myself in that cell; the prostitutes chewing away at sticks of gum, the female hoodlums looking me over.

I angled my body ever so slightly toward the door, just enough to lend some thrust when I opened it.

"Don't do it," the officer murmured.

I looked from him to the open alleyway behind me. My fingers clenched on the handle.

The dumpster and the dog were a few feet away. I could use them to barricade the path once I fled the shop.

One long alley led to a street with half a dozen shops selling purses and T-shirts. A couple of zigzags down narrow streets, and I could be on the pier. I could even hear the bell buoys clanging in the distance, calling the fog home.

The dog whimpered at me and backed up a few steps before it sat on its haunches, eying me as though to say, "You know what to do."

Yes. Yes, I did.

I knew it was ridiculous to run. It showed guilt better than a bloody glove at a crime scene. But I had a record. A small one. Three days in a small town jail for possession of a controlled substance.

I'd been eighteen, schlepping my wares on a street corner. They'd arrested me under suspicion of prostitution until they found the ounce of marijuana in my pocket and realized I wasn't selling my body at all.

Duping people with false readings wasn't a crime, but holding a stash of psychedelics certainly was. If they wanted to arrest me, they'd have to run off a few donuts first.

So I fled. Even though they might very well shoot at me, I ran. Right past the dog and the dumpster.

They followed, of course. I heard them barreling along after me, swatting aside the garbage cans I tipped as I fled, awkwardly and noisily, because the cowboy boots I'd put on to complement my flowing tissue style dress that morning had large, clunky heels.

Outside, my foot crushed a styrofoam cup. It stuck to the toe of my boot and made a ridiculous clicking sound with each step. I took a second to fling it off. When I did, I stumbled into a pile of discarded cardboard stacked in the alley next to one of the tackle shops.

I grabbed for the fire escape closest to me and used the rung of the ladder to steady myself. My breath wheezed in my throat and set flame to my lungs.

I couldn't see the officers behind me, just hear the rattling of tin and plastic, cursing as they no doubt splashed into the pile of vomit I'd barely skirted.

The docks were still a few blocks away. The pier had a way of swallowing people whole. If I could make it there, I could disappear.

No time to zig zag. Best I just barrel straight for it. Once I exited the alleyway, I slowed to a crushingly casual pace that wouldn't draw attention. I kept my face directed ahead, no matter how badly I wanted to look over my shoulder to see where they were. Nothing spelled guilt the way a runner did when casting glances over tense shoulders.

I had to stop dry heaving my air.

A gaggle of teenage girls in their high-waisted, pleated jeans and midriff tops snickered behind their hands as they darted judgmental gazes over my figure. I figured I looked pretty vogue in my mid-thigh dress and boots, but the wreath of flowers I'd jammed into my hair for the day's performance was unique enough to stand out.

Running and doing my best to blend in might help, but all the officers had to do was look for those flowers and my white dress. I stood out in the crowd. One harried glance around me showed a busker belting out his rendition of *New Orleans is Sinking*.

I speed-walked to the small cluster of drunken girls swaying in front of him, caught not by the music but by the charismatic smile he tossed their way as he dug into the tune. I shouldered between a couple of them and ditched the crown of flowers by stuffing it into his guitar case.

I ignored his annoyed glare and edged up to the old factory-turned-brewery where he'd set up. It was early evening, and the sun hadn't set. That meant I was still too exposed.

I braced myself against the brick wall as I stooped to dig into the gaping space in my boot and ankle, plumbing the depths for the baggie I had smuggled into the session room. I angled my face toward the wall and away from the street so I'd blend in better.

"I'll give you a dime of 'shrooms for your jacket," I said to the musician.

The black coat in question was slung over the back of a camping chair he'd set up to hold a few items. The thing was dingy and lopsided and weighed down by a knapsack bursting with clothes. Dude was homeless, apparently.

He stopped strumming long enough to run his gaze over my legs. The girls huffed with long-suffering indignation and headed back toward the brewery entrance. Perfume wafted back at me, heavy enough to make my sinuses hurt.

"Portobello or shitake?" he said, holding my gaze cautiously.

"Funny." I pulled out the baggie and tossed it into his case next to the flowers. "You want them or not?"

I mentally counted the time it would take for the officers to find me wearing the gauzy dress and daisies. They should have rounded me up by now. Even though it didn't feel right unloading the contraband on the poor guy, if I didn't get the hell out of there, I'd never be able to deny possession.

He kicked the case closed with a thunk and grinned, then reached to pluck the black zip-up sweatshirt from the chair.

"It might smell a little," he said.

I caught the sweatshirt when he tossed it and nearly retched at the stink it wafted at me as it reached my fingers. He wasn't kidding. Cats must have birthed a dozen litters in the hood alone. But I shoved it on anyway and jammed my hands in the pockets.

I was about to thank him, but he had already picked up the case and was packing up his stuff. Apparently, a nice trip out of town was better than he'd hoped for in a night's work of playing Canadian rock to drunk youths with no cash.

I ceased feeling sorry for him when he pulled out a much nicer, much cleaner American Eagle hoodie and yanked it down over his scruffy T-shirt. His grin with clean, white teeth made me suck the back of my own. A grifter. A con. Using the trappings of the homeless for pity. I should have recognized it.

"Enjoy your trip," I said and turned away as he picked up his case and headed for the brewery door, leaving behind the filthy rucksack and chair.

I had to hold my breath at the stink of the jacket as I pulled up the hood to cover the pink ombre of my hair. My breath came in gasps as I bent my head and threaded my way toward the docks all while trying not to breathe in the coat's stink.

I'd have to wait till dark before going home and get up early so I could head to the shop and clear away any dope that still sat in my Buddha urn in the darkest part of the back store. If the cops didn't get me now, they'd return to the shop in the morning. They'd want to know why I'd run.

But by then, any incriminating evidence would be gone. There'd be nothing to arrest me for. There'd be nothing...

I didn't see him until I slammed into him.

"Ms. Duncan?" the voice said. "Ms. Brie Duncan?"

His grip went round my elbows to steady me as I looked up into the face of the Hugo Boss officer and all I could think was *shit. They know my name.*

I shook him off; the hood falling away. He swept me with a studious gaze, his eyes so brown they might have been made of chocolate.

"Why were you running, Ms. Duncan?"

I blinked as my mind trundled forward on a hamster wheel of thought. I inhaled deep, deciding the best offense was defense.

I dragged in all the air I could manage and then I let loose.

"Help," I screamed. "Someone help me."

I yanked out of his grip, pulling the jacket tight across my bosom.

"Someone help me! I don't know this man. He has a gun."

He cursed and lunged for me as I shouted, pinning my arms against my sides as the second officer, dressed in his grays, came round the corner.

"Police," Hugo Boss barked out to the general vicinity.

He dug into his jacket with one hand as he held me with the other. Then he lifted his badge over our heads with a practiced flourish. "Nothing to see here."

I glared at him and shook him off, taking several steps backward. He let me go with an irritated expression riding his handsome face. With a quick movement, he shoved the badge back beneath his suit jacket. No one had so much as stopped to gawk. City folks. Nothing fazed them.

"Why did you run from us?" he asked.

I pulled away and squared my shoulders. "Wouldn't you run if someone you didn't know barged into your shop and pulled a gun on you?"

He canted his head at me. "We didn't declare ourselves?"

He flicked his gaze over his shoulder at his partner, who shrugged.

Crossing my arms over the stinking jacket, I planted my feet wide. "The gun you had pointing at my head certainly declared your intentions."

"So you ran because you were afraid?"

I remained silent. Best to say as little as possible.

"And because you were afraid, you stole some homeless guy's stinking shirt and pulled it on so, what? You'd repel a uniformed police officer and his partner?"

I lifted my chin defiantly, but at least his shoulders sagged just a little.

"We had reason to believe your shop might be in danger," he said without pressing the point.

He hadn't declared himself, and he knew it. What I wore or how I acquired it wasn't the point. But I understood what he said in the things he didn't say.

My shop was in danger. Not me. Careful, careful wording.

"What makes you think I'd be in danger in my own shop?" I asked, purposefully framing myself as a victim. I'd learned a thing or two in the foster homes I'd bumped around in. Like never admit guilt. Always toss the hot potato right back before it could burn you.

I caught him looking at the uniformed officer and, in his face, I read he was the one in charge, that he wasn't so much asking permission of the uniform, but showing his intent.

"Maybe we should go back there," he said. "It'd be easier to explain what's going on."

The hush in his voice indicated he didn't want to drag the scene out any further, but I knew there was more to it than that. Once they were in my shop, they'd poke around ever so casually.

I wasn't entirely sure I had returned my Buddha urn to its hallowed place in my apothecary galley. In fact, I might truly have left it on the counter when I'd made the mocha blend for poor Sherry.

I shook my head, still clutching the jacket together, thinking I needed to get rid of it soon or be sick. "If my shop is in danger, I'm not setting foot back in there until you tell me what's going on."

He jerked his chin toward the hoodie I wore. "Don't you want to peel off that foul sweatshirt?" he said with a knowing glint in his eye. "I mean, I know it's depositing a stink right now on your skin that you won't be able to wash off for days."

"I want answers," I said, holding my ground.

He huffed but reached ever so tentatively toward the sleeve as I tugged it down over my fingers.

"Maybe it's best if you come down to the station, then," he said.

I knew what would happen if I went in for questioning. They'd find a reason to hold me. Didn't matter what the charge would be. They'd find something. They always did. At worst, they'd fine me and I didn't have the cash because I'd already spent what I had on three months' interest on the mortgage instead of the payments I owed.

But it wasn't just the lack of funds. They'd eventually want to check my shop, and I was already imagining the mess I'd have to clean up when the surrounding shops started buzzing to would-be clients that the psychic medium witchy poo next door had been arrested.

No. I didn't plan to go along peacefully at all. And I didn't plan to let them ruin the reputation I'd spent the last three years building.

So I did the only thing I could think of.

I fell into a seizure.

CHAPTER THREE

I FELL TO MY knees as the attack took me, letting my palms support my weight as I hung there, chest heaving theatrically as I let unseen forces buck through me. I knew the detective wasn't buying it, but he dropped to a crouch next to me and laid his palm on my shoulders.

His body beside mine held an impatient tension. I sensed he was about to yank me back to my feet, drill me with that hard stare of his until he forced me to confess I was faking.

Then, I saw ghosts. Three of them.

All women.

The image streaked across my mind's eye the way a sudden stink hits your nostrils. I pulled in a sharp, terrified drag of breath as the vision train-wrecked through.

He might have doubted the seizure, but he knew the authenticity of fear when he heard it. He probably felt it in the way my body flinched away from his touch and went truly rigid as the throes of sudden vision took me. Maybe it was the way I scrabbled away from him, oblivious to the way my dress fetched up and revealed more than it should.

I hyperventilated for real then. My skin felt all tingly with shock. I dropped onto my bottom and crab walked away from him. The image of the women burned be-

hind my eyelids, a black, haloed thing that lost defin-
ition and faded. I had to blink several times to regain
my composure.

He reached for me slowly, making sure I watched the
movement as though I was a cobra about to strike and
when I didn't do more than hiss, he gave my dress a
gentle tug, pulling it back down over my knees.

"Nice show," he said, and I wasn't sure if he meant my
seizure or what I might have revealed of myself with
that undignified hiking of skirts.

I just sat there, blinking as I tried to slow my heart
rate down to something that wouldn't hurt my ribs. I
hated him in that second, for raking my dignity with
a callous comment. What kind of man made a woman
feel humiliated when she was so obviously terrified?

"They're dead," I said before I could think about what
slipped past my tight lips.

He canted his head at me, those chocolate colored
eyes narrowing. "Who's dead?"

I pulled my hands back to my sides and pushed up
into a more distinguished position, curling my body
over my knees as I laid my chest on my thighs. I could
breathe better that way, at least.

"All of them," I said. "They're waiting."

I wasn't sure what I meant, but it was the impression
that still lingered in my mind as I met his gaze. It asked
the question his mouth didn't.

"Ghosts," I said and shuddered because I was supposed to be pretending. It was something I was very
good at. Sometimes I even fooled myself, but this was
not that. I'd never seen ghosts before. Even if I told my
clientele I did. "I saw ghosts."

I lifted a shoulder as though to indicate it happened
all the time.

"Sometimes they just come to me." I tittered with a subtle underlay of nervousness. "Sorry."

Maybe he believed me and maybe not, but he cupped my elbow, urging me to stand. I yanked my arm away because I didn't want him touching me. His reaction was to smother the cocky smile that tugged at his mouth. At least he'd holstered his gun at some point, which was encouraging.

I smoothed down the layers of my tissue-style dress and shook out the hem to fluff it up. It was going to take a few moments to gather my thoughts and collect myself, and the inconsequential act of rearranging my skirts gave that to me.

I tried to remember if I'd sipped on any of that mocha coffee or stuck my finger in my mouth without thinking after handling it. There was no way to be sure. The shit show back at the shop was a muddle of chaos. I'd be lucky if I could remember the name of the client.

Sherry, my mind whispered. Poor soul.

I must have taken too long to recover, because he shot a curious glance at his partner. My seizure had gained me a moment or two, but the effect was waning. I couldn't waste what remained if I wanted to gaslight my way through this.

"I'm feeling a little shook up," I said. "It's all too much. Do you think we could do this another time?"

His scruffy jaw seesawed back and forth as he slipped his hand beneath his suit jacket.

"I'm afraid this can't wait, Ms. Duncan."

"Call me Brie." I smiled as nicely as I could and let my hand slide into the space between us. It hung in the air, extended in introduction as though I hadn't just given them chase through back alleys like some Dickensian pickpocket. The sweatshirt slid off my shoulder.

He didn't put his hand out to grip mine. "I'm Detective Garder. This is Officer Farrell."

"Garder," I said. "Interesting surname for a cop."

"How delightful," he drawled. "I've never heard that one before."

He said it with just enough dryness that he effectively shut down my thin veneer of charm.

I reacted before I could stop myself, even knowing I was on thin ice.

"Anyone ever tell you, you're a bit prickly?"

"No," he said. "But I have been called a prick plenty of times."

He ran his palm down along his suit jacket as though searching for something, then gave up.

"These ghosts of yours, are they newly departed, or do they come to you because of proximity?" He ran a thumb over the scruff on his chin, then crossed his arms over his chest and rested one elbow on a forearm. "I mean, I'm not a medium or anything..."

His tone was just this side of mocking, and I reacted automatically.

"I'm not a medium either," I said quickly, retracting my hand and pinning it to my side. "Not strictly."

The folks around the docks knew my shop. Someone might overhear and get the wrong idea and think that was all I sold. Caution was the best.

"Seeing spirits is just one facet of my power." I lifted my chin. "It's not something I enjoy, detective. It's something I try to control."

I hugged my elbows. The stink of the jacket wafted up at me.

"This time it got away from me," I said.

He nodded slowly. Someone brushed by him too closely, a big man carrying a crate of fish that smelled more than a day old, but despite the heft of the load and the weight of the man, Detective Garder didn't shift one inch. He was either too stubborn to give or was just so muscled beneath that Hugo Boss suit that his stance made him as movable as an oak. Or a mountain. I decided mountain was a much more apt description because he seemed chiseled out of rock and had about as much charm.

While he didn't give an inch from the torso down, he offered a subtle movement of his head, directed at me as though it were a bow of respect.

"My apologies," he said. "I'm not up on all the spiritualist vernacular."

There was a moment, just one, when I thought he was lying, but he slipped his hands into his pockets in a way that made him look less threatening, and the insight was gone, replaced by a careful posture that was so studied in human nature, I knew it was deliberate.

He rocked back on his heels, the color of his eyes melting to a golden hue as he examined my face.

"I've always wondered what prompted that sort of thing. Do the ghosts have some sort of consciousness or is the environment a trigger?" He jerked his chin toward my chest, where my amulet had fallen free of my neckline. "I mean, do you need that sort of thing to call to them?"

I had the feeling he was fishing, but I wasn't sure which answer he wanted to dredge from my lips or what he planned to do with it once he got it. I figured the best answer would be none. Keep deflecting. Keep redirecting. I was not at fault here.

I stuffed the amulet back beneath the sweatshirt. "I'm not sure what you're implying or what you're looking for, detective."

"No special answer, just curiosity." He looked over his shoulder at detective Farrell.

I took the break in eye contact as a chance to excuse myself and took a step sideways, out around him because I knew trying to get past that mountain would end up with me on my ass.

"I think I'll be on my way," I said. "Book an appointment and we can discuss further if you like. Maybe I can call to your mother. See what she says about your choice of vocation."

I didn't know his mother was dead, but I guessed at it based on his apparent age and the fact that most mothers would be anxious about their loving sons becoming cops. I was rewarded with a quick, understanding grin. He knew what I was doing as well as I did.

I smiled back and made to depart. My heart rate was still ticked up, and I knew the only thing that would bring it back down was for me to make sure my urn was safely stashed away and I was inside my shop and out of direct line of that knowing stare.

He let me get a few feet away before he spoke again. His voice wafted over me like the smell of cinnamon.

"You never asked why we wanted to question you."

I looked over my shoulder at him. He hadn't moved. His hands were still in his pocket but he leaned back on those heels with his chin lifted, a dare, if I was brave enough.

I swallowed, trying to find the words. He studied me for a long moment before pulling a notebook from beneath his jacket.

He flipped it open. "Most people demand to know why we would dare to interrupt their day."

He hadn't said most innocent people, but the inference was clear. I was guilty of something. He just wasn't sure what.

"You said my shop was in danger," I said. "I know it's not."

He took a step forward, tentative, as though he wasn't sure if he should press on. That, too, seemed like a calculated movement.

"You're the real deal, aren't you?" he said. One more step, equally tentative, his expression gathering a cautious thoughtfulness. "There probably aren't many, but you are."

I held my ground, not wanting to confess to anything. If he wanted to believe I was 'it', then let him.

"I might need your insight," he said. "If you're amenable."

"I'm not sure," I said, trying to wrangle the possibilities that collected at the words. Was he trying to trick me? Did I have anything to gain, to lose? And what did he need insight on? "I mean, I need to change..."

I looked down meaningfully at the stinking sweatshirt.

"We're investigating an incident," he said, as though he'd read the question on my face.

When he closed the distance between us, garnering a bit of privacy with the proximity, Farrell closed in as well. A two-foot buffer stood between us and the crowd milling around.

Garder nudged his partner with his elbow. "We could use her."

I didn't like the sound of that. "For what, exactly?"

He sighed heavily. "A murder investigation." He jerked his chin toward the docks. "A new one. At the pier. It's why we came to your shop."

He paused just long enough to make my eyebrows lift before continuing.

"We thought you might be injured. The victims are all psychics from the area. Three of them," he said. "All women of ... power."

He let that sink in, watched my reaction, and seemed to get what he wanted when I couldn't hold back the gasp of surprise. My legs went to water.

Within the ten-block radius around the docks and the tourist blocks around it, that there were five psychic and magic shops. All women. Like me, they all claimed to be that real deal. I knew better.

I'd lived my early years with a woman who did awful, horrible witchcraft things in our basement that left me trembling in my bed.

When I got shipped off to my last foster home, it was a relief.

"You saying some of my colleagues in spirit have been harmed?" I asked.

"I'm saying it might be helpful if you took a brief glance at the crime scene for us."

My gaze flicked from him to Farrell. This was unusual, and I could see from his expression just how strange. His scowl made it clear that it was unwelcome, too.

"The crime scene is active?"

I tried to imagine which of the women in the dock shops had been murdered and thanked my lucky stars I was a relative newbie. I wondered what sort of frauds they'd perpetrated to make someone angry enough to murder them.

"It's active," he said. "And that's precisely why you might be helpful right now. Nothing has been disturbed."

I knew without looking that I'd be useless, but if the lookie-loos around the crime scene saw me mulling over evidence with the police, it might lend an extra air of credibility to my work. I could use that sort of street cred. My bank account would thank me.

I peeled off the sweatshirt, thankful to have it off me, and dropped it into the nearest trash bin.

"Okay," I said. "I'll give it the once over to see if anything speaks to me. But I warn you—a crime scene might not be the best environment to call to my powers."

It was good groundwork, but he didn't acknowledge the comment. Instead, he nodded to Farrell, who headed back the way we came.

I followed along, quietly assessing the back of Garder's shoulders, how broad they were, the gait that had me double-stepping to keep up. He wasn't a desk jockey, that was for sure. He either worked out or had a natural inclination to muscle that might only turn to fat once he hit middle age.

And it was a tremendous amount of muscle, judging by the way they moved beneath his clothes.

I was so busy studying him that I wasn't aware we'd made it to the docks until the sudden odor of fish wrapped around me, signaling the threshold of the piers and the end of the tourist district.

The piers were perfect places in the summer months to ply my trade as tourists ambled about, seeking entry into quaint shops. I made sure mine was as attractive as I could while still indicating to those who were looking for the sort of thing I sold that they had to check out the interior.

Since the tourists dried up in October, I had to make sure that in the winter months, the store looked innocuous enough that the locals would still patronize me. Specifically since during the lean times, I had to rely on séances and medium services and the selling of trinkets and candles.

If I could help the police, it would be one more revenue stream to keep me afloat.

I was planning the new brochure when he stopped short. I smacked into his back and stumbled a step, my boot splashing in briny smelling water from a puddle left over from a rogue wave. A burble of seaweed popped beneath the heel.

He snagged my elbow, steadying me while Farrell lifted a band of yellow tape that cordoned off the entire scene, complete with grizzled looking police officers and what I presumed was the medical examiner judging by the way he was high-stepping his way along the wharf, carrying a large black briefcase.

A tall redhead followed in his wake with a bush of hair held back in a ponytail.

"It's over here," Garder said and waited till I ducked beneath the tape. He let it go and gestured that I should follow the other officer. "We won't keep you long. Just take a quick peek."

We dodged through piles of crates and boxes as we threaded our way along the dock. Container ships loomed over us, smelling of diesel and smoke. The area had been cleared, apparent from the lack of dockmen or workers ambling about when normally it would teem with them.

"What should I be looking for?" I said and then clamped my mouth closed when I caught sight of a thick iron hoist hanging over the edge of the dock.

A blue tarp draped whatever hung from its fat hook. It fluttered at the edge, lifting with a warm breeze in a wave that invited me to draw close. The tips of several fingers peeked out from the bottom, suggesting there was more than one person cloaked by that tarp.

And if the pool of blood beneath the tarp was any sign, they were all dead.

CHAPTER FOUR

THE WOMEN HUNG BY their feet. Three of them, all hooked together from the largest hoist on the pier like filleted fish. Their hair dipped into a puddle of water beneath them as they stared into the distance toward the bell buoy with unseeing eyes. If I took in just their gazes, I might be inclined to think they'd died peacefully.

I retched, dry-heaving painfully as I caught sight of them, wishing with all my might that the officer who had flung the tarp off their bodies had heeded the too-late warning shout from Officer Garder that a civilian was on scene.

Garder stomped over and grabbed the edge of the tarp by the grommet hooked over the junior officer's finger.

"You need to pay more attention," he said. "These poor women deserve some dignity."

The officer's gaze dropped to his shoes encased in rubber galoshes.

"The photographer is here," he said in defense. "He needed pics for the file."

"Yeah, well, so is the psychic." Garder jabbed a thumb in my direction as I stood my ground in a briny puddle, demanding my stomach obey my desperate and silent commands to remain as calm as a summer sea. He looked me over with a critical eye. "Go find her a cup of coffee or something, assuming she can keep anything down after that."

It wasn't unkind, the way he said it, but it made me feel two feet high.

The junior officer's eyes drifted toward me, and his shoulders squared with an almost defiant jerk. He had the kind of look that appealed to younger girls, pretty with perfect features. A flick of his eye over me indicated he preferred those kinds of girls, too.

He didn't linger for one moment over my bare calves or generous bosom the way most men did when they saw me. I caught a chill from the look he gave me. Several other officers were elbowing each other as I stood there, cowboy boots rolling edge to edge as I considered what in the name of hell I was going to do to help without putting myself at risk.

I thought I heard them whispering about my dress and ran a hand over my backside to make sure I hadn't inadvertently jammed the hem into my underwear the last time I'd gone to the restroom. Because I'd done that before. Too often to count.

"What in God's hell are you doing just gawking?" Garder barked at the junior officer, who still hadn't leapt to obey the command. "Coffee. Now."

Garder might have missed the glare he sent me when that happened, but I didn't. I lifted my hand in the universal gesture that indicated I was okay. I couldn't have put my lips to a fragrant mug of anything at the moment anyway, let alone a milky bit of java, and the last thing I needed was an enemy, even if that enemy was a soft-looking rookie.

That boy was the kind who held a grudge, even when it was misplaced. I read that in him as he shuffled away with one more direct glare in my direction.

I tried to let it go, giving him my best you-impressed-me smile to cover my anxiety about what was no doubt going to happen next. It might have worked if he'd held my gaze a moment longer, but he stumbled over a coil of hemp rope and, instead of ending up having his ego salved, he found one more reason to glower.

I gave it up for a lost cause.

By the time I gathered the courage to look back toward Garder, he was looping the edge of the tarp back over the bodies, fidgeting with the tatters of the bottom so it covered up everything but the grayish skin of the fingers peeking out from beneath.

Those few seconds of revelation showed me enough to know what the tarp hid was pretty damn close to the image my mind had fed me earlier. I didn't need to recall it to know how horrific it had been.

I knew the women, too. I hung back while Garder messed with the tarp as it resisted his efforts, and I mulled over the awfulness of what lay beneath, trying to call up some sort of useful tidbit.

Those women were three of the five psychics that surrounded the half dozen blocks of my shop. When I'd set up two years earlier, they'd come calling to make sure I kept to my area. There was room for us all if we were careful. I had the feeling they ran the circle like a crime syndicate, and I was careful to stay in my territory, never canvassing on their turf.

"You see anything that might look familiar?" Garder said from beside me and I realized I'd lost track of him and the image beneath the tarpaulin for a few moments. He'd come up next to me before I could recover.

I jumped, startled.

"I'm not sure what I should look for," I stammered.

The creepiness of seeing their bodies hanging there, coupled with knowing that I'd seen their shades before I knew about this crime scene, was wearing me the way a tag does at the back of a new shirt.

I wanted to rip the thing off and never deal with it again. I wasn't sure why I'd had the premonition. That had never happened to me before. As much as I wanted to discount it as a bit of mania on my part when I'd thought I'd get arrested, I knew in my heart it was something different.

He rustled his scruff with his thumb and index finger as he studied me. Too intently, I thought, to be just curiosity.

"You know the women?" he said.

I nodded. "I recognize them, if that's what you mean."

"Recognize, but don't know."

I shrugged, hugging my torso beneath my ribs. I didn't want to think about that image again or the premonition because both were too unsettling, and while it had got me out of the mess I'd been in, I would not count on it happening again or being something I could exploit. Hell, I didn't want to exploit it. The damn event wasn't something I wanted repeated.

"We aren't chummy or anything," I said. "Just peers."

"You do the same sorts of things?" he said and reached out sideways, but some instinct prevented me from turning with him.

Someone passed him a styrofoam cup. Steam curled over its rim. He pushed it toward me.

"One of them professed to be a witch," I said as I accepted the cup. It would warm my hands. They felt unnaturally cold. "The other two were fortune tellers. Tea leaves, tarot cards, that sort of thing."

"But that's not what you do," he said.

"Is there something specific you want from me, Officer Garder?" I said, hedging away from exactly what I did. That way lay nothing but trouble. Best to keep things on the track he'd steered the train onto.

He cast a knowing glance along my hands. I was sure they were trembling.

"For shit's sake," he said in a voice filled with annoyance. "She's cold." His nod to the junior officer who lurked nearby indicated he was talking about me to him. "You might be used to seeing awful things, officer, but she's a civilian. Can't you find her a blanket or something?"

Desperate not to look like a bother or get stuck in any cop's memory because I was being a pain in the ass, I turned to the young cop. "It's okay," I said. "I'm fine."

The officer's mouth pressed into a thin line but he spun on his heel and left, presumably to get an impossible to find blanket, but more than likely to escape the bullishness of his superior officer.

I would have liked to toss the hot coffee into Garder's face for making me feel like a burden when all I wanted was to get the hell out of there, just one more unremarkable citizen never to come to mind again during a traffic stop or innocent drugging. I supposed it was too late for either.

Garder's steely gaze landed on me again.

"I hope you're just cold," he said, "and not in shock. Shock is much worse."

I was in the middle of explaining I was just feeling chilly when he pulled off his jacket. The fabric of his shirt strained against his chest as he moved to drape the coat over my shoulders.

I shrank into the warm interior. Yup. Cold, thank God. Shock would have meant a trip to the E.R. and I wanted this over as quickly as possible.

As much as I enjoyed the feel of the residual heat of his jacket, the smell of the coffee, strong and black, was making my stomach roil. Saliva filled my cheeks a little too quickly.

"I think I need to step away for a moment," I said.

"Sure." He shuffled backward, giving me room to pass.

I thought he was hesitant to do so, but obeyed some training he'd probably had somewhere along the line that told him he needed to be nice to women. Little late, I thought, but I'd take it. My stomach was definitely squeezing enough to make my skin tingle.

I tried to push by him, but he evidently thought better of letting me escape again and gripped my elbow with steely fingers. On any other day, under some other circumstance, I bet I'd have enjoyed that touch, but now, I knew he wouldn't see me as anything more than a criminal he found useful.

Even the way he guided me away from the crime scene showed he didn't trust me. That knowledge, coupled with the awful sweep of nausea over my body, made me speed up. In response, he stepped up his pace, too. I wanted out of the vicinity as badly as he wanted to get rid of me, it seemed.

We stopped a respectful distance away and thankfully, the shivers that threatened to shake my body hunkered back down. The flapping of the tarp was nothing but a bit of static in the background.

"Take a few minutes to gather yourself," he said. "When you're ready, I want to show you something."

I peered up at him from beneath his heavy jacket and caught his eye. The emotionless way he watched me was a good sign that it wasn't over at all. He was going to take me back to the crime scene like it or not, or he would visit my shop again and make my life a living hell.

One more flash of those dead women streaked through my mind at the thought of that. I nodded hastily. I needed more space than he was giving me, from the crime, from the stink of that coffee, from him.

I shoved the cup back into his hands before fleeing to the side of a building beside us, where I could lean against the bricks. It was all too much. The smells of brine and salt fish, the diesel fumes, and the overpowering male scent of sweat mixed with cologne. A seagull watched me from its perch atop a filthy dumpster covered in fast food wrappers and fish guts.

I rolled off the wall and curled over my abdomen, making sure my head was between my knees. I breathed in slow, deep inhalations until I felt like I could move without puking up my breakfast.

The gull squawked, forcing my eye to its beady black one. It hopped once, flapping its wings and shrieking at me.

"What's your problem?" I said to it.

It spread its wings in threat as it hopped again and settled back onto the pile of rubbish.

"Don't worry," I said. "I'm not interested in your rotten fish."

Just saying the words made my belly spasm. I clutched it with one hand while I tried to hold Garder's jacket away from my face.

The gull squawked at me again.

It took a moment to realize it wasn't threatening me, but something off to the side. Something just out of my peripheral vision.

I looked sideways along the line of buildings and the lot that provided the fishermen and dock workers with storage facilities. Several large coils of abandoned rope filled the space, along with blue barrels for water and oil and shaves of ice. Gray plastic fish crates with cracks and holes, discarded as useless, lined the wall of the building.

But there, right at the corner of the building.

The dog.

Big. Black. Gorgeous and terrifying at the same time.

"Hey you," I said to it.

It stared back at me with yellow eyes. I remembered a comment one of my foster parents made about a dog that kept sneaking into their yard. Something about not being able to trust a dog with yellow eyes. They hated it when I brought home strays and always sneaked them off to the local shelter.

Truth was, I'd never met a dog I couldn't trust. People, men, other women? That was another story.

"You lost, boy?" I said, judging by size alone, that it was male. "You follow me here? You hungry or something?"

I pushed off the building and took a step toward the stray, heading toward it with the thought that I might find an I.D. tag. At the same moment I moved, its tail ducked low, and it spun on its feet, soundlessly darting away. It whipped around and bolted behind a pile of old and faded gray crates.

By the time I got to the end of the building, I couldn't see it anywhere.

"What are you looking for?" Garder said from behind me. "Thinking of running off again?"

I whirled around to face him. His jacket arms spread out beside me like wings as the breeze took them.

"Are you always so damn suspicious?" I said.

He shrugged. "I'm a detective. We wear suspicions like they're jeans." His arm snaked out for me and his hand slipped into the pocket of his jacket. He pulled out a piece of gum from inside and unwrapped it. "Besides. Everyone's guilty of something."

"Well, I'm not," I said as I lifted his jacket from my shoulders and held it out to him.

When he reached for the collar, his fingers whispered against mine, lingering for the briefest of seconds. I had to fight the urge to curl my hand in his.

"We found something," he said as he shoved one arm then the other into the sleeves. "Or rather, they want to clean up the scene and I want to show you what I found before they do."

I nodded with a sigh. Apparently, my price for the credibility I hoped to gain from this excursion was going to be the expensive butter chicken I'd bought from a high-end restaurant the night before. That would teach me to spend money I didn't have.

"Here," he said once we'd crossed the lot to the edge of the docks.

He'd brought me to the offending hoist, I realized, but someone had freed the women from the hook, so they didn't lurk over my head as I squatted with him to study a mass of coiled red and black tubing.

There was something peculiar about it. Maybe it was too small to be rubber, or maybe it was the stink emanating from it, of sizzling fat and scorched earth. My stomach lurched threateningly, but I held on. Barely.

A movement caught my eye to the left, and I looked to see two separate ambulances parked, jostled in between several forklifts as though they'd had to wedge themselves in. Their lights flared and cast intermittent red glows on the water beyond.

The medical examiner was slapping the closed door of one, and the other had yawned open its back doors to receive the last mound that lay on a stretcher covered in black. The redhead leaned against the side of the ambulance, watching Garder with an annoyed expression.

"What do you think?" he said, pulling my attention back to him.

"I think I'm not going to sleep tonight," I said and sighed.

"You might just have nightmares," he muttered and stood up, hitching his hand beneath my elbow and yanking me along with him. "Those are the worst."

I eyed him from beneath hooded lids. He looked entirely too jaded to have nightmares. Every inch of his face seemed cut from stone, from the sharp angle of his jaw to the solid chunk of cheekbone. The shell of his ear blended into the hardness of that facade where the lobe was fleshy and fat. The scruff of beard softened the rest of the edges.

A gal could find satisfaction in making that roughness more pliable. At least some other gal might. I doubted I was his type. Probably liked them soft and yielding. Someone he could bully, who would be his little domestic goddess, fulfilling his every whim.

I got lost in the fantasy of making him meals and having him smile for me and then dumping the contents of the plates onto his head. When he spoke to me, I jumped. His eyebrows raised half an inch at my reaction, and a smile tugged at the corner, but he pulled the mask back in place within the barest of seconds.

"There," he said, circling his hand over the surrounding area, drawing out a symbol in the air. "Do you see it?"

I looked down at our feet. I did see it. What I was looking at was not tubing. It was viscera. Bowels and entrails and blood.

They had the peculiar appearance of sausages that had burst their casings, and little buds of meat bloomed along the edges. Brackish looking holes gaped in places, and where there was a large area of tissue, it was burned and black.

That was the last straw. I fled for the building, my cowboy boots clacking against the concrete like a taunt. I barely made it to the corner before the heaving overtook me. The taste of half-digested butter chicken threatening to take me as I dropped to my knees.

The vomiting took me with a violence I'd not suffered since I was a kid and ate far too many marshmallows topped over butterscotch syrup and ice cream. It wracked my ribs and tore my gallbladder. I swore the violence of it even yanked my spleen inside out.

An unexpected draft of cool air struck my neck, merciful and welcome.

"You get used to it," said a quiet voice next to me and I realized Garder had lifted my hair back from my face as I puked. Great. The man was a saint now.

"God," he said after a moment. "Did you eat the entire Thai menu?"

Maybe not a saint. More like a demon. I gagged on a hunk of chicken and coughed around it.

"Fuck you," I said.

He chuckled. "Not with that mouth," he said. "I'll wait till you've brushed, thank you."

I shuddered as the last of the spasms wavered through, all while he grumbled about having to babysit me. When I thought it finally was over, I sat back on my haunches and breathed slow and deep to calm my stomach. He still had my hair lifted into a coil over my neck but dropped it to settle over my bare shoulders. The locks fell against my neck with a wet slap and I realized I'd gotten some caught in the stream before he'd arrived to help.

"I guess that leaves you off the hook," he said.

I put my palms on the ground beside me so I could look up at him without falling sideways. That brown gaze traveled my face, lingering for one second on my mouth. I swiped at my lips, self-conscious, and grimaced when I felt a smear of fluid coat my hand. Great. I must look a picture. No wonder he kept staring at my mouth.

"What do you mean?" I asked.

He pulled a kerchief out from his pocket and passed it to me.

"I wasn't sure if you were the killer," he said. "But puking like that, I'm guessing you're innocent."

I almost laughed, but he was deadly serious as his gaze held mine.

"You're not joking."

He lifted one of his coffee-colored eyebrows. "I don't joke about murder."

When it seemed I would not use the hankie, he took it back and ran it over my hands for me, all while I stared at him with sudden understanding.

"This was a test," I said. "You didn't think I could help at all. You brought me here to see my reaction."

He sank back on his haunches and held the kerchief by one corner, pinching it with two fingers. He looked left and right, then with a shrug, tucked the filthy thing between two coils of rope that sat beside the building.

"I think you might be able to help now, if that's any consolation," he said.

"Why?" I said instead, incensed that he'd think such a thing as me being a killer. A sadistic killer at that. "Why would you think I would murder anyone?"

I forced myself to recall the image of those dead women, hung by their feet, their bellies sliced open and empty. I'd glimpsed the muscle of their ribs during that moment, like deer skinned and cavities left broken open.

I almost retched again, but I was too empty to do anything but heave. He watched me with a cautious air and leaned back to avoid any resulting splash back.

He was safe, though. I was done.

And I was angry.

"It would take a hell of a lot of muscle to do that to them," I said. "You have to know that."

He said nothing, just watched me intently. I knew he was doing the same thing I did to folks, just for a different reason. His quiet assessment infuriated me more.

"Why would you suspect me?"

"The viscera," he said, as though I should have understood without asking. "Didn't you see it?"

I fell onto my bottom, feet splayed out around the puddle of sick. I wished I had the energy to get up and get away from the stink, but I didn't.

"Of course I saw it," I said and waved a weak hand toward the pool of vomit I'd left between us. "There lies the evidence."

"But did you really see it?" he said. "Really. Did you notice anything odd about it?"

I stared at him, watching the way his eyes hooded as he studied my face. His gaze fell to my chest, and at first, I thought he was doing the man thing and checking out my boobs just like all the other policemen.

I had the insane insecurity that they might not be as full as he'd like or that he might find them lacking. But then I felt my necklace laying heavily against my dress as I swayed toward the wall.

My mother had willed it to me, and it had been waiting for me in the safe deposit box I'd been granted, along with her ephemera and rundown apartment in the city's center.

The amulet was always a gaudy-looking thing, cast pewter tied off with a brown leather thong. I knew it was unique with its inch across circle engraved with a maze leading to a tiny star in the middle.

It took me a lot of Internet searches to discover it was called a Hecate's Wheel, and while I didn't care why my mother had owned it, I decided it was odd enough to lend me an air of mystique. I even used the symbol as my logo on business cards and signage.

When the stone fell against the bare swell of my breast as I moved to look down, I knew he hadn't been looking at my cleavage at all, but at the amulet.

"Oh, my God," I said as I understood exactly what had bothered me about the viscera besides the fact that it was a pile of other women's intestines. "Someone burned a mark into them."

He nodded with a ghost of a smile that lacked any humor except for how long it had taken me to figure it out.

"Not just a mark," he said. "A symbol."

His eyes pinned to mine as I plucked the necklace from atop my dress to drop it between my breasts. But he didn't miss the movement. His gaze trailed from the collar of my shirt back up to my eyes.

Not just a mark. A symbol. My symbol. The one I wore around my neck every day.

CHAPTER FIVE

I TRIED TO IMAGINE someone hunkered over the concrete of a fisherman's wharf as he arranged a woman's viscera into a big enough landscape that they could sear a symbol into the tissues, and I immediately wanted to vomit again.

Garder lunged for me as though he thought I was going to pass out.

"Hold on," he said and laid a cool hand against the back of my neck, as if trying to use sheer will to keep me from giving in to the urge to retch. "I don't think I can hold back your hair this time."

I waved him off. "Don't worry. I don't have anything left."

"Damn good thing. I don't have a second pair of shoes with me."

I stole a look at his feet and grimaced when I realized I'd managed to hit him with a spray or two the first time.

"I'm sorry," I said and lifted my gaze to meet his. He was irritating and cocky, but I would have tried to avoid puking on him if I could.

The brown somehow melded with a honey color around his pupils, making his eyes look like molten chocolate with swirls of butterscotch. Something inside my chest went warm, and then all but purred when he ran his hand down along my arm to find my elbow.

He put just enough pressure to urge me to stand with him, his firm grip helping me find my feet.

"Only a fool wears fancy shoes to a crime scene," he said.

It was the first really civil thing he'd said to me, and when he squared his shoulders, pulling his hand back to his side, I gave him a tentative smile. He regarded me with something akin to sympathy.

"Are you okay?" he said.

I nodded. "I think so."

My fingers went to my amulet and traced the edge. "It's not every day a gal sees the kind of things I just saw." I shuddered and remembered my vision. "And I've seen it twice today. What do you think it means?"

He sighed. "The symbol, you mean? I don't know, but I remembered your shop and the sign outside." His gaze dropped again to the amulet. "It was too much of a coincidence to ignore."

He looked back over his shoulder to where the photographer was taking pictures again. The flash went off even though it was midday and there should be plenty of light to illuminate the shot.

I watched the photographer maneuver around the puddle of reddish and glistening coils, astounded that he could get that close without wanting to throw up everything in his stomach. He wore a cap that was pulled down over his ears and fingerless gloves as though it were mid-November instead of the middle of August.

Policemen were weird, I decided, an insight that was solidified when the photographer laid down on the ground, stretched out prone, to snap another shot of the viscera from the side.

Garder mumbled something about the guy that sounded very much like he shared my view.

I stole a look at him. He was staring at the sight with a furrowed brow, his eye drawn to the puddle of blood which the photographer was now surveying and comparing to the images on his camera.

"It was my mother's," I said because I wanted Garder to realize what sort of degree of separation he was dealing with in case he was inclined to recall his original suspicion that I was guilty. "The amulet, I mean."

He turned back to me with a distracted look at first but then that intense gaze narrowed like a gun sight focusing in on a target. "And the shop sign?" it wasn't a complete accusation, but it had the same heaviness.

"Branding," I said with a shrug. "It's unique. Draws in customers like flies to honey."

"Just to be clear," he said. "I really was worried for your safety."

I cupped my elbows, hugging my arms against my chest. For some reason, his comment, innocent and casual as it was, did something to my throat. It closed up on me, making it ache all the way down to my sternum.

Even in my foster homes, no one really said they worried about me. They scolded me, they yelled at me, some of them even starved me, but no one had said my welfare concerned them. Not even my mother had done that.

It made me uncomfortable enough that I backed away, unsure how to answer without sounding like a peevish child.

"I'm fine," I said. "Except for a headache. If you don't need me anymore, I'd like to leave."

He started to answer when the photographer came over to us and tapped his shoulder.

"Got a good shot," he said. "They're clearing the scene now. Do you need me any longer?"

The photographer gave me a long look, much the same as the junior officer had, and I stood my ground, defiant. I hadn't gone through five foster homes by being demure.

"You got a problem with me?" I said as I faced him with a lifted chin and a direct stare.

"It's not the norm to let civilians on site," he answered with a flare of annoyance but it disappeared when Garder sent him a withering glare. Instead, he shrugged and leaned closer to Garder, pressing a button on his DSLR.

"I took them all with a wide enough angle you can see the whole thing from above," he said. "Nasty fucking stuff."

I thought he muffled a gag. Because I was a little pathetic, I let a smug smile cross my face.

Garder looked the screen over for several seconds before he nodded then turned to me. "Is there anything else you can think of to tell me before I let you go? Anything about the women or the scene that stands out to you? Professionally, I mean."

The photographer rolled his eyes behind Garder's back and I had the urge to find something useful enough to make those eyes roll right out of his head. Not because I didn't like that it was in reaction to Garder, but because it indicated more what he thought of me.

"Just one thing," I said. "The women were all fakes."

The photographer snorted but Garder just let the faintest of smiles play across his lips. I expected both to some degree. In fact, I'd counted on it. It was clear Garder had some sway here, enough that the others deferred to him. But I didn't need his protection. I squared off against the photographer with my fists clenched against my sides.

"There was something else in that mess on the ground beneath them," I said, drawing from my experience with people and their reactions to insinuate I knew more than I did. "Something that spooked you."

The photographer blinked at me, trying not to give away anything, and he no doubt thought he kept it pretty close to his vest. But he'd been acutely involved in photographing the mess from the ground level, all from one specific angle. There was something there, all right, and a casual observer might miss it.

I hadn't. it was my stock and trade to notice things. All I needed to infer my otherworldly knowledge was right there in the way he made sure to lay the camera on the ground just so and fire off several shots of one angle when he didn't bother with any other. That it spooked him was evident by the way his hand shook as it held the camera out to Garder.

"The killer didn't just arrange the viscera, did he? He left something for you to see."

"Doesn't prove you're the real thing," the photographer said, but I knew I'd been right. His eyes trailed to the camera display window, and I followed his gaze. He hurried to move the image forward to the next with a harried click on the right arrow.

Part of any successful grift was guesswork. The other parts were risk and luck. I didn't need any of them to know what had bothered him. I saw the image before it shifted. A flash and no more as it moved across the LCD display.

A number. Drawn in blood. The number three.

"He numbered the kills," I said. "Either that, or he's planning two more murders."

The photographer took a sharp intake of breath.

I turned to Garder.

"May I go now?" I said.

Garder nodded but he didn't let his expression shift from stoic lawman to astounded believer for one second, even though I could feel the photographer draw away as though I'd burned him. I inwardly smiled. Not bad for a cheat and a con.

"Well?" I said.

"We have what we need, I guess," Garder said, digging into his pocket and holding out a card for me. "But I might come by if we need you again."

His words might have indicated need, but the real meaning was clear. He might come by if he found something else to connect me to the murders.

"Please don't," I said, but I took the business card just the same, if only to continue to appease him. "This was enough to give me nightmares for a month."

I spun on my booted heel and strode through the crime scene to the tape and lifted it high enough to duck under. It took several steps past that before my breath began to move in a regular rhythm and by then, I was starting to decide that helping the police was a fool's bargain.

Whatever credibility it could lend me wasn't worth seeing more blood and gore, or of witnessing the last moments of horror those women had to endure.

I wasn't exactly new to violence, and it wasn't the brutality of the murders that bothered me the most. No. It was the flash of memory that played behind my eyelids as I'd looked down at those entrails.

The scene nudged my belly into reaction and roused a memory of dark rooms lit by black candles that cast an eerie yellow light. I smelled the moldy stink of wet concrete and smoke. My stomach had recoiled at an aroma not present today, but dredged up from that memory.

I knew I'd seen entrails like those before. I'd been a kid, maybe five or six and had stumbled into my mother's basement room after waking from a nightmare. At least, I'd thought it was a nightmare.

I'd only known it was the stink of burning fat that roused me when I opened the door to find her with hands clasped over a broad copper bowl. Smoke rose from the sizzling guts in that vessel and I remember pissing myself as I stood in the open maw of the basement door, watching her and listening to her monotonous chanting.

A small dog laid off to the side on a raised bed of earth she'd brought in from the garden. There were still sticks and rocks in the clumps of dirt.

A memory long buried but now exhumed, one that still made me sick if I let it settle too long, and so I didn't.

Instead, I walked the streets with a dull ache in my temples. The busker was gone and the crowds had begun to thin now that the crime scene was being cleared. The bar where the girls had flirted with the musician had grown louder and drunks hung around the perimeter, swaying to the music that crept out into the street. The smell of perfume hit me like a mushroom cloud as I passed by.

I threaded my way past couples who had come out to enjoy an evening dinner on the outside patios that lined the streets where the docks turned to a boardwalk for tourists. Sunset was still a few hours off, but in August, those tourists made the boardwalk part of their dinner plans. They were as plentiful as the seagulls and just as frustrating to get past when you were in a hurry.

And I was in a hurry. All I could think of was getting back to my shop because I realized I'd run so fast to get away from Officer Garder and his buddy, that I'd left the store unmanned. Probably unlocked.

I doubted the police officers locked the front door behind them when they'd barged in, and now I wondered what sort of shape I'd find it in.

I prayed I'd not lost my entire inventory to thieves.

As I drew near, I realized losing my inventory would be the best of scenarios.

The front door had been vandalized. Graffiti scrawled across the surface in muddy streaks. Fraud. Fake. Charlatan. Words that would blast to bits a hard-earned reputation that was just beginning to blossom.

I halted in front of the door with a sigh that made my belly ache all the more. It felt raw inside, like someone had scraped out the contents with a shovel.

Who would do such a thing? I stood there with my heel rocking sideways as I bit down on my lip so I wouldn't let go the tears that had been building ever since I'd seen those poor women. I didn't think I'd crossed anyone. I'd given good readings and had the thank you cards to prove it.

But someone was evidently mightily displeased to vandalize the storefront that way. It would take me hours to clean it up, all time I'd lose from the business. Hiring a cleaning crew might take days. I couldn't let the graffiti stay there 24 hours let alone days.

I scanned the walls of the building, grateful that at least most of the damage had been done to the door and windows. Maybe with the right materials, I could make quick work of them.

The worst of the accusations were written on the door. I could clean that while it sat opened to the inside and still man the shop for calls or quickie sales. I started to run my gaze over the rest of the façade, triaging the cleanup in my mind, when the smell hit me.

That was when I decided not to touch the handle at all. The stink was strong and earthy. I suspected feces and leaned in for a better look. Sniffed at it like a fool.

But it wasn't covered in the same kind of mud and feces that smeared my storefront. And based on what I'd witnessed the last few hours, I was pretty sure I knew exactly what it was.

Blood.

CHAPTER SIX

A RIVER OF BLOOD dripped from the lintel of the shop and looked like someone had dabbed it on with some blunt, rag-tipped pole you might see in a bad Passover movie.

I had taken great pains when I'd opened to make my storefront look nothing like the cliché most people would think of when they imagined a spiritualist shop. Under my mother's care, it had been a dump that she used to sell second-hand books and ephemera that barely kept us afloat when my father died.

When I returned home from Canada after her death to claim the lot of lousy things she'd left me, it was the building that held me here. Beneath the crusty exterior, I'd seen through adult eyes the classy lines of a sturdy, if aged, building. It fit into the patina of the old area because it had been built before the docks brought mass copies of Bombay Company furniture to the citizens of the city.

The over one hundred-year-old building needed a bit of love and a whole lot of cash to get it into shape. I'd put in a ton of sweat equity to stretch out the mortgage so I could transform it into the swan it became. I knew right away how I'd fit into the area too, how I'd earn my living, how I'd capture the tourist trade and the locals as well.

Those other spiritualists were mere charlatans, is what my shop and exterior said. It was time for the real deal to come to town.

I'd painted the storefront's intricate exterior moldings a rich purple that would stand out but cast an imperial appeal. Even the dentil moldings that ran along the header of the door and along the top of the two windows that flanked the broad entrance wore the same shade. The straight, square columns on either side of each window held aloft ornate corbel moldings and, despite a distinctly rococo style, they reminded me of Egyptian columns.

But it had been the windows themselves that spoke to me. Like an old owl's eyes, they stared into me from the face of that store. They let in enough light to flood the space.

I could save a pretty penny on electricity if I wanted, but I strung white fairy lights around the sill and hang gauzy curtains. I hired someone to paint the symbol from my amulet in the middle of both. Two gargantuan stone planters squatted on either side of the door, and I filled them with herbs and sacred plants.

I topped it all with a sign made of individual golden letters like you might see above a fancy chocolate shoppe: The Alcove. My chalkboard sandwich sign had a snappy, sassy declaration. *No need for an appointment*, it said on one side, and *I already knew you were coming* on the other.

I was proud of my little shop because working on it day after day had built something within my soul as well. Not just because of the sweat and tears I put into the shop, but what I put into each client that came after. Seeing the healing take place in them might not have exactly removed all that childhood horror, but it did fabricate a nice wall, and painted a thick patina over it.

To see all my hard work so defaced was like a kick in the teeth.

Anger bubbled up my throat. As true as those words about me might be, my storefront didn't deserve such an assault. The fury at seeing it vandalized remained for all of one heartbeat. Then I heard a sound coming from inside, and the fury evaporated, replaced by cold, hard fear.

In that moment, the certain panic rose that I might not just be dealing with a regular disgruntled customer or delinquent teen. What if the noise from inside was being made by the same person who slapped blood across my lintel and scrawled the graffiti across my windows in black, fragrant shit?

Maybe the blood had come from one of those poor unfortunate psychics, and the killer was here to continue his vendetta.

My pulse went into overdrive.

I bent to dig into my boot and yank out my phone at the same time as I fished into my bra to extract the business card Garder had given me. I wasn't surprised to see my hands shake as I dialed each number and waited for the call to connect as I fled to the back of the building.

A large red dumpster in my back alley could hide a full grown woman if she could wedge herself between the stinking metal and the rickety fence behind. I fully planned to become whatever size woman could shove herself into that tight space.

When Garder answered, I was crouching near the dumpster in the back alley, terrified to go into my shop or stand out in the open. My own cowardice made me sick but after what had happened to those other women, I wasn't going to take a single chance.

"Garder here," came the strong voice, almost too loud. It boomed out into the alley and I hurried to turn off the speaker.

"I need help," I whispered into the phone. "Someone is here. At my shop."

A noise came from the mouth of the alley just to the right where my door shouted to every passerby that just inside, a fraud and charlatan shilled her wares. It sounded like someone had tripped over my chalkboard sign.

"Hurry," I said. "They're still here."

The phone went dead and I told myself it was because he'd shut it off so he could head over at break-neck speed. He might not like me but he had a duty to serve and protect, right?

I repeated the assertion to myself the entire time I crouched there until a large orange cat strolled out of the front door with a mouse in its teeth.

It tossed the vermin up into the air and watched it smack to the cobblestones between its legs. A lazy paw smacked down on the whip of tail when the mouse shook itself free of shock. Then the feline bit down on the mouse's neck and tore off across the street.

By then, Garder came panting up with his gun drawn. I hissed at him to come toward the alley instead of blustering through my front door.

He hunkered down as he ran, much like I'd seen in crime shows, but seeing it real and live put a sort of tingle down my spine.

I had the feeling when he found nothing inside but a few gauzy scarfs, I'd feel pretty damn foolish, and if I'd indeed left that coffee urn sitting on the counter, I'd feel worse than that.

He was all threat and caution as he came toward me. Those thickly muscled thighs strained at the material of his slacks and the look of utter violence on his face made me shiver. Not entirely from fear.

"Where is he?" he said as he pushed in next to me, shoving me aside so hard I nearly fell onto a pile of take-out containers. Served me right to eat so much Chinese takeout.

"Front or back?" he barked. "I have a couple officers standing by at the corner."

I pointed to where a smaller cat was streaking across the alley at the intersection. The mouse's tail dangled from its mouth like a frayed string and bounced along merrily as the cat ran.

"Not sure how many of the damn bastards broke in," I said. "But I think they got the best of my stock."

Any other time, I might not have cracked a bad joke or even chuckled at it afterward but I was so relieved, so adrenaline soaked, I couldn't help the nervous laugh that erupted despite the scowl he sent my way.

Relief eased the tension from my shoulders and I heaved myself to a stand, grateful to be moving.

I didn't notice the black look he was giving me until I stretched my shoulders out, rolling them up and down as I angled my neck. The movement showed his full expression, pinched and serious. The chocolate colored gaze had gone yellow.

Chagrined, I tried to move past him, but his shoulder butted into mine, preventing me from extricating myself from the tangle of debris behind the dumpster.

"You called me here for a stray cat?" he said.

I arched my back to ease the kinks.

"Two stray cats," I said because I didn't like his tone.

He holstered his weapon beneath his jacket and the look of threat on his face shifted to annoyance as he realized there was no real danger. "You called me and several other officers to your shop for two mangy cats after we'd just cleaned up the worst homicide mess we've seen in years."

His voice was flat but his gaze certainly wasn't. It could have lit me on fire.

"Well, I didn't know it was a stray cat when I called." He wouldn't bully me. I refused to let him. "I only just saw the damn things when you came running, guns ablaze." I tried to make it sound reasonable, but he was having none of it.

"If this is your way of getting me into the sack," he said with a dry tone that made my ire rise, "you should know I'm not into damsels in distress."

I wasn't sure why I took such offense to that, but I did. The damn man didn't deserve my good natured ribbing and he certainly didn't warrant the thought of me jumping into the sack with him.

He didn't deserve much more than for me to shove my way past him and leave him standing there with his gun in his hand. Which is exactly what I did. At least, I tried to.

He laid his palm flat against the dumpster as I tried to push by him, effectively barricading me in.

I met the starkness of his gaze with all the haughtiness I could muster under the circumstances.

"I heard noises from inside. I was scared." I couldn't help the defensive jut of my chin as I spoke. "After what you showed me today, and after seeing the mess someone made of my shop, I think it's entirely within the realm of possibility that I was being hunted."

His jaw seesawed back and forth for a mere second before he got it under control. When he spoke next, it was with a note of suspicion.

"What mess?"

I jabbed the air with my index finger in the direction of the street.

"My damned store," I said, matching his tone. "Someone covered it in dirt and blood. I would think an observant detective would have noticed it."

He recoiled as if I'd slapped him. I started to feel guilty until he spoke again.

"Seems to me someone called me with terror in her voice and said she needed help, then shrieked at me to run into the alley."

"I didn't shriek."

He crossed his arms over his chest. The muscles of his biceps twitched and he sighed heavily, reluctant to concede the truth as we both knew it.

"You're right," he said, with a grudging tone. "I wasn't as observant as I could have been. We're downwind here and..."

He let the words trail off as though he'd said too much and wasn't sure how to recover, then he finally just sighed and pulled his hand back off the dumpster so I could get by. "Let's just say I wasn't paying attention the way I normally would."

His gaze on me was intent enough that I had to look away.

"So what do you make of it?" I asked, taking the opportunity to fumble my way past him.

I gestured to the front where the sun was already sinking below the rooftops. Whatever the mess, it would have to wait till morning now. I sighed as I imagined getting up at the crack of dawn to get down here before any customers could see the mess.

He raked both hands over his buzz cut and scratched back and forth thoughtfully. "We should check inside just to be on the safe side."

His hand went beneath his jacket, and I presumed he wasn't positive I was in the clear.

"You're nervous," I said.

"Alert," he corrected and swept me behind him as he headed to the back door. "Stay here. If someone comes out besides me, run. Don't wait."

I nodded resolutely and then waited anxiously as he swept through my shop. It took him about twenty minutes to give the all clear and by the time it came, I had already imagined dozens of scenarios where he'd found my stash.

Unfortunately, I didn't think of any reasonable excuses for having it except to blame it on whoever might have entered the shop while I'd been away.

I decided to saunter in at his call as though everything was on the up and up. Surely, there'd be reasonable doubt there if he'd found it.

He was looking over a display of crystals when I entered and snapped on the overhead light. During the day, I kept it low lit. But I still felt the creeps from the afternoon and wanted light. Lots of it.

"Didn't your mother ever tell you to look with your eyes and not your hands," I said as I headed toward the counter.

Yup. I sure did leave that cannister out. I grabbed it with both hands and carried it toward the apothecary galley between the back of the shop and the main store front. I kept it in its own locked compartment and planned to return it there out of sight of inquisitive eyes.

"My mother died when I was two," he said.

I spun on my heel to face him. I'd not heard him follow me, but there he was. Not a foot away. I wasn't sure if his stealth was a bonus or not. I laid the cannister on its shelf and closed the door, all under his watchful eye, and decided that under the right condition, that stealth could be very handy. I was sure I'd appreciate it at some point. Not now, though.

"I'm sorry to hear that," I said.

He shrugged. "It was a long time ago."

I twisted the lock to make sure it clicked. "Back when the dinosaurs roamed, huh?"

"Not exactly dinosaurs," he said and showed me a grin that transformed his face from shaggy, stern detective to scruffy, sexy regular guy. Not sure I was happy about the way it made my heart stutter.

He squeezed past me in the tight space, making my heart speed up, and I thought when he caught my eye on the way that he'd done it on purpose.

He ran his hand along the beaded curtain that separated the shop proper from the back room, my inner sanctum where I performed my most therapeutic magic. The beads made a rattling noise as they clicked together.

"I suppose it doesn't matter how old I am," he said. "To you young whippersnappers, I'm sure anyone over thirty is ancient."

"I'm twenty eight," I said, feeling an unexpected sting of offense that he would consider me young and immature. "Not so far off from thirty."

I leaned against the cupboard and let myself drink him in. Now that the most offending of evidence had been put safely away, I could appreciate that he really had the most amazing eyes.

One of his hands tangled in a long thread of beads as he leaned in toward me. A hint of mint escaped his breath and I had the feeling the short tug he gave was to test the curtain's sturdiness.

I had a flash of image, of those beads hanging over his shoulders as I wrapped my legs around his waist. By the way his gaze went to my throat, I thought he might be thinking the same thing. My throat ached with the desire to taste his breath.

"Twenty eight," he said with a cocky lift to his eyebrow. "Still young enough to partake in the world of psychedelics then."

There went the fantasy. I snatched the beads from his grip and tossed them back into the veil of curtain where they clacked angrily against the other lengths of beading.

So he had snooped around while he'd been alone in my shop.

I spun on my heel, heading to the front of the store to see the bastard out. "I don't know what you're talking about."

He caught my hand and jerked his chin toward the cupboard behind me as he leaned against the door-frame, one foot hooked over the other, arms crossed over his chest.

"Your little happy Buddha coffee cannister," he said. "I'd say he's grinning like a fool because he has something other than coffee filling his belly."

I went into defense mode, one trained in me after long, miserable years of answering to things I'd not done to people who would never believe me, and careful, calculated years of planting confidence in folks who wanted to but shouldn't.

I blinked innocently, pasting on the wide-eyed wonder I always seemed to manage each time a client's loved one slipped into our world from the ether, and I could barely believe I'd done the magic one more time.

"My coffee cannister was sitting out in the open, Officer Garder," I said and pulled my hand back. "Easy reach of anyone in the shop."

I tapped my finger into his chest and couldn't help noting how solid it was beneath his Hugo Boss. I swept the thought aside the way I'd yank a cobweb from the ceiling.

My hand curled into my fist and I buried that into my armpit as I crossed my arms over my chest and stared him down.

"Anyone could have put anything they wanted in it," I said. "In fact, anyone could have stolen me blind because two police officers barged in the front door and left it unlocked when they dragged me off to a crime scene."

"First of all," he said, raising one finger in tension-filled space between us. "We didn't drag you off. You ran. We chased. Second, we pulled the front door closed and locked it. Procedure. We need to contain the area. A locked door is a quick way to do that."

He pushed himself off the door frame, coming to his full height over me. "You left the back door open. Third—" He dropped his hand on my shoulder in a casually intimate movement that had me both wanting to pull away and lean closer at the same time. "I don't care if you indulge a little."

His gaze trailed over my mouth and down my throat, where it eventually moved to the cupboard behind me. "What you do in your spare time is of no concern to me. Three women are dead in the most horrible way imaginable and I'm starting to believe you're the only one who can help us figure out why."

I almost couldn't breathe as he looked at me. It took an effort of sheer will to pull my eyes from his.

"Then you are most definitely screwed."

He gave me a long look that might have made my heart flutter except he spoke and ruined everything.

"You're the one with blood on your door with a killer loose," he said. "If anyone is screwed, it's you."

CHAPTER SEVEN

WHEN I ARRIVED AT the shop at sunrise the next morning, my neck prickled with premonition. Someone had been there ahead of me, someone who just might still be lurking about. I thought of Layne's comment that the blood on my door put me at risk and I froze at the sight of my shop.

All signs of the vandalism from the day before had disappeared. The blood, the dirt, the stink of filthy graffiti, all gone. I was met with a clean slate of purple paint and glossy windows that caught the orange of the sunrise and cast it back at me with a reflection of the clouds over the rooftops. Drops of water clung to the leaves and flowers in my planters even though there hadn't been a heavy dew and we'd had a long five-day stretch without rain.

I spun on my ballerina slipper heel and scanned the area, my throat tight with nervous energy. If this was someone's idea of a joke, I didn't find it the least bit funny. Relieved as I might be that I didn't have to clean up a horrific mess, I had the feeling someone was toying with me.

The only thing I saw besides the regular shops and lampposts going dead for the day was the smoke stacks and white facade of a new pleasure cruiser big enough to dwarf the quaint shops that surrounded the pier.

I braced myself as I reached for the door handle, hoping to find it still locked and not broken or jimmied open. It resisted my grip. With a sigh of relief, I fumbled for my purse over my shoulder and pulled out my key.

I was jiggling it into the stubborn lock when someone came up behind me. Instinct bade me twirl around and flatten myself against the door, but I wasn't ready for the man that stood there, cleaning his hands on a gritty towel as he watched me.

I let go at least a ten second stream of obscenities. Very un-crunchy granola of me. Detective Garder—Layne—raised both eyebrows as though he'd never heard such words before. That just ticked me off more.

"You scared the bejesus out of me," I said to him, but even so, I relaxed against the door. "You make a habit of creeping up on unsuspecting women?"

The white T-shirt he wore was wet enough to reveal a cord of muscles in his stomach. The scruff on his chin and jawline had been scraped clean, and I wasn't sure I preferred the school boy look to the day old whiskers of the day before.

He canted his head at me as he flung the towel over his shoulder. "You don't strike me as the unsuspecting type."

I only barely managed to keep from flipping him an F-you finger.

"You can't just sneak up on a gal like that. Not after what happened yesterday."

He crossed his arms over his chest and I tried oh-so-hard not to let my eyes trail down the sculpted curve of his biceps.

"I don't sneak," he said. "I watch. I serve. I protect." His gaze dropped to the pulse in my throat, hammering away like nobody's business. "But sometimes I do admit to chasing women through the streets."

"Fuck you," I said. "I'm entitled to a bit of a scare."

His grin cracked open a delighted expression that didn't seem the least bit sorry that he'd scared me.

"You'd think a good psychic would know I was coming."

I razed him with another stream of curses just in case he wasn't aware of how I felt about that remark.

"That's some mouth on you." He ran both hands over his buzz cut, back and forth as though he couldn't scratch at it enough to relief a deep itch.

"I've been told my mouth is my best feature," I said, knowing full well it was leading and coy. I just desperately wanted to see him off his heels. Even for a second.

"I'm more an ass man," he said, but the way his eyes glued themselves to my lips, I was pretty sure he had taken the bait, and the heat crept all the way up my neck in response. I was about to toss out a ridiculous jibe about all men being the same, but he jumped like someone had poked at him with a stick.

It was abrupt enough and poorly timed enough that I flinched. He swore and maybe even let go a little girly squeal, but that happened so fast, I couldn't be sure.

When he started flapping at his tank shirt and started running his hands down his jeans—my God, he looked even better in jeans than the Hugo Boss—I realized he was either spontaneously combusting and was on fire and trying to put it out, or he'd encountered the nest of earwigs that lived under my planters.

I quirked an eyebrow at him and did my best not to laugh. Earwigs were the devil, and I wouldn't reserve that punishment for the worst of humanity, let alone a cocky detective who had no right being at my shop at that time of the morning. It gave me the heebie jeebies, and it wasn't beneath me to smirk. Just a little.

"Spiders," he said as he peered at me. "Your shop is loaded with the little fuckers." He shuddered visibly enough that I didn't doubt his paranoia. "Cobwebs everywhere. Cripes."

I knew I should say something, but I wasn't sure I could open my mouth without laughing.

"You're welcome, by the way," he said as I struggled to straighten the smirk to a flat line of indifference.

I managed to nod but not much else, but evidently, that was enough for him to reach toward me, his chest coming close enough that I sucked in a breath. For an insane moment, I thought he was going to run his hand down my arm, but his arm brushed past me instead. The door rattled as he twisted the knob.

The door behind me swung open, and I stumbled at the suddenness of it. He caught me, with one warm hand on my waist. I was acutely aware that my tank top had ridden up and his palm was on my bare skin.

"Should have seen that coming too," he said with a half grin as his gaze dropped to my mouth.

Another flush rose on the heels of the first one. I chose to ignore the bad psychic humor and stammered out some awkward question about what I should be grateful for and realized before he even answered that of course, it was for the work he'd done on my shop.

Because some part of my brain had noticed the sweaty brow, the washcloth, the buckets of soapy water that sat at the corner of the building. Noticed it, registered it, and immediately shoved it under the mat of my psyche because I did NOT want to like this guy.

"Must have been a lot of work," I muttered because he was eliciting all sorts of emotions I did NOT want to feel. And considering I'd got up early to make sure the facade was cleaned up before any potential customers might decide to meander by, I should have let him hear the gratitude in my voice. Instead, I just kept going. Like a ninny. "Guess I got up early for nothing."

He scraped his hands down over his Tshirt, smearing it with a greyish bit of filth that I knew would never come out. "I wouldn't say you got up for nothing," he said. "You got to enjoy a good long look at an arrogant well-dressed detective acting all work-a-day Joe. Score one for the witch."

That did it. My gaze dropped to my shoes, ashamed. When his fingers touched down on my chin, tilting my face up at him, I let him do it.

Whatever expression tried to play over his face, he controlled it quickly. "I would have torn the whole building down with my bare hands if it could have kept you from seeing that," he said in a hushed voice, and held my eye for a long moment, then some sort of switch turned off and his tone was all business. "No one should have to deal with that sort of vandalism."

The moment, the tension, got too awkward, and he shouldered his way past me, ruining any opportunity to apologize or explain that I wasn't good at compassion. I'd never had it.

"You got a bathroom in this place?" he said, and stood for a moment, taking in the shop before striding all the way in.

He peeled off his shirt as he went to show long lines of muscle in a back marred only by a palm-sized scar over his left shoulder. Several black tattoos surrounded it and banded his shoulder cuff. I'd never seen a scar beg for my touch so badly, and I wasn't aware I had stopped dead in my tracks to stare until he swung around to face me.

He stopped short, as though he didn't expect me to be so close. His nostrils flared and for a second, I thought he inhaled, maybe just a little bit, then the moment was gone and that expressionless mask settled back over his face again.

"Bathroom?" he said, running his hands up his arms in a scrubbing motion. "I can't stand the thought of the little bastards crawling over my skin."

I nodded, unable to do much more than that as I pointed in the direction of the chalkboard sign over one of the doors that said: Power Room, using a deliberate misspelling as a euphemism most customers still didn't get.

He grunted and disappeared behind the door, leaving a wake of aftershave and the best kind of perspiration.

I waited till I heard water running before I let go a long breath. I had to get a grip. It had been a while since I'd had a good roll in the hay, but really. It couldn't have been so long that I'd pine for a man who was an arrogant SOB on his best days.

I strode to the counter, running my hand along the smooth epoxy that covered the wooden top as I mentally calculated the months it had been since my last relationship.

I couldn't come up with anything in the last year. Ouch. That would explain the gob-smacked staring at Garder's body. I had to fix that issue like yesterday because if I didn't, I was going to end up getting my ego crushed. Men like that didn't find girls like me attractive, and girls like me deserved better than that anyway.

I willfully smothered down my frustrated lust and settled in to work. I had a full day of work ahead of me. Sherry was coming back to pick up that spell I'd offered and I had to gather some herbs and leather and string. I had a neat little calligraphy kit and wax seals in my apothecary gallery that made that sort of thing look authentic.

It was all in the details when you wanted to cast a spell. Customers didn't expect them to look ancient and all, but they always remarked on the scrolled parchment and wax seal when I added it to their package.

I was busy pulling all the materials from the cabinet when Garder came back out, fully clothed, thankfully, to save my dignity. His hair beaded with water and he smelled strongly of the patchouli and lemon soap from the pottery dish on the sink.

He paused in the doorframe long enough to pull his phone from his pocket when it chimed. He chuckled as he checked out the screen and then typed furiously before pocketing it again and making his way to the counter.

I watched him from beneath hooded lids as he ran his hand along the counter much the same as I had a moment earlier. I smiled at the thought of the physical echo. I never got tired of people taking pleasure in the display top. It had cost me a pretty penny to ship and was completely worth it every time someone noticed it.

"It's made of wood that's been cracked and cratered by nature," I said of the counter top. "A Nova Scotian artist gouges out the rotting wood and fills the grooves in with colored epoxy then runs clear over top all that. I don't know how he does it, but the work is really stunning."

He knocked on the top with his knuckles.

"It's gorgeous," he said then turned to the door of the shop when it chimed to indicate someone had come in—a redhead who stood taking in the shop with a sharply assessing gaze.

She looked vaguely familiar and I puzzled over where I might have seen her before, thankful to have my mind settle on something besides the man next to me giving off so much heat I felt like testing him for fever.

"I'm not open yet," I said over Garder's shoulder.

"No worries," she said, flicking her hand in my direction and then to encompass the shop contents. "I'm not a believer."

The nonbeliever, so tall she might have gone eye to eye with Garder, crossed the room as soon as her eyes landed on him. She wore a plaid shirt tied into a knot at her stomach and a white tank top beneath. A slouch beanie was stuffed into her front jeans pocket and she fiddled with it as she entered the shop.

It took looking at her hands to recognize her from the crime scene. One fingernail—her thumb—was painted a bright violet.

"Shit, man, you weren't joking," she said without directing her gaze toward Garder. "This place is like taking a trip to La La Land."

She traveled the shop with her eyes and finally landed on Officer Garder's face. She waggled her eyebrows and nodded some sort of wordless communication that made my back go even more rigid than it had at the La La Land comment.

I told myself it was her dismissal of my vocation that bothered me the most, not the way she headed to Garder with a direct beeline that indicated she knew him. Really well. Really, really well.

When she cozied up next to him I realized she wasn't quite as tall as he was after all, but given heels instead of the flat leather boots she had on, and she'd easily tower over him. Her clothing, casual as it was, still couldn't cancel out her model-gorgeous looks. That auburn hair tumbled down her back in a long plait tied at the back of her nape and her full lips were so perfectly a match for Angelina Jolie's that I found myself running a finger over my own in comparison.

I hated her instantly.

And I kept hating her right up until the moment she spied the counter top.

She squealed. Literally squealed. And then I couldn't find the energy to hate her any more.

"This," she said, stabbing the wood with her finger. "This is the most beautiful thing I've ever seen."

She leaned over the wood and ran her fingers along a seam filled with white bubbles until they splayed out over the tributaries of seams.

"It's like there's a river in the wood. Fuck." This last word was said with a note of wonder. She looked up at me with black eyes that were such a contrast to the coloring of her hair and skin that I could barely keep from staring. "You have to tell me where you got this."

I let my glance slip to her hand as it lay on the wood. Blunt nails. Clean but trimmed almost to the quick. Small fingers but strong looking wrists. She might be beautiful model material, but she was a worker bee. Someone who understood hard labor.

"It's Canadian," Garder said before I could answer.

She looked at me in amazement at his comment, checking for confirmation. I nodded.

"No shit," she murmured. "Fucking Canadians."

She cocked her head at me.

I didn't know what to say to that so I said nothing.

"Parrish," Garder said.

"La-ayne," she said, drawing out the first letters into a full syllable and making a full stop in between the second. "Fuck man, lighten up."

She ran her hand over his buzz cut and water flicked off the ends. "You need to let your hair grow. You look like a fucken boyscout."

He grabbed her wrist so quick I doubt even she knew he was going to put her into an arm twist until she was spun around and arching up onto her toes.

At first, my hand went for the stapler I kept on the counter, fully intending to bring it down onto Garder's head if I had to. But before my fingers touched down on it, she laughed and laid her forehead against his, looking him in the eye. Whatever this was, it wasn't assault. She'd expected it.

"What did I tell you about cursing like a sailor in front of people?" he said then caught my eye as he let her go. "She has a bit of a swearing problem."

She sagged against the counter.

"You're my fucking problem," she said as she dug into her bra with one hand, pulling the shirt away with the other, just enough to make a large gap between the fabric and her skin. I could see all the way down to her toes if I bothered to look. I didn't doubt Garder could from his vantage.

I checked his reaction. He didn't avert his gaze respectfully as she inspected beneath her shirt, but there was something different in his expression as he followed her hands with his eyes. Intimate, but not sexual.

My shoulders eased up the death grip they had on my spine.

"Sweet baby Jesus," she said as she grimaced and scooped below the cup. When her hand came free of the shirt and bra it was with a handful of crumbs.

"I had one piece of toast this morning. One." She sucked the back of her teeth in annoyance as she held out her hand. Her quick scan of the area put her up on her tiptoes as she leaned over the counter. "You got a garbage can or something? Goddamn toast crumbs got all up in my business."

"It's just crumbs," I said and gestured to the floor. "I haven't swept yet."

Her auburn eyebrow cocked into a perfect triangle.

"Sweet," she said then reached up under the hem of her shirt. A few vigorous shakes of her bra made her moan in relief as more crumbs fell out onto the floor.

"Sheesh, Fienes," Garder said, rolling his eyes. "You couldn't do that before you came in?"

"It wasn't itchy till now," she said as though it was something he should completely understand.

She grinned as she looked at me. White teeth, but a cap over the left front one. I wondered how it had got broken.

"You ever get toast crumbs in your bra, blondie?"

I almost answered but I caught the look Garder gave her and clamped my mouth shut. There was no way I was going to let him imagine me that way and react with that expression.

She didn't miss my response, though. She leaned right in with a conspiratorial look as she tapped her temple. "Bitch, ain't it? I'm thinking of just burning the bras and going commando."

Garder all but groaned. Parrish was pretty well endowed, so I imagined it bothered him.

"I hate you too, Layne." She squared her shoulders. "Now. You said to come pick you up. I'm here."

Garder turned to me and started explaining for some reason. "Parrish Fienes is the assistant M.E." He gestured toward her but didn't glance her way. Instead, he kept his gaze on mine, intense enough that it made me uncomfortable. "Fienes, this is Brie Duncan. She's helping with the psychic murders."

Psychic murders, as though they had so many these ones needed a label. Parrish laid both elbows down onto the counter and studied me with unabashed curiosity. I waited, giving her my own brand of study.

"You the real deal?" she said, finally.

I didn't need to answer. Garder snagged her elbow and yanked her away from the counter.

"You promised me another look at the women," he said. "Let's move before your boss can get in and raid the staff fridge."

He tugged her along with him and while she let him hurry her along, she cast a look back over her shoulder at me.

"I'll see you later, Brie," she said. "Maybe I'll come back for a reading and see if you can convert me."

Usually, I would take that challenge, but I didn't think I'd be able to slip past her bullshit radar and I had to admit I didn't want to take on the task. Besides, I didn't think I wanted to visit any traumas she might be hiding behind. I had a feeling they were as vast as my own.

I followed the two of them to the door, though, intending to lock it behind them.

"See you," Parrish said with a wave.

I waved back and set my attention on Detective Garder, who nodded at me, his gaze lingering long enough to turn that molten honey color again. A sweep of heat rushed my chest at that look but thankfully, he turned away before the full flush of it hit my face.

They ambled down the sidewalk, heading toward a car parked just a block away where a few meter-free parking spots existed for service vehicles.

I was left alone to putter around the shop and get ready for Sherry to pick up her spell. That meant I had to gather multiple things from cupboards and shelves.

It was a meditative thing and part of the job I enjoyed the most. I could check out my brain and settle into making something that would have an old world feel but still look interesting. The parchment and wax was part of that design and I had multiple seals to use depending on the need, but I usually impressed my brand on each seal.

Black wax seemed the most fitting this time, and I was pressing the amulet's shape into a glob of hot wax when the doorbell rang over the shop door.

Apparently, I'd been so engrossed in Officer Hottie that I'd forgotten to actually turn the lock.

"Sorry," I said peeking up from my work, my fingers still wrapped around the seal's handle. "I'm not quite open yet."

The man who met my gaze was already several feet inside. I had time to notice he was as tall as the door before he lifted a rusty scythe to chest height.

"Perfect," he said. "Because I doubt you'd want anyone to see what I do with this."

CHAPTER EIGHT

THIS WAS A SCYTHE the size of a cartoon grim reaper's, but it looked far more deadly. I took one look at him and knew I was dead. Soul's Harbor was a tourist trap in the summer, and while it fostered a few farmers, the surrounding area was more fishery than agriculture. I couldn't think of any other reason for him to be brandishing a scythe in my shop except that here was a man who wanted to kill another psychic.

I held up my hands, already scanning past him to measure the distance from where I stood to the door and out into the street, where I was willing to bet I'd be safer than locked inside with him.

My mind ran over the amount of time it had been since Garder and Parrish had left. Would they have got so far away that calling them back would be useless, or would screaming like a banshee be my best bet? Should I take my chances and head for the back room? And where in the hot blue blazes had I left my cell phone, anyway?

"I'm not sure what you need," I said, hedging as I inched sideways.

Apparently, my feet had decided for me and were heading for the back room. I had my doubts that the beaded curtain separating it from the shop proper would make an excellent barrier, but I knew the nooks and crannies of the place. I could navigate it much faster than he could.

"It might be best if you came back in a half hour?"

He advanced on me, bobbing the scythe up and down in his grip as though he was testing the weight of it, the sturdiness.

"I can't come back," he said. "I need to finish this right now."

That was far too terrifying. My heart rate ticked up enough that I felt it in my throat. Even so, it wouldn't fuel my legs with any oxygen. Some part of me was yelling at my legs to move, but it was a heavy sensation, one that might have been slogging through water. I had the feeling I was gawking at him, wide-eyed and paralyzed, but couldn't do more than blink.

I'd heard about the effects of adrenaline but never suffered it myself until that moment. They weren't kidding when they say you are frozen to your spot.

I had just given up on it all and piss myself, hoping to disgust him enough to leave me alone, when a croak moved through my throat. It built to a full-throated sound that shouted out a series of bald curses, but it didn't sound like it was coming from me.

It took me several seconds of opening and closing my mouth like a suffocating fish before I realized it wasn't me yelling at all. Someone else was doing all the shouting. From outside the shop. Loudly. Enough that it caught the man inside's attention.

"Fraud," someone shouted. "Don't go in there. She's a fraud. She steals you blind."

The man in the shop swung around, the scythe sweeping a graceful arc through the air as he moved. The movement wafted the smell of grass at me. At the clarity of the aroma, my brain finally registered it had a life's purpose and messaged my legs to move damn you, move.

Although they'd freed themselves of the paralysis enough to lift my feet, something else held me back. Doubt.

What if running triggered some predatory instinct in the intruder? What if he liked the chase, the thrill of the catch?

So despite the strain of wanting desperately to run like the wind, I forced myself to move slowly to freedom. I edged away from the counter. One step. Two. Three.

My skin prickled with fear. The back of my neck went clammy. Just a few more feet and if his attention was diverted enough, I'd have gained enough ground to run for it and bet I could out-pace him.

The shouting continued and by the time I'd made it halfway across the distance to the back room, the door flew open with enough force to hit the wall on the other side. The man in the shop dropped the scythe to his side as whoever had been outside barged in.

It was a perfect opportunity for me to bolt, finally, out back and run for safety. Call the cops. Call Garder. Call someone.

But something stopped me.

Whoever this rude intruder was, he didn't deserve to come face to face with a murderer. I couldn't just leave him there. I was a charlatan and a cheat, but I was no monster.

I swallowed my fear and swung to face them both, praying that the man with the scythe would think twice about committing any sort of violence if he also had to take out a man to get off Scot-free.

I smothered the nagging thoughts that he'd killed three women already by reminding myself he'd taken them one by one, not all together. There was nothing to indicate he'd kill me with a customer in my shop. That was the only thing that kept me from fleeing out the back way.

Even so, the fear was strong. I had to force myself to recall those women as they hung from the hoist because the very act of the assault done to them was clear enough evidence to me he didn't like witnesses, the killer. He wanted to savor the violence.

While it wasn't a soothing thought to imagine the man in my shop just a few feet away from me, hunched over a vulnerable belly with a blade, it did at least bolster me enough to pull in a long breath as the intruder slammed the door closed behind him.

I had time to think that here was the culprit who'd vandalized my shop before he cleared a chair of pillows, sweeping his arm across the seat and flinging the cushions to the floor. They landed with soft sounds that were a stark contrast to the gritty, flushed look of him.

He was skinny, this one. His mop of strawberry hair looked greasy, and it stuck up in mats that indicated he'd not been sleeping well. He would be handsome if not in such a rage.

He gave the barest of glances to the scythe man, and for a second, I thought there might have been some silent communication, but then he stormed across the shop and left me gaping at him in stupefied confusion.

He stabbed at me with a filthy finger, got in my face, and spit sprayed over my shoulder.

"You," he yelled. "You fucking fraud."

I recoiled instinctively in the face of that anger. I wasn't typically easy to scare but I was in the shop with two men. Alone. Whatever his intentions were, I didn't think they included cutting my belly open. He didn't even have a knife. The worst he'd do was hit me maybe, and although I didn't relish a blow to the cheek, the vandal didn't deserve to end up dead at the hands of a killer.

That didn't mean I would be so foolish as to stay there with two angry men. My best bet was to position myself so I could get out and try to draw him along with me. Maybe try to get them both out into the open air where the owners of the other shops might be arriving to open for the day. Witnesses. I needed witnesses.

I so badly wanted to check the time to see how close it was to the other stores opening, but I still couldn't remember where I'd dropped my phone. So I held up my hands, compliant, surrendering for the moment.

"Please," I said in as soothing voice as I could muster, inching away for each step he took, aiming myself toward the front of the shop. "I'm sorry you're upset. I'm sure whatever is bothering you, we can work it out."

I knew telling him to calm down was going to accomplish the exact opposite. I was acutely aware of the first customer and just where he was relative to where I stood.

Too close, was what my mind was telling me. Had he advanced along with the second man? Had I misjudged and the two of them were working together?

My throat clogged up. I saw my mistake for what it was and that feeling of being a deer in the headlights slammed back into me. I could barely blink let alone move.

"Please," I said but didn't get any further before the vandal lunged toward me.

I couldn't get out of the way, I was so busy trying to work out why he would paint my door with blood and filth instead of paint if he was just an innocent vandal, or where he would get blood in the first place, whether or not he was part of a murderous pair that I didn't manage to even throw up a hand to defend myself when he grabbed for me.

And then it was too late. He had his hands on my neck.

A shriek tore from the congestion of my throat. I hadn't expected him to touch me, let alone wrap his hands on my neck. I was dumbfounded. And still I tried to reason with him. Like a fool, I couldn't fathom any other way through.

The whole world funneled down to that one foot of distance. Any other worry or concern I had evaporated when my teeth clacked together so hard I bit down on my tongue.

He was shaking me, not strangling me. Not that it was much better. I felt his fingers digging into my skin and knew there'd be a bruise if he didn't flat out kill me.

Something fell with a thud to the floor behind us. I heard the scuffling of shoes on wood.

The hands wrenched away from my neck, hooking on the leather cord of my amulet as they released.

"Let it go," said a male voice from behind my attacker. Raspy, as though he'd smoked cigars from the time he was a toddler. But raspy as it was, it was filled with command and I expected the intruder to do exactly as he said.

The thug yanked harder on the amulet. It chafed into my skin and I had to step closer to him to put slack into the necklace.

"Move," scythe man said to me. "Duck. Run. Doesn't matter what you do. Just get out of the way."

I didn't question the order. I ducked just as the scythe man shoved the intruder, and it gave me just enough freedom to spin when he let go the amulet. My feet moved automatically, with every intention of getting clear even though I had no idea where I was going to run to.

I'd lost my geography of the room. Was I facing the curtain or the door?

I fell to my knees, and decided to crawl out of reach. Anything...I'd do anything to get away.

To hell with the man and the killer. They could have each other as far as I was concerned. When I thought I was safely out of range of both of them, I rolled to my feet and grabbed for the nearest thing to protect myself. It turned out to be the handle of the scythe.

It was heavy, awkward to hold until I found its fulcrum, where it rested neatly and well-balanced in my grip.

I squared my shoulders and planted my feet. Come at me, I thought. Just you come at me.

But the two were not interested in me anymore. The vandal, small as he was, gave a quick feint and a snap of a jab. He neatly avoided the round house swing from scythe man, but in doing so, he fell against one of shelves filled with candles.

It toppled over, him falling with it. He stared up at the scythe man, his face filled with rage and fear. When he climbed over the pile of pillar candles to stand, one of them rolled beneath his feet. He fell hard on his ass.

Scythe man pinned the vandal with a gaze that made me quake. There was something primitive in it, something predatory and violent.

Strawberry held his ground, mentally at least. He was still trying to get to his feet amid the mounds of rolling candles.

"Thou shalt not suffer a witch to live," he said, "only to raise her on the third day."

Oh, great. Misquoted Bible references. Just the thing to make you look like a rational human being.

"I'm not a witch," I said, feeling the offense through my terror.

Scythe man looked at me over his shoulder.

I squared my shoulder defiantly at his what-the-hell look.

"Witches are for Halloween," I said. "I'm a woman of power. There's a difference."

"You're a fucking con is what," Strawberry yelled as he struggled to his feet. "That's all. Nothing more."

That earned him a backhanded cuff from Scythe man's elbow when he finally stood. As he reeled from the blow, his feet found solid purchase and he used the momentum to propel himself toward the shop door.

He turned to look over his shoulder when he reached the threshold. "You'll regret this," he said. "You'll end up dead if you're not careful."

Dead. I stared at him for a moment, not sure whether I could memorize every detail of his face but knowing, just knowing this man who had vandalized my shop...he was the killer.

He darted a hateful look at the man with the scythe and curled his lip. "She's a fake," he said as if he needed the man to hear it one last time, then he slipped out and fled across the street.

I watched him go with a vague impression that I was trembling. I raced across the store to see which direction he'd gone but there was no trace of him. I turned slowly, in a daze to face the man I'd thought was a killer. I didn't realize how tightly I was clenching the handle of the scythe until the customer eased it out of my grip.

That was when I discovered it wasn't a scythe at all, just a fist-thick walking stick clenched in my knotted fist. I blinked at the cane in confusion.

"You can let go," he said. "He's gone."

I lifted my gaze from the stick that wasn't a scythe at all to his eyes. Black, I noted. Totally in contrast to the bramble of wheat-colored hair. The posture I'd mistaken for aggression was just the muscle of a man who had a body hardened by manual labor. But really, a man that muscled shouldn't need a walking stick, now should he?

I stole a look at his leg, thinking maybe he had a sore foot, trying to remember if I'd seen him limp. A wash of nausea swept over me as I realized how foolish I'd been. How had I mistaken such a simple thing as a walking stick for a dangerous weapon?

I breathed in shallow gulps as I realized how badly the whole murder thing was getting to me. Like hallucinating the ghosts before, the blink back to reality was dizzying.

I dragged my gaze from the customer and his walking stick with great effort and lifted it to the window in an attempt to release the last of the adrenaline.

Sunlight streamed through the windows and the streets had begun to fill. Several tourists with disposable coffee cups were gathered in front of my window, peering into different shops, waiting for them to open.

"Thanks," I mumbled and let him take the handle of the cane.

I didn't have the energy to hold onto it anymore, and I figured if he'd protected me from the freak, he wasn't likely to kill me. The shame of letting the adrenaline of the last day get to me and presume he was a murderer put a knot in my throat. Or was that the knowledge that I'd just been attacked?

I sagged backwards and caught the edge of my gorgeous wooden counter. My palm struck something small and hard. My cell phone. I almost laughed.

"You alright?" he said, and he didn't look the least bit threatening now that I wasn't quite so terrified.

I was aware I was shaking my head instead of nodding, but I said yes anyway and tacked on a, "Thank you."

He shrugged. "No problem."

I put my fingers to my temples, feeling a dilly of a headache coming on fast and hard. "I'm not sure what you're looking for, but I don't think I can help you today," I said. "That took all the stuffing out of me."

I thought he might argue, but he plunked his walking stick on the floor and tapped the wooden boards three times.

"I'll come back another time," he said.

"I can book you if you need something special." I scooped to pick up one of the candles.

It smelled of frankincense and myrrh. I'd labeled it the Baby Jesus Candle, and it was one of my best sellers. I held it out to him.

"Please," I said. "Take this as a thanks."

He pulled his shoulder back, not a jerk or a spasm, just a subtle enough movement that I pulled the gift back against my chest. Maybe he'd had a bad encounter with fire. Perhaps a candle had accidentally caught something alight during his youth. Because he was nervous about it. Sometimes people were. It usually came down to some childhood trauma.

"I'd rather not. I'll just come back later." His gaze fell to the candle and then he grinned, backing away a step. "Can't take the smell."

That explained his aversion. So many people now were allergic to environmental scents that I felt foolish for shoving the thing at him without considering that. I dropped it onto the counter. He was already heading to the door. A moment more and he'd be gone and I really felt like I owed him.

Wait," I said and rounded the counter to pull out my appointment book from beneath. "You want a reading? Free of charge as a thanks."

He stopped at the door, his hand on the knob as the door yawned open.

"Sure," he said.

I knew my book was empty the next few days and an hour of my time wasn't too much to ask for a guy who had helped me out. I noted a date for him, a few days away to give us both time to prepare, and crossed the store so I could close and lock door behind him when he left.

I hadn't lied. I really was all in. He stood on the other side for a long moment, watching me and I smiled tentatively. He tipped the cane to his forehead the way a gentleman might tip his hat, and then he shouldered his way through a cluster of young tourists that had gathered at the hemp shop across the street.

I found myself smiling as I watched him make his way down the street, prodding the sidewalk with the walking stick with each step.

After the awfulness of the day before, it was encouraging to feel positive about something, that there was good still in the world. I was happy to be reminded of it.

But even as I scanned the area around me, feeling chuffed that I could repay a kindness, I noticed the dog again.

Except this time it wasn't sitting there, watching me.

It was dead.

CHAPTER NINE

I'D SEEN TOO MANY dead dogs in my day to mistake the corpse of the stray as it lay on the sidewalk. As badly as I wanted to run to it, I had to fight back all the memories that wanted to flood in when I saw it lying there, not moving.

I struggled to wrestle those recollections where they belonged, back in the recesses of a fogged over memory, blanketed with audio wool and darkened by shadows so thick you could coat a street with the tar black of them.

I was not waking in the middle of the night to a sound that scared me and had me padding from my bed to the top of the basement stairs. Without a daddy anymore to make me feel safe, I was scared all the time, worried that whatever had taken him from me would take me too.

This was not the basement of my childhood.

This was the middle of a street with streaks of sunlight slanting down onto buildings and early walkers.

This time, I might be able to do something for that poor dog.

Even knowing those things, I still couldn't force myself out into my shop. I felt the same paralysis I had on that night so long ago when I'd found my mother in our basement crouched over the body of a small puppy she'd bought from a pet store.

I smelled again that strange scent of mingled wet cement and scorched wax. The stink of burning hair. I nearly gagged on the cell memory of those smells as I tried to make myself take a step over the threshold and into the street.

I'd told myself back then I would intervene when I could. If I just got old enough, I'd help whoever or whatever was suffering, and yet here I was clutching the door frame as that stray lay there, alone on the sidewalk.

My eyes stung, and not just because I felt bad for the poor beast. My hand trembled enough that when I finally was able to let go the door frame, I had a hard time letting it hang without shaking. I had to tuck my hand beneath my armpit and take several deep breaths.

Maybe I was wrong about the dog. Surely pedestrians wouldn't just walk by it like they were if it was dead. After all that had just happened, I had to be imagining things.

I advanced one step and leaned forward, hoping to get a better view.

I recoiled at what met my gaze.

Its mouth hung open. The poor thing's tongue dragged on the ground.

Dead. Yes. Undoubtedly so. That great enormous beast that had shadowed my doorstep for the last few days, that I'd left bowls of food out for and buckets of water to drink, took at least three quarters of the sidewalk and yet people just walked right on by.

When a woman, obviously a tourist by the way she was dressed in expensive sneakers and huge shopping bag, stepped over it as though it wasn't even there, rage boiled in my chest.

"Have some respect," I shouted, clutching my throat instead of the door behind me.

She tossed me a confounded glance but she didn't so much as double back to look at the body she'd just goose stepped over. I almost barged at her, furious, but two steps forward and I knew I couldn't do it.

Cell memory was in the driver's seat right then, and residual adrenaline from my confrontation with strawberry hair was riding shotgun.

I should go out there, but I couldn't.

But what if someone decided to report it and it got picked up by DNR and tossed into a burn pit or something? I couldn't live with myself if I let that happen. I even left food for the seagulls though they were pests and my neighbors sent me cease and desist letters over it.

The thought of that stray being dishonored so got my muscles moving, but instead of running out into the street, I retreated and tore back across my shop to the counter.

I grabbed my phone and with shaking fingers, texted the only person I could think of who might be able to stop that from happening.

"Not on my watch," I said to myself as the text sent. I waited, my foot tapping, for a response. "Come on, Garder."

His reply was taking too long. I leaned backwards, looking out the shop door. I couldn't see the dog from my vantage and had to inch back toward the door.

I glanced at my phone again. He had replied: I'll be there in ten.

Ten minutes. It wasn't long but it felt like an eternity. My chest had broken into a sweat while I'd stood there. I could smell my own perspiration. A splash of water. That was what I needed. Cool, wet water on my face, under my arms. I'd feel better then, less like puking or passing out.

Now that the worst was over and I knew Garder was on his way, my legs were as solid as wet teabags as I headed for the bathroom. I barely recognized my face when I looked in the mirror. The skin had a pallor to it that unnerved me, and my pupils were so large I worried Garder would think I'd been smoking up while he'd been gone.

I ran the cold faucet long enough that the water that streamed out would be icy cold. I dipped my hands in and splashed my face, then wet a paper towel and ran it beneath my shirt, swiping over my armpits and between my breasts.

I felt much better then. I even looked passable. My hair could use a bit of water to refresh the putty I'd put in to separate the strands, but that was just vanity and a dog was dead, for Pete's sake.

I opted to run my damp hands through my hair just to feel the coolness on my scalp. I blew out a bracing breath just as my door chime rang. When Garder called out for me, I shook out my hands and left the bathroom, bracing myself for the inevitable growl and glower.

"I didn't know who else to call," I said partly because it was true. The other part didn't want to admit why I'd thought of him in the first place.

In the back of my mind, I told myself it was because on the heels of the intruder's attack; I considered filing a report, but I knew that wasn't true. The man had been worried about his wife, was all. I didn't expect him back, not after the nice walking stick man had run him off so effectively. Besides: I was pretty sure all my reaction had been amplified by the stress of the last few days.

"Where's the body?" he asked, scanning the shop with a narrowed and expert gaze. "Did you call 911?"

"911?" I asked, bewildered. "I don't think they'd do anything for him."

"Well, no," he said. "It would be too late to do much to help him, but it is standard procedure."

"Really? I always thought the dog catcher picked them up." I crossed the shop. "And I just didn't want to think about what might happen to him if they did."

"The dogcatcher?" I could swear his nostrils opened wider, that he took in a little extra air as though he thought he could smell the answer. "What are you talking about?"

I pointed toward the door. "The dog. You had to have passed right by it."

He ran his fingers up and down his midriff, scratching thoughtfully.

He rocked back on his heels, giving me ample view of his chin and the way it lifted in egotistical study of the way I stood there with my hands wringing together. I noticed for the first time since he'd entered the shop that his brown eyes were melted into liquid honey.

"I'm confused," he said. "Ten minutes ago I got a text that said, 'he's dead. I need help'."

I felt foolish at the way he said it and I squared my shoulders defiantly because if I balked I knew he'd make me feel guilty. There was nothing to feel guilty about.

"He *is* dead. And I *do* need help." I stormed my way to the door and pointed toward the street. "That poor thing is just lying there."

I realized my hand was shaking again and it was visible in the way my arm trembled. I pulled it back and hugged my elbows.

"I can't just leave it. You have to help me bury it at least."

I watched as that smoldering look of annoyance transformed to concern.

"There was no dog out there," he said and approached me, a bit too cautiously I thought. The floorboards creaked beneath his weight. He stopped several feet away, as though he was afraid to come closer. "And there certainly isn't one lying dead on the sidewalk."

If he was teasing me, I didn't like it at all. Instead of replying, I pushed the door open so he could see out into the street and if that wasn't enough, I'd shove him outside and kick his ass all the way to the sidewalk.

"Come over here," I said, gesturing him over. "He's right there. Just look."

I waited, keeping my cool despite the temper riding the edges of grief. "Well?"

He sighed heavily but approached all the same. He held my gaze with his and something in his eyes made my throat constrict.

"There aren't many people who can order me around," he said with what sounded like a note of threat, but he leaned out the doorway, his broad palm resting on the frame to support him.

"You're that much of a bully, huh?" I said, trying not to let my gaze linger on the way his shirt stretched taut as he moved, outlining his back muscles against the material. Now that he was here, I was feeling less panicked about the dog, at least, but his proximity was making me antsy.

A thoughtful sound rumbled from his pursed lips as he retreated back into the shop and leaned against the door frame, facing me. One foot crossed over the other as he echoed the posture with his arms.

"A bully takes advantage of powerless women," he said with a twitch of the corner of his mouth. "I prefer to let powerful women take advantage of me."

I let go the same thoughtful sound at the way he said it. Was it an invitation? An innuendo? He certainly looked as though he was struggling not to smile. Mocking me, I supposed.

"So," I said. "Tell me what you saw."

"A pretty hot looking tourist in butt-cut shorts," he said with a sensual drawl in his voice. He craned his neck to peer back out into the street. "Maybe I should go arrest her for indecent exposure."

"The dog," I said flatly, directing his attention to the real issue, tired of the game already. I just wanted to get the dog taken care of and then go home. I didn't have a single appointment in my book and the whole morning had drained me. "Are you going to help me get it out of the street?"

"There's no dog out there," he said. "Trust me. I have great eyes and a pretty good nose for foul play."

When he turned back to me, humor and something else danced in his eyes. His gaze dropped to my throat and I had the feeling that I should be lifting my chin, exposing the skin to him. I shook off the sensation and leaned past him to pan the street.

I saw the backside of the tourist he spoke of about a dozen yards up the street. Her shorts were cut so high, I could see the curve of her ass beneath the hem. A dock worker strode with purpose toward the docks, his insulated bag of lunch swinging in time with his steps. He stopped mid stride to watch her sashay up the street.

I turned away, annoyed at the bald look of lust on his face. Shopkeepers along the block were putting their sandwich board signs out for the day and chalking them.

But the space where the dog had lain was empty. Pedestrians walked right over it without so much as a pause.

"He was right there," I said, swinging my gaze back to Garder and throwing my hands up in surrender. "I swear, Officer."

There was something about the way he was watching me that made me feel guilty.

He pushed off from the door frame and laid his hand on my shoulder. It was warm and comforting, and downright annoying.

"Please," he said with a sober note that was both throaty and commanding. "Under the circumstances, I think you better call me Layne"

"And what circumstances are those," I asked, plucking his fingers from my shoulders. Damn his hands were so rough, like a laborer's might me. It was all I could do not to imagine them running over my bare skin.

His mouth twitched. "It's alright if you want to see me again, Ms. Duncan, but you don't have to keep making up emergencies to do so."

Hot humiliated fury burned in my chest at the words. I wanted to say he was the last person I wanted nosing around my business, but the flush in my neck that climbed as high as my cheeks said otherwise.

"Well, Layne," I said, borrowing the energy from the flustered reaction to shoulder past him into the open air of the sidewalk. "Maybe you don't see anything now, but that dog was there." I spun to face him in challenge.

His hand burrowed into his pants pocket and came out with a package of gum that smelled strongly of mint. He unpeeled the piece from its wrapper as he watched me so intently I felt a squirm start up in my spine. Somewhere over the docks, a seagull shrieked in hunger, but Layne remained silent.

I fidgeted, no matter how badly I wanted to keep still. It was a shrewd tactic, one I'd employed myself often enough. You wait and the other person eventually gives in, spilling words into the gap of silence. Great if you want to get them to start talking. Horrible if you were on the other end and didn't know what to say.

So because I knew saying nothing gave me an edge, I started to pull the door closed to abandon him inside the store behind a barricade of glass and steel. Let him decide whether he wanted to follow or end up getting jammed between the doorframe and door when I hauled it closed.

The door whistled shut just in time to avoid catching on his arm. I didn't smile to myself. Not even if it eased the dread feeling weighing down my shoulders. That would be uncharitable. And I was a cheat and a con, but I was not a monster.

But now that the desire to hurt him had lifted, I wanted to satisfy myself that I hadn't been seeing things with the dog. I didn't exactly want the stray to have met an unfortunate end, but neither did I want to have to confess to hallucinations, not when he already thought I was in the habit of making myself any mocha coffee. The ghosts and the scythe were bad enough. I felt I also owed it to myself to know for sure.

I pressed my fingers to my forehead, feeling the pressure of the headache growing with each step to where the stray had lain. I felt Layne behind me, a heavy, heady presence that dogged my steps.

By the time I stood in the middle of the sidewalk, with people breezing past me, wafting perfumes and aftershave and fragrances of morning coffee from broad rimmed travel mugs, I was dizzy.

"He was right here," I said and swung around in a circle, scuffing my soles along the pavement.

There was no blood. No wet spot of any sort to mark fluid. There was just this hanging, cloying scent of boiled eggs and cabbage.

"Sulfur," Layne said, almost to himself.

"What's that?" I said, my brow squeezing together as a pain lanced across my forehead. Reflex sent my hand to my head and I held onto the front of it with a cupped palm.

His hand ran over the small of my back, too intimate for a detective, but also so comforting, I couldn't bear to move away. Without thinking, I leaned on him just briefly enough to feel the warmth of his chest. And when I realized with horror what I'd done, I jerked away, almost twisting my ankle on the uneven crack in the sidewalk.

"You moved it," I said, looking at him. "You must have. Before you came into the shop."

He shook his head. "Why would I bother to move a stray dog when I thought you were being attacked?"

The comment sprung loose the fact that I had been attacked, and the truth of it must have been written all over my face because he gripped my elbow, his fingers caressing the inside as he said, "What is it? You smell afraid."

I lifted my gaze to his,and the barely disguised anger in it flustered me. "I don't know how to say this,"

"Just say it."

So I did. I explained about the vandal right there in the street with my shoulders shaking until he pulled me in against his chest. Neither of us said anything for a moment while I collected myself. I felt his heart beating fast against my cheek. I left out the part about seeing a weapon where a walking stick had been because it was all too confusing.

"I'll have to find him," Garder said of the first man. "Get his statement."

I pulled away at the note of brisk efficiency in his voice. I avoided his eye, feeling awkward that I'd leaned on him now that he was back to the suspicious detective. I rubbed my arms and hugged them against my chest.

"He'll be back. I made him an appointment but I didn't get any information. Just booked him as Knight in shining armor. I'll get you the time and date."

He made a sound low in his throat that sounded distinctly displeased. It annoyed me that he would be put off by my assessment of a man who had saved me probably from certain death.

"So how did you get here so fast?" I demanded. "You said ten minutes. It was more like five." I didn't say that if he was so close he might have caught the guy. I wasn't the kind of girl to rub it in no matter how badly I wanted to.

He fidgeted, his eyes dropping to the sidewalk and scanning the area around my feet as he answered. He paused to take the gum from his mouth and press it into the wrapper that was still in his fist.

"I was on my way back here, actually," he said.

"Now who couldn't wait to see who again?" I said and started to give him my own brand of cocky smile, but he turned away to toss the gum in its wrapper toward the open-mouth trash bin nearby. It missed.

He didn't shift his gaze fast enough for me to avoid seeing the expression that crossed his face. A grim line to his mouth that had nothing to do with not hitting the target with his wrapper.

"What's going on?" I said.

He leveled me with that direct stare and I grimaced as I caught the scent of sulfur again. The trash bin must be ready to be collected.

He shoved both hands in his pockets and rocked back on his heels.

"I was coming to see you because another psychic has been found dead."

CHAPTER TEN

THE WOMAN DIED HOLDING onto her own intestines. Whoever had pulled her from her shop and dragged her out into the back alley and sat her up like a macabre yuppie camper in front of a campfire had done it without leaving another mark on her except for the slit from sternum to pubis.

I gagged when I saw her, but I kept it together so long as I skirted to the side and kept her in my peripheral vision. It was so much worse seeing her propped up against the wall of her own shop, with her shirt flapping open at her sides, than it was seeing the first murder scene.

I didn't think Layne knew it was as bad as it was when he asked me to accompany him. I was sure he didn't expect the scene to still be fresh and the woman bared to her observers when we arrived because he swore in a way I'd not heard from anyone in all my days.

"Cover that up," he barked at the uniformed officer taking notes.

Unperturbed, the policeman looked at Layne from the side. "Can't," he said. "M.E. said not to disturb the scene and since it's out of sight of the public, we just cordoned it all off."

I noted the cars pulling in tight to obliterate the view from the one gap in the street where buildings didn't obscure. Several flunkies were hauling out screens from trucks and standing them around the scene.

We were at the apex of a three-way crossroads, with the building spanning the breadth of the connection. On either side, the streets bustled with activity, but the buildings that lined them kept the area where Iris sat looking at her entrails private.

It couldn't be coincidence.

Layne looked at me with concern in his face, and I realized I was muttering to myself.

"I'm sorry, Ms. Duncan," he said. "I didn't expect this."

He guided me away so that I was at the edge of the yellow tape.

"Brie," I said. "Just call me Brie. If we're going to be picking through other women's secrets, you best use my given name."

"Brie it is, then," he said, not unkindly. "We'll do what we need to here and when I need your eyes, I'll come for you." He leaned down to peer into my face. "Do you need to sit down?"

"I know her," I said. The familiar flood of water into the back of my cheeks told me I was going to vomit again if I wasn't careful. "Iris. That's her name."

I tried not to think about her eyes when I said that. They'd been so wide, so terrified. I shuddered.

His warm palm ran to the back of my neck and he exerted a gentle pressure. Something in my body went slack.

"It's okay," he murmured, and I realized he was trying to force my head between my knees. "You won't faint, but if you need to puke, mind the shoes."

I was grateful for the bad joke and hinged forward. The blackness I hadn't realized was taking over my vision peeled back like a blanket. The prickling in my skin abated. I sighed out a relief I didn't know I needed.

"Better?" he said.

I nodded at my feet.

"I don't think I can look at...that," I said, refusing to say the word *her* because if I thought about what I was seeing in terms of humanity, I didn't think I'd be able to sleep ever again. I didn't want to think about Iris as a person right then. I just couldn't.

"You don't need to look at her," he said and I noted he used the pronoun when I couldn't. Maybe he was used to the sights of dead bodies and violence, or maybe he refused to let what the killer had done to her take away her humanity.

Whatever the reason, right then, I admired him for it.

I peered up at him. The concern in his expression echoed in his eyes as he met my gaze. There was something moving in the depths of the brown, a molten sort of motion that made me think of gold being melted and reshaped.

"She was a good woman," I said, thinking even if she was a fraud, it didn't mean she was a reprobate. "She welcomed me to the community when I came home."

He crouched on the pavement next to me and I eased myself down onto my bottom so I could let the trembling tension in my thighs dissolve.

"What was her specialty?" he said quietly, and I realized just how good he might be as a detective under the right conditions. His voice soothed me.

I thought about the woman's shop, pulling to mind the signage outside. She had a cute logo of a woman peering into a dark tunnel.

"Medium," I said. "She called to the dead for people."

"Was she the real deal?" he asked.

I glanced at him, trying to assess what he was rooting for and decided he wasn't testing me, just looking for information.

"Real deals are rare," I said with a defiant lift to my chin just the same. "And even they aren't foolproof."

"So you told me before. It's not always a controllable gift, is that what you said?" He started to reach toward my ear but paused with his hand hovering beside my temple.

"You have a gum wrapper stuck in your hair," he said. "Do you mind if I take it out?"

I shook my head and waited poised, as he extracted a crinkled bit of paper and showed it to me.

"I have no idea how that got there." I reached for it but he pulled it away, just out of reach.

"Some magic is practiced," he said. "Ten thousand hours or something like that."

I narrowed my gaze at him. "There wasn't a gum wrapper in my hair at all, was there?"

He wadded the paper and tucked it into his pocket. "Just a bit of sleight of hand," he said. "Good distraction. Works for kids. Can't tell you how many times I've managed to escape a crying jag with that little trick."

I tried to imagine him comforting a child and was surprised to find it wasn't a long walk at all.

"If she was the real thing, I should know," he went on. "That kind of detail can make all the difference. Is the killer taking out frauds or is he dissatisfied with a service, or does he really believe the women had power?"

He pushed himself to his feet and held out his hand for me to take.

I shook him off and shrugged before attempting to rise on my own steam. I wiped my backside with my palms, hoping I hadn't sat in something awful. A vague sense that I'd missed something niggled the back of my mind, but I couldn't place it.

"So you believe in her," I said. "In the real thing being possible."

I toed the asphalt casually, trying not to give away that I didn't believe it in the least or that I was fishing for how he'd think about me if he discovered I was a fake too.

"Any information can be the thing that cracks open motive and motive can crack open a case. I don't want to see any more women die."

It wasn't an odd answer, but it wasn't exactly an answer to my question, either. I wondered if he was the sort that believed in ghosts or bogeymen, but he didn't look the type. Too practical. Too cloaked in the everyday horrors of the world to have time to wrap himself in the make believe of the other.

I knew one thing was certain, though. If he didn't believe in magic, he thought the killer did. He would not have involved a civilian like me otherwise.

I didn't need to agree with him, and I didn't think he expected it. I turned away so I wouldn't catch any of the activity around Iris in my peripheral vision. He didn't miss the subtle angling of my body.

"You don't need to look at her," he said again. "I'll have them cover her."

"If I don't need to look at her, how can I tell you what you need to know?"

It was too late, though. I'd seen a good deal. Part of what made me good at reading people was the fact that I took in a lot of information and processed it pretty damn quickly. Just like I had the first tableau at the docks. But there were differences in this scene, and if I noticed them as a layperson, he was sure to as well.

For one, that tableau was carefully concealed with tarps and I'd only got glimpses of the women, but I'd caught sight of their viscera pulled out and coiled beneath them. Iris had been propped up in front of a propane brazier with a rack over top.

I was willing to bet there was a number there somewhere, too. Just the way there had been with the first scene.

I watched Layne watching me, his jaw working the three squares of gum he'd shoved in a moment before.

"What I need from you is what you think he's after. What can you see in the tableau that might indicate his motive?"

A flash of Sherry's husband went through my mind and I shoved it aside impatiently. This act was one of intention and premeditation. What happened with Sherry's husband was no more than an irate man confronting a fraud. Maybe if he came back, I'd mention it to Layne or file a report. For now, there didn't seem to be a point, and with another woman dead, adding my trivial customer issue didn't seem right.

"You're thinking it's a he," I said. "You're sure it's a man."

He shrugged. "I've never known a woman to roast someone's insides on a barbecue pit."

My jaw tightened as I pushed aside the flash of memory that told me exactly the opposite. If I concentrated, I could still smell dog hair burning.

He watched my reaction and presumed my nervous shuffling had to do with his comment. When he apologized for being so graphic, I waved off the worry.

"It's alright," I said. No sense raising that old welt to the surface of my skin anymore. I was free of the trauma. My therapist in Nova Scotia had said so. "No one ever died from the truth."

He sighed heavily as he glanced past the yellow tape. "Doesn't mean the truth doesn't hurt," he said. "Look. Parrish is here. I need to go. You'll be okay? Why don't you rest a bit, then go for a coffee? We'll be here all day and you can come back when you're ready. We'll talk then."

I dared one look over his shoulder and saw Parrish's orange bandanna bobbing about the crime scene as she inspected Iris's body with her hands on her hips. Even from this distance, I could make out her glaring at the corpse like she thought the woman committed the atrocity to herself.

When I didn't say anything, Layne made to head toward her, and I hooked his arm before he could get too far.

"There is something," I said. "It might not be important, but it's something I know for sure. I smelled sulfur."

He nodded. "Me too. And wet dog. That's a pretty distinctive smell. Hard to miss, really."

I hadn't caught the scent of animal at all but I had the sulfur. It was a pretty strong scent and I presumed he'd smelled it too, but he might not know the significance of it.

"It's used for transformation," I said, peeling the information from the mental folder I kept when I'd researched everything I needed to open a psychic shop. "Witches burn it to cleanse an area before they cast a spell, and if they are seeking to bring about a change, they burn it during the casting."

He nodded as his expression lit up. He stuck his fingers in his mouth and pulled out the wad of gum and stuck it to the bricks, jamming it into a hole in the grout of the brickwork.

"Sure," he said. "That's helpful."

I smiled for him, grateful for the comment in light of the selfish motives I'd had in agreeing to help in the first place. I watched him stride away, hugging my torso. He faced me for several steps at first, his gaze on mine, before he showed me his back. When he did, I leaned against the building and let my legs slide out from beneath me again.

I knew each of the dead psychics claimed to be as real as I did. Did that mean I would be on the kill list eventually? And how long before that someone sought me out?

I thought of the vandalism on my shop and the man who had tried to strangle me with my own amulet. My fingers went to it as I sat there. I rolled it absently between my finger and thumb, feeling the etching of the design as I pressed deep into the surface with the pad of my finger.

Maybe I was being too nonchalant about the attack in my shop. My instincts were usually pretty good and I'd trusted them for years because they never steered me wrong. What made this time any different except that I didn't want Layne to think I was the victim of my own mocha coffee when I knew I'd been seeing strange things. I never saw strange things. Ghosts, scythes, dead dogs that weren't there. Was it too much of a coincidence that the man who vandalized my shop was in a rage at a fraudulent psychic that I was willing to put myself in danger just to avoid looking like a druggie to a man I didn't care about?

I peered across the lot, watching Layne and Parrish work together. It was obvious they knew each other better than lovers might. Their body language indicated two people who were aware of each others' space and the way they nodded simultaneously as the other spoke, without even looking at each other, indicated they shared some sort of wavelength of thought.

I liked Parrish. I had a good feeling about her. If she trusted Layne then maybe I should too. In the meantime, I went back to my shop and tried to work as though nothing was out of the ordinary.

I managed, but by day's end, I found I couldn't prolong it any longer and returned to the crime scene, knowing Layne would want to talk to me. And to be honest, I was edgy enough after deciding to tell him about Sherry's husband that I didn't want to wait.

Several clusters of rubberneckers hung around as expected, eking the last bit of sunshine before the clouds overhead ran them out of the vicinity.

Layne kept his promise about having someone cover Iris. She was now hidden behind a make-shift barricade of sorts. From where I sat it looked like an old fashioned coat rack that someone had draped a tarp over, effectively cutting her off from view of myself and the street without contaminating the crime scene.

I noted that three officers were erecting poles around the perimeter too, and a fourth was shaking out a vinyl square of material. I sat cross-legged with my back against the building as I watched until a cold spot popped up on my arm. Rain. They were tenting the area because it was starting to drizzle. I looked upward and several more droplets fell onto my face.

I closed my eyes and opened my mouth without thinking. I caught at least a dozen drops of rain that way before I felt someone standing over me.

"A lesser man might crack a blue sort of joke," Layne said from above me.

I opened my eyes to see him looking down at me. His arms were crossed and those eyes had gone all molten honey again. I was beginning to think I was losing my mind.

"A better man wouldn't have mentioned the joke at all," I said.

"You tell her?" said a familiar female voice from just behind him.

Parrish. She had crept up on us the same as Layne had me and was wiping her hands on some cloth that might have been red at one time. Now, beneath a smear of filth, it was a soft pink.

"Haven't had a chance yet." His gaze dropped to my mouth and I realized it was still hanging open.

I clamped it closed and rolled onto my hip so I could push myself to my feet. I hated having him looking down on me. It was too perfectly metaphoric.

Even if I didn't feel at a psychological disadvantage, both of them had a way of standing when still that made me think of a wolf in a dark wood waiting for prey to come slinking out of a hole.

I wiped my hands on my jeans as I faced Parrish, more to disguise the shiver that ran through me when I imagined that image.

"What is he supposed to tell me?" I asked her.

She elbowed Layne in a way that made him twitch like a kid and the predatory posture disappeared.

"We found sulfur," he said, earning a glare from Parrish as though he'd dismissed her comment altogether.

"Sulfur," I said.

He made a quick gesture at Parrish with his hand that he thought I couldn't see. It was a cutting motion, designed to tell her to shut up. I decided to let him think I hadn't seen it.

"Quite a bit of it," he said. "Parrish, here, had to tell me what all the yellow powder was around the brazier. I had no idea what color the stuff was. I always assumed it was black."

"A lot of people think that," I said, taking in the strange way he was looking at me, as though he had more to say but wasn't sure how to broach it. I knew that was the case when Parrish kicked his foot.

"And there was something else..."

"A number?" I asked and quirked my eyebrow, expecting him to continue, but it was Parrish who finished, either eager to pass on the information or too impatient to wait.

"No number," she said. "But the bastard stuffed a small statue into the woman's fucken entrails, for Jesus' sake."

CHAPTER ELEVEN

I WASN'T AWARE THAT I had passed out until I came to with Layne's face an inch from mine. I started at first, not sure why he was so close, and exactly why in the hell I was lying in his arms looking up at him. He put a steady hand on my shoulder, effectively calming me like he was some sort of psychic whisperer or something.

The smell of mint wafted over me, and I noticed he'd shoved another piece of gum into his mouth and was chewing it so fast it made squeaking noises. When he caught me opening my eyes, he made an equally swift movement to shift the wad to his cheek. Those cocoa-colored eyes filled with black pupil.

I blinked several times, trying to clear the stupefaction from my oxygen-deprived brain.

"You passed out," Parrish said in an echo of my own thoughts as my surroundings came into focus.

She stood behind Layne, and I could see her now, hovering over his shoulder as she peered down at me. A chunk of her auburn hair had come loose from her bandanna and she flicked it off her shoulder with an annoyed movement.

"I think she can figure that out for herself, Parrish," Layne said without taking his gaze from mine.

"Tell her what else happened," she said and this time, he did glance at her. I caught the look that passed between them when he all but made that same cutting motion with his hand.

The scent of his aftershave took over that of mint and cocooned me as it mixed with something else. Pheromones, I supposed, because it wasn't something that I could place as a fragrance. It wasn't unpleasant, but it wasn't commercial either.

"Let her get her bearings at least," Layne said.

I had my bearings. Unfortunately, once I'd registered that I was lying in his lap with Parrish lurking like a crow behind him, I'd got every single one of those bearings.

I was still on the edge of the crime scene with a very dead Iris somewhere behind me as I lay in Layne's lap. The stink of fish clung to my nose, and the image of a brazier and her burned intestines scorched into my mind's eye. Pretty good bead on my bearings, actually, and I didn't like it. Not one bit.

A fact that seemed lost on Parrish, who almost seemed to take some perverse enjoyment out of my reaction. I wasn't sure if I hated her for it or had found a kindred spirit.

"You had a seizure," she said in an awed sort of gleeful tone that made me decide on kindred spirit. "Guess the thought of stuffing a statue into a woman's gullet was too much to take standing up, huh?"

Right. The statue. I'd forgotten why I'd have lost consciousness in the first place. But that was what had done it alright. Crammed into a woman's gullet. Sure. That was enough to make a gal pass out.

I still felt woozy when I thought about it. I must have looked as bad as I felt because she put the back of her hand on my forehead and shook her head at me.

"Just a bit clammy," she said. "Can't say I blame ya, but you'll be alright."

She eyed me like she thought I was milking it and should be up on my feet already. The childish desire to pick at me a little longer rode her features so clearly, I could almost imagine her as a kid teasing a sibling. I bet she had several, and all of them afraid of her.

Even Layne must have thought she was going to goad me a little longer because he cut his eyes at her.

"What?" she said with a canted head and eyebrows that climbed at least an inch higher. "It's true. She'll be fine. Eventually."

She leveled her gaze on me as I tried to extract myself from Layne's lap and arms. Keen, those eyes. They roamed to just the right places, finding the hands that trembled as they tried to find a place to land with enough purchase to roll free.

She ignored the obvious giveaway of my legs shaking as I got to my feet and crouched there as I tested my legs.

"I puked the first time I saw something like that," she said, watching me perch on my toes as I considered pushing myself to my feet. "Well, maybe not exactly like that, to be honest. For me, it was a guy who had painted the walls of his living room with his own shit before he cut his throat. So don't feel bad about passing right the fuck out. I don't think anyone has seen an ivory statue wedged so far up—"

"Parrish." Layne's voice was a bark, and she clamped her mouth closed even though her eyes warred with the fact that she'd just given in to an order she obviously didn't want to submit to.

My palms met the asphalt on the outside of my knees. I thought I might be able to get up finally. Layne was already on one knee, his hands out to catch me.

I glanced at them and brushed his hand away. Parrish stuck hers out toward me then, indicating the state I must really be in if she too thought I needed help getting up.

I eyed her for a long moment before deciding that leaning against the building beside me might be the best plan in the end. I didn't need either of them or their help. I could use the sturdiness of the brick to climb my way to my feet.

With a shake of my head at her still outstretched hand, I situated myself so that I leaned against the building and decided, if my legs could hold me, that it would be prudent to stand.

Layne stood with me as I rose, and Parrish supervised with her hands on her hips. I was a little weak, but she was right. I'd be fine. At least physically.

Her nod of approval when I stood for several moments without collapsing was all I needed to tell me I'd made the right choice. I blew out a long breath, testing the strength of my resolve as well as the steel in my spine.

Both of them watched me and I realized so long as I braced myself against the building, neither of them would give up playing nurse maid. I pushed off the wall and shoved my hands into my pockets when I managed to stand there without swaying. I refused to look in the direction of the crime scene. That way lay madness.

Parrish's eyebrows settled to a normal height, though, so I supposed I must have looked a little less likely to faint again. She angled her gaze toward Layne, running it up and down the length of his frame in an assessing way. Like a sister might.

"You got grease on your fancy pants," she said, jerking her chin toward his backside.

To his credit, he just squared his shoulders. I stole a look and saw the stain spread about two inches over the left cheek.

"People are going to think you pissed yourself," she said and I knew she was trying hard not to laugh.

He shrugged. "You think I care what people think?"

She murmured something to herself, and he flipped her a gesture that made her throw up her hands.

"Okay, Mr. Boss, I'll let you pretend you don't care what people think." She eyed me. "Feeling better?"

I nodded. "Much."

I inhaled to prove it to myself and when all the oxygen didn't make me dizzy, I angled myself in a way that I couldn't catch sight of the crime scene from my peripherals.

"How long was I out?" I asked.

Her posture shifted. It was subtle, but she moved just enough that she wasn't looking me in the eye. Since she towered over me anyway, it shouldn't have been necessary but her movement worried me.

I turned my attention to Layne, who was checking his backside for what had to be a very wet bit of material.

"Layne?" I said. "What's wrong?"

"It's nothing," he said, but I noticed the secretive glance he sent Parrish's way.

"It must be something," I said. "Neither one of you will look at me."

"You didn't exactly pass out fully," she said. "You sort of...moaned a bit and mumbled."

"Mumbled?" That didn't sound especially unnerving, at least, not enough to warrant the looks they were giving each other.

"Yeah," she said with a shrug. "Sounded like you were talking to the vic."

Layne eyed me, and I was aware I was chewing my bottom lip at the close scrutiny. I decided only someone who had something to hide would be tearing her lips to rags so I stopped. I faced him with a shrug equal to Parrish's.

"The power isn't always controllable," I reminded Layne.

He nodded and took my elbow. "So you said the first time we met," he said. "I think we've had enough for the day. Why don't I see you home."

It wasn't a question. He wanted me off-site. Though I wanted the same thing, it still stung. I felt as though I was being dismissed.

I let him guide me toward the street, but I felt Parrish's eyes on my back until we turned the corner. I had the feeling she watched us for a long while after that before she returned to her work, and even then, I could swear I felt her eyes burning through from my spine to my sternum.

Something wasn't quite right.

"Why wasn't there a number?" I said. "I was sure there would be one."

He shrugged. "Maybe one person dead didn't need to be counted. Maybe it's obvious."

I thought about that but it didn't fit, and I guessed he did too because he pulled out his notebook and wrote something in it as we walked.

"Did I say anything useful when I was 'mumbling'?" I said. The nagging feeling that prickled against the back of my neck wouldn't let go. Even though the sun was still out and the streets had filled to normal with tourists and dockworkers, a chill went through me.

"You might have mentioned a few strange things."

"Like what?"

The reluctance in his voice to give up any information filled the silence that came when he didn't answer right away. I shouldn't take it personally, I knew. It was probably a habit that came from having to keep evidence under wraps from general public.

But I was good at silences. I waited and eventually, he continued without me prodding him.

"Parrish is more suspicious of people than I am," he said, "so don't think anything when I say what I'm going to next."

"And what is that?"

The farther we got from the scene, the more the lingering dread lifted. It didn't wash away entirely, but my shoulders started to swing more naturally, and the sensation of having a heavy shroud holding them tight against my ribs eased up. Asking the hard question of what I might have done while I was passed out didn't bother me as much.

He guided me around a broad puddle with a gentle coaxing of his fingers on my elbow and, surprised that my body responded so automatically, I snapped the question at him again.

He withdrew his hand from my arm as though it burned, and I instantly regretted my reaction.

"I'm sorry," I said. "Nerves."

Both of his hands raked the top of his head as he dragged in a long breath without breaking stride. It felt like he was trying to outpace something. Then, he paused on the sidewalk to face me.

"It's fine," he said, but didn't look me in the eye. "I shouldn't expect more from a civilian."

That he might have expected a less reactive response from me at all was a surprise. Disappointing him wasn't something I'd considered until that moment. I wasn't sure what to do with my hands now that we weren't walking, so I crammed them each into my opposite sleeve cuff and gripped my forearms. I felt steadier that way.

"When you asked for my help I didn't think it would be like this," I said, trying to explain and he waved my words away like a mosquito buzzing too close.

"To be honest, I didn't either. I shouldn't have involved you." He sighed heavily, a man who felt backed into a corner. "I understand if you want to forget it all."

I barked out a dry laugh. "Like I could."

Someone jostled past us and pushed me against him. He caught me by the arms and steadied me. My amulet swung free of my collar and lay on my shoulder between us. He plucked it from my sleeve and tucked it very chastely against my throat where it slid down between my breasts again. It felt warm from his touch, sending a little jolt of electricity through my sternum.

I caught his eye as he pulled his hand away and my breath hitched.

"Listen," he said. "I have an ulterior motive for pulling you away from Parrish like that."

That awful dread rose up from the shadows of the dark closet I'd stuffed it in and I did my best to shove my full weight against the door.

"She was about to spill some nasty secrets, wasn't she?" I said, aiming for lighthearted banter to counter the tension in the air. "Like you wear women's underwear."

He chuckled, and the closet door in my mind clicked shut. "Is there something wrong with laying a woman's panties over your face while you relax with a tumbler of whiskey after a hard day?"

I didn't expect the humor from him and it caught me by surprise so much that I laughed. Snorting kind of laugher, the kind you release when you've been pent up with an awful trauma for too long.

We were outside a pizza place that whispered of wood smoke and oregano, and oak planks railed the tables and chairs on their outside deck. I leaned against one as tears of relief and exhaustion brimmed over and ran down my cheeks. His joke hadn't been that funny, really, but the cork holding in all my emotions popped free at the unexpected humor, and I couldn't stop laughing.

He grinned at me and waited for the whole mess of cry-laughter to subside before he hooked his arm behind my back, easing me off the wall because a couple had dropped their butts into the chairs on the other side. We started up the sidewalk again, walking slower, his palm resting gently at the small of my back.

His hand felt good there. Natural. I decided to let it stay.

"Maybe we both need a break," he said with a sigh. "A bit of fun to forget everything we've seen the last two days."

"You were thinking a lovely boink and bath vacation to the Mediterranean?" I joked and leaned closer to him without realizing it until my shoulder fetched up beneath his. His body went rigid at the contact, and I realized my thoughtless mistake too late to do more than shiver as though I was cold.

He relaxed then, but we had reached a traffic light and he paused, waiting for the light to change. He pulled his arm away from my waist and I took the opportunity to slip a few steps sideways, my cheeks flaming. I had put a good two feet of distance between us when he spoke again.

"You make me sound like an opportunistic lech."

He didn't sound offended. Maybe I could salvage the awkward moment after all. I pointed an accusing finger at him, lacing the action with a playful smile so he'd know I wasn't serious.

"Aha!" I said. "So you were thinking of taking advantage of me."

"I know a good opportunity when I see it," he said without a hint of anything more. "So, yes, your delicate state is a good chance to coerce you into coming to a party with me."

"Me?" I said, the confusion at the abrupt change in topic wrinkling my brow. "You want to take me to a party?"

He shoved his hand into his pocket. "I hate fancy things and well...I have to go and I need a plus one." He scuffed his shoe along the concrete. "The person I usually take to these things isn't available and I don't have time to find someone suitable."

The backhanded invitation and insult made my throat hurt. "What about a social app?" I said. "Tons of willing girls there."

He had the grace to look chagrined. "It's a fancy affair," he said, ignoring the weight of hurt in my tone as though it didn't matter. "I'd have to vet her first and..."

"You don't have time." I hated the bitterness in my voice.

He shrugged. "You want me to lie? I need a plus one, and you need a bit of a break. Sounds like a fair exchange to me, unless you'd prefer to sit home alone and enjoy some of your coffee."

The statement came out nonchalantly but I knew it for what it was. He was reminding me that he hadn't done a single thing about the illicit drugs he'd found.

"So by coerce, you really mean blackmail," I said with a tight voice. "Isn't that just as illegal?"

He didn't blink when he responded. "I asked you out," he said. "That's not extortion."

"You're in the middle of a nasty case where four women have died."

He walked toward me, pursuing me with an almost predatory stalk.

"If I stopped living every time someone in this city got murdered, I'd never do anything but work. It's important for our mental states to live our lives when we aren't working. And this is a very special occasion. The MVP Charity Dinner."

I'd not heard of this event, so it must be something new. Something fun. A place that I might be able to forget everything for a few hours. Maybe find a few more wealthy clients. I chewed the inside of my cheek, wondering if it might be a good idea or entrepreneurial suicide.

"It's this weekend," he prodded.

It was already Thursday. I calculated all the things I'd have to do for a night on the town. Waxing. Shaving. Buying a new dress. Dusk was already settling over the skyline and that meant the shops would be closed. I was down to one day if I wanted to buy something.

"Formal?" I said, already arranging three separate to-do lists for relevant affairs.

"Very formal," he said with a grimace and a shudder. "The kind of stuff women like." He all but rolled his eyes.

It had been a long time since I'd gone out for anything except a pizza. The invitation was pretty alluring, if I put aside the fact that he'd just blackmailed me.

I looked down at myself and the jeans and tshirt I'd pulled on that morning.

"I'll see if I can rustle up some decent duds."

I caught him scanning me too, his gaze lingering on the swell of hips that filled out a bit too much of my low-rise jeans. His throat moved as he swallowed and when he met my eyes again, his had shifted into that golden yellow color I'd begun to associate with warm honey.

Flustered, I pulled my gaze from his to the light. It had changed, finally, and I used the chance to get out from beneath his scrutiny. I crossed with him on my heels and walked briskly down the street, my mind racing. He caught up to me easily and we remained silent until we passed the bus stop I usually took to get to work.

We were very close to my apartment building, then. The shock of the day had seeped out and I had the feeling I'd sleep like the dead when I finally hit the hay.

And it was that thought that reminded me. I stopped a few blocks before my building and grabbed his elbow, forcing him to stop too.

"You said I said some strange things when I fainted," I said. "You were going to tell me what they were until I snapped at you."

He dug into his jacket for a piece of gum. He unwrapped it as he spoke.

"It wasn't much, really," he said and popped the stick into his mouth. "At first, it was a lot of mumbling to Iris. Parrish already told you that bit, but the other stuff. It was odd because it was almost like you were somewhere else. Seeing and hearing things we couldn't."

"Like?"

He shrugged as the gum moved around in his cheeks. "Mostly you talked about dogs. Dead puppies. Dogs coming back to life. And the really creepy thing, the one that had Parrish's hackles up, was that you said you could hear hounds howling."

I froze at the words. Hounds howling. Dead puppies. Reanimation of stray dogs. I remembered now. I knew exactly what had taken over me during the time I'd fainted dead away at the crime scene.

And the mental image was enough to tick up my heart beat. Adrenaline soaked my tissues and tried to urge me into run. All I wanted all of a sudden was to be in my own bed with the lights on and the television playing M*A*S*H reruns full blast.

It unnerved and the brief respite was gone.

"I'm close to home," I said around the tightness of my throat. I was close enough that I could see the dumpster in the back alley of my apartment building. Just a couple more blocks and I could lock myself behind my door and hide in my room. Alone.

"No problem," he said. "I'll see you to the door."

I didn't want him with me right then. I didn't want to risk the panic attack and explaining myself when what caused it couldn't be talked away. Hadn't I spent years in therapy trying to do just that to exactly no avail?

"I can make it the rest of the way."

He stiffened and backed up a step. I knew he'd taken offense but I couldn't help it. I might not have wanted to hurt him but I had lost all ability to chatter about nothing.

Those memories when they came weren't just creepy recollections that made my skin shiver as though something stood behind me. They were a gut punch and it took a great deal of willpower to push on without wanting to hunch over into a ball to protect my insides.

"Sure," he said in a tight voice. "I'll leave you alone."

"I'm fine," I said, hastily trying to patch over the awkwardness. "I'm just tired and I know you've had a hard day too. I'll be fine. Really. I don't need an escort."

I was already walking away, faster than I wanted to.

I was aware he watched me, but by the time I'd made it across the street, I didn't sense him standing there anymore. I checked behind me to see he'd disappeared, probably turning the nearest corner so he could leave me to my own devices.

It was just as well. That was the thing about those memories. They had a life of their own and when they came, they controlled me. Like it or not.

I picked up my pace, eager to get home and lock myself in.

I felt almost resentful as I rounded the corner, thinking while he and Parrish had the luxury of feeling no more than a little creeped out by what they thought were my visions, I wasn't spared the same benefit.

He and Parrish were just on the sidelines. They might feel their skin prickle and their heart rate tick up at a grown woman ranting about hounds howling and puppies dying, but they weren't involved. They hadn't lived through what I had.

I'd spent a good many years burying those memories in the back yard of my psyche. That too, ignited the resentment. I'd spent too much time to let an investigation I had no stake in exhume them. Maybe I needed to back off. Maybe I needed to tell them both it was too much for me.

It wasn't like I was going to get much more than a bit of street cred out of the deal. And with the memories coming back fast and hard, if I couldn't get a handle on my own emotions, that cred wasn't going to net me any useful coin.

I was still mulling over how I'd find the words to tell Layne I was done with the investigation when I felt a prickling across my neck that crept up into my hairline.

I glanced over my shoulder in the dark, expecting to see him still watching me even though I knew he was gone.

The street was empty. The prickling sensation continued. If someone had stood behind me, running a finger up along the minute hairs of my nape, I wouldn't be the least bit surprised, it was that physiological.

My heart rate ratcheted up.

I didn't know how I knew it, but I knew it.

Someone was out there watching me.

CHAPTER TWELVE

MY HEART RACED, AND my fight-or-flight response kicked into overdrive.

There was an old saying my mom used to drill into me on the nights I cried and whimpered from nightmares that seemed more real than shade. She'd tell me that only fools feel no fear.

I didn't fancy myself a fool, but I wasn't completely ignorant either. After the things I'd seen her do in that basement, the things that sent me crying to my bed in the first place, I'd become the sort of chick who liked to see what was coming for her.

I watched the needle during blood work even though I nearly passed out every time. I left my bedroom door open at night so I could see what was coming for me if someone broke into my apartment. And if something was gunning for me, you best believe I was going to see it coming.

So, I kept glancing over my shoulder, panning the sidewalk, and twisting to look behind me as I hustled up the street. I wished now, with every shadow threatening to grab for me, that I'd not balked at Layne's offer to see me to my front door.

If I'd just found a way to chill out, he'd be walking with me right then, and I was willing to bet even the killer would walk on by at the size of the good detective.

Because Layne was big. Even his shadow was monstrous. He would have been the best deterrent to violence next to a gang of thugs and several belt-fed weapons.

And I'd forced him to leave me alone on the poorly lit street.

I knew the neighborhood as well as I could for having lived there a couple years, but in the dark, everything took on a dangerous tinge. The railing leading to a basement apartment looked like a cage. The bicycle with its solar powered headlight, locked in its parking spot next to a crouching shrubbery, had a demon's glare.

Everything smelled off. My skin prickled.

I took another furtive glance sideways as I came up abreast of the abandoned lot that stood between my apartment building and the old school.

The private school had fallen into disrepair when the board of directors closed up shop last year, and now the lot, filled with teeter totters and basketball nets, served as a playground for no one. Any local families with kids sent them to the fresh new public school after the pandemic ate up all their savings. I hadn't seen a teen selling drugs in it for weeks.

I watched the lot carefully as I passed by. The floodlights that used to illuminate the area had been broken, either with rocks by kids or a pusher who wanted some privacy to peddle his molly.

I thought I caught sight of a shadow moving in the well of darkness that surrounded the space. My feet sped up on their own, a response to the way my heartbeat increased. I could hear my own rasping breath.

I was a block away from my front door. Almost home free. If I was calm and collected, I'd get to my front door without making a fool of myself by tearing along the neighborhood like an idiot on a bad drug trip.

Usually, cars ran the streets at all hours, but not tonight. Tonight, everything was silent. The cars lining the streets in parking spaces were dark and empty.

Most accidents happen near the home. People get slack, complacent. They let the safety of their environment lull them into a false sense of security.

I was right in the killing zone, if the statistics were to be believed.

A growl come from within those shadows. It didn't sound like anything I'd ever heard before. Not in the city growing up for sure, because the worst growl then came from rutting tom cats. And not in the wilds of Nova Scotia when I'd gone backwoods camping with bears and coyotes on the prowl.

No. This sound wasn't like any of those things. Even a citified desk jockey wouldn't have mistaken that sound for anything remotely natural.

I didn't wait to see what came out from those shadows that could make a noise like that.

I ran.

I tore off in the direction of my front porch.

The light I'd left on in the living room that morning beckoned me. My footsteps were loud enough that it drowned out any noise from around me and I panicked because I couldn't tell if I was being chased or if I was just a lone, idiotic woman running headlong up the sidewalk with no one behind me.

I couldn't help it. I screamed as I ran. I knew I'd feel ashamed later if it turned out nothing was following me, but I needn't have worried. No one came to my rescue.

No lights came on in the buildings. No cars moved on the street. It was as if I was in some bubble of alternate reality and I hollered like a banshee as I streaked down the sidewalk.

The growling kept rumbling through the air, cresting over me like a shroud being pulled tight against my face.

I was in full-fledged terror by then and a little thing like shame wasn't about to stop it.

I made it across the street. I could see my front door. I leaped for the curb.

Too fast, way too fast. I fell before I got to the sidewalk.

The curb met my cheek with a painful crunch that stole my breath. I couldn't scream. I couldn't even catch an inhalation of air. I rolled onto my side, using my hand to prop me up enough to look behind me finally even as I pushed at the asphalt with my feet.

Big mistake.

I saw what it was then: a huge, moving, man-sized shadow with glowing eyes.

Whatever my assailant was wearing, whatever light was catching his eyes and making it reflect like an animal's, it certainly managed to make him look inhuman. He smelled like detritus and dirt and the funk of death.

And if I could smell that, then he was far closer than I'd thought. Less than a dozen feet. If I didn't get up soon, he would be on me.

"Please," I said, hoping to appeal to some humanity within. "I don't want any trouble."

I held up my hand, supplicating. It masked his form for a second, but then he kept approaching and the shadows of his form leaked out over the sides of my palm.

I shoveled at the pavement as I tried to get up. I couldn't stay there any longer. Whatever time I had gained myself from running away was now running down. I had to get up.

But I couldn't.

Some force pinned me there. My own fear probably, clogging up my muscles and short circuiting my normally quick synapses. I took another look at the approaching figure, the way his arms didn't look right, too long and too stiff to be natural.

I dug deep into the well of my own God-given sense of determination.

I thought of the moment I'd decided I didn't have to live with my mother's strange and frightening practices. The way I'd packed up my entire life as a kid with all the mindset of an adult. How I'd shoved clothes and food into a back pack and slung it over my shoulder, an eight year old believing she could live on her own much better than with a mother who killed stray puppies in the basement and cooked their entrails on a little stone altar.

I'd believed in myself then, and I'd eluded capture for three whole days. I could get the hell up now.

But I couldn't. I just couldn't. All I could do was flatten out on the sidewalk on my shoulders, whimpering as whatever was after me drew closer. My mind flashed to the man in my shop carrying the walking stick that I'd imagined was a scythe. My savior, my angel. I wished he was there right then.

The noxious scent of sulfur permeated the air, cloaking me in an odor that curled my lips back.

Sulfur. Layne had said they'd found sulfur at the crime scene. Sulfur. One of the main ingredients in spell work.

"Who are you?" I demanded in a voice that sounded far braver than I felt. "What do you want?"

I didn't really care to be honest; I just wanted to distract him, gain myself time until I could connect my brain to the pathway of my legs.

He took his time. One arm jutted out to the side in a half-moon curve, and I was certain he was sniffing the air as he approached, locating me the way a blind cat might scent out a mouse.

I choked on the sob that tried to escape and it was that sound, the desperate, pathetic noise of a coward that told me I was done for. If all I did was turn into a puddle of terror, then I wouldn't live through this one, no matter how determined I might have been as a kid.

My body had all but decided it wasn't worth saving and left me to fight the immobility of my own limbs. I felt cocooned in something sticky and invisible and I was pretty sure it wasn't just my own terror.

Still, he kept coming, swerving first one way and the other, raising his face in profile now and then the way someone lifts their nose to the currents to make out the faintest of smells. The way a blind man might use his other senses to carve out form and structure from his other senses.

That was when I realized the truth.

He couldn't see me. He really was scenting me.

I tried to remember if I'd worn patchouli that morning or if I'd been in too much of an exhausted daze to think about putting on fragrance at all. I tried to recall getting out of my shower and doing all the regular things I did as part of my routine and couldn't even remember turning on the faucet.

I didn't have to work to lie still. The terror was doing a good job of preventing much more than a few small inhalations. No. It was the way my terror clawed out a desire to scream that took the most work. I felt my stomach tremble with the effort of it as I fought the urge. Because if I did, he'd home in on me like a stealth missile.

It was right about the time that he began to phase out of sight like a 60s television signal that I started to think I was hallucinating.

Maybe someone had put something in my coffee.

I almost laughed at the irony of the thought, and I might have convinced myself of it if the man hadn't phased back in—mere inches away from me.

I sucked in a breath and he cocked his head sideways at the sound. He wasn't deaf, not at all, and I was beginning to believe he wasn't truly blind either. He'd just lulled me into staying perfectly still so he could reach me without having to chase me.

Stupid. I was so stupid. I started to hyperventilate and it seemed to fuel my muscles. I inched backward on my elbows, my eye on that thing that was phasing out of shadow and into something more solid now.

Those eyes that glowed, they didn't look human. His arm, the one curved outward, lifted up over his head.

He was going to strike.

I tried to scrabble to my feet, freed from the agonizing paralysis. The movement released my amulet from beneath my shirt and it struck the sidewalk. My shoe caught on its cord. I choked as it went taut. I ducked to release it from the tangles beneath my foot.

The thing in front of me roared, a deathly, horrible sound. Its breath cascaded over me in a wave of putrid mank, carrying with it a tsunami of decay and the certain stink of sulfur.

There was no rational thought then. I was far too hyped up after the whole day. My stress limit was overtaxed and I was spent. The pain lancing up through my jaw and into my temple was the only thing that cut through the miasma of panic.

Just when I thought I'd lived my last moment, a flash caught the corner of my eye. Before I could process what it might be, something collided with the thing in front of me. It growled as it struck the shadow and I knew then the shadow was corporeal, not shade.

It wasn't human, either because as the huge stray dog that had stalked my store the last few days tore into the flesh of the thing, it made no sound of pain or fear.

It struck back, and the dog yelped in pain.

Chapter Thirteen

My relief that the dog was alive was short-lived. I staggered to my feet as the beast and the dog roiled together on the ground, one colossal mess of moving shadow. One moment, I could make out dog and fur and teeth, the next all I saw was blackness and that unearthly glow that made up the cavernous eye sockets.

The sounds they made together made the hair stand on my arms.

I thought of all those dogs I'd let down in my childhood, the ones I couldn't save, and I resolved to do what I could for the one that had risked itself for me.

The trouble was, I didn't know what to do. I had no weapon, just my phone and footwear.

I stooped to pluck one shoe from my foot, thinking to sling it hard at whatever was tearing into the poor stray.

I hurled it at the bulky, moving shadows but missed by several feet. The shoe clattered off to the side and struck a car tire.

The dog yelped once as whatever it battled must have ground down through its skin. I scanned the street, praying someone had heard the noise and would come to investigate. A light went on down the street. Someone came to the door and called to their cat.

"Thank God," I said.

I waved my hands over my head.

"Help," I yelled at her, not caring anymore who saw what or if they believed I was crazy. Something was out there fighting with that poor dog and that something needed to be stopped. "Please! I need help."

If she heard me, she gave no sign. There was no way she hadn't heard me, but I yelled again, this time shrieking so that the pitch would carry better.

She paused, looking my way. Her head canted in my direction. I all but sobbed in relief.

I fumbled in my pocket, searching for my cellphone, hoping to heaven I hadn't broken it when I'd fallen.

I waved my other arm at her as I dug into my back pocket.

"Call the police," I said. It's killing him."

I gestured frantically to where the dog and the beast still rolled around together. My fingers met the plastic of the case and I hauled it out so fast I dropped it on the sidewalk. I groaned and yelled all in one breath.

"Hurry," I said, dropping to my knees to feel for the phone. "Please."

She turned from me and picked up her cat by the belly.

I swore at her loud enough that the entire neighborhood should hear.

As though she didn't care, she turned on her heel back into her house. The door closed, shutting off the light from inside the foyer. She jerked the drapes of her window together right about the time when my palm dropped down onto my phone.

I scooped it up and turned it over in my hands to find the screen. I swiped and swiped across the black surface and realized I hadn't just cracked it; I'd knocked it dead.

The dog howled, a long, keening sound that made me drop the phone again. It clattered against the asphalt as I scanned the area in front of me, trying to see through the darkness to the stray.

He had to be alright. He just had to.

I caught sight of the dog finally, a large unmoving lump in the middle of the street. The sounds it made as it lay there lifted the hairs on my nape. But its attacker was nowhere in sight.

I froze. My skin prickled with electric tension. Wasn't that always how it went down in the movies? Killer disappears just seconds before the poor damsel gets her throat cut?

I swallowed my fear, noting that the sound of my throat moving was too loud for my ears to hear anything else around me. I swung my gaze left and right, desperate to see the attacker and desperate for it to be gone. There was no sign of it.

I thought I heard the normal sounds of the city again. A car horn blared. A cat yowled.

The return of those normal sounds made me realize I hadn't heard them at all over the last few moments.

Confused, I swung in a circle, panning the entire neighborhood for evidence that things had shifted, that I was really alone with the stray and the thing I'd seen was truly gone.

Some man yelled at his wife or his kids and a car door slammed. A siren sliced the air several blocks away.

I dragged in a breath and glanced toward the dog. I wasn't sure what was going on, and my breath was so loud in my ears I couldn't hear my own thoughts.

The dog tried to get up and staggered. I approached it with my hand out.

"It's alright," I murmured. "Everything's going to be okay."

My foot crunched down on my cell phone and the dog's massive head swung toward me when I swore. It leveled its eyes on me and then lurched to its feet as it met my gaze. Its lips curled back as it growled low and rumbling and full of threat.

Then the sounds of the city around me warped like waves in a wind tunnel. The peal of the siren and the blare of the car horn abruptly cut short, sucked up like a vacuum had Hoovered its way over the entire street. The stray dropped its head to shoulder height, and all I could make out was the sound of its threat rumbling through the air toward me.

"Oh fuck me," I said, the words slipping from my lips because I realized the dog wasn't growling at me at all.

It was trying to menace whatever was right *behind* me.

My breath caught in my throat as I worked up the nerve to steal a glance over my shoulder and failed. I was facing the wrong direction. And I wanted...badly...to see what lurked behind me. But to do so just might ignite that thing into action once it noticed I was looking. Once it knew I knew it was there.

The dog leaped, taking the decision from me. Out of a sense of terror, I ducked sideways.

I spun on my feet, nearly toppling backward. The flicker of its tail disappeared into a blur as it hurled itself at its attacker.

I stared through the darkness, trying to see which beast had clamped down onto the neck of the other. It didn't take long to realize that while I might not be able to make out what the attacker was, I did know the dog was the one losing.

If I didn't do something fast, any chance I had of surviving was going to bleed out like the poor stray. I swallowed hard and gathered what courage I could.

I pitched myself at the ball of shadow and fur. I had no idea what I was going to hit it with but it was too late, I was already bringing both my clenched fists down onto the back of its...shoulders?

My hands struck flesh and bone, hard enough that it reverberated all the way up to my elbows. I gasped in pain and recoiled, all rational thought gone to the face that it was really and truly solid, not a shadow at all. Not my imagination.

A corporeal body that let go of the dog.

A physical body with claws and teeth and furious eyes as it whirled on me.

Its teeth had all the vigor of a lion's. Thick, long and sharp, they glistened in the lamplight for a full heartbeat before a sound ripped through its throat.

Then they snapped together with a nasty click.

By some miracle, I was already moving, and those teeth rattled against each other audibly as the thing bit down on air instead of my arm.

Not a man, my mind whispered. Not a man. Not a man. Not a man.

As if I ever really thought it was anyway.

I scrambled to catch myself from falling as I sprinted to put distance between us. The stink of sulfur rose heavy and cloying in the air. I struggled to stay focused on the light of my porch as I staggered, half running, half limping toward my stoop.

I couldn't do anything more for the stray. Not now that I'd seen what had been chasing me.

I was dead if I didn't move.

I got about three steps before a second shadow rampaged into the street from behind a parked car. It came at me like a locomotive. I shrieked without meaning to because by then I was nothing but a bare electric wire hanging loose.

Before I could even consider jumping out of its way, it shoved past me.

"Run," the intruder yelled in a voice so graveled the speaker might well have swallowed a handful of sharp-edged stones. "Get the hell out of here. Now."

A smart woman might have kept running. A smart woman would have hidden behind a locked door and not come out till daylight.

I'd never been accused of being smart.

I spun on my heel to face what was going on. It wasn't because I felt brave. It was because whoever had decided to interfere on my behalf couldn't be just left to deal with the horror while I cowered behind my locked door safe and unharmed.

The two slammed into each other with enough force to elicit grunts and growls from both. While the stray had only a mouth and teeth to fight, this new intruder had arms and legs and he used them like a warrior might to wrestle his opponent into a grip that bowed his head low.

Blow after blow rained down on the creature. My savior seemed less and less human as he joined shadow with the beast.

I was mesmerized as the two fought.

I'd been to a dog fight once, an illegal, back alley, high stakes barking and snarling mess. I'd been invited for a night on the town by a new boyfriend who I hadn't realized was part of a criminal element until he tried to get me to hustle bids for him. His idea of a hot date was to introduce me to the world of organized crime, apparently.

I'd hustled, all right. I didn't feel the least bit ashamed of using my boobs to distract the handler who guarded the pit. When the dogs escaped, they were so enraged and rabid, the entire mob of gamblers swelled into a wave of panicked limbs and feet.

I called the cops on my phone outside the bathroom and I packed up and moved the next day.

Never underestimate a man who will force an animal into fight or flight aggression. And never leave an animal lover an opening to kick that man's ass.

This fight, even though cloaked in shadow and only occasionally lit by the streetlight as they shuffled and fell and danced away, was much like that. And it sounded like it too. It was enough to make my stomach clench with anxiety.

I stood there, helpless, thinking of those poor animals and the full-throated threat of their growls. I knew as I watched that whatever happened in the next few moments, one of these two would be dead without intervention.

I couldn't be sure the one who survived would be the one on my side.

The comprehension ignited me to action. I ran toward the sounds of exertion and pain without considering what I might do when I got there.

I was within reach of the back of one of them as it wrestled with the other. The stray dog jumped between us. It growled at me, low in its throat, crouched as though it would strike if I took another step.

"Okay," I said, and lifted my hands in surrender. "I'll back off."

Backing off didn't seem to be enough. The dog advanced on me and as it moved, an overpowering smell of sulfur permeated the air along with its every step. My amulet burned against my skin.

Darkness crept into the corners of my vision. Real darkness. The kind that comes when you are about to pass out. I felt lightheaded and everything in front of me swam in pools of wavering trails. Neither of the fighters seemed human in the narrow light of my blurred vision.

"Not now," I said, not knowing what I meant by it except that it was so not the right time to pass out.

I weaved on my feet as the dog went in and out of focus. The sounds of fighting leveled off. One of them roared in impotent frustration and another in pain.

My throat went tight in fear. Out of some absent-minded habit, I plucked at my amulet.

So hot.

It burned my fingers.

I yanked my hand away, pulling it free of my neck and flinging it to the ground.

The dog was gone and there was only one bulky bit of shadow lying on the sidewalk in front of me, draped in weak light from the streetlamp. Not the creature, thank God, but a man. My savior.

And the closer I got, the more familiar he looked, and by the time I reached him, I knew exactly who it was.

Chapter Fourteen

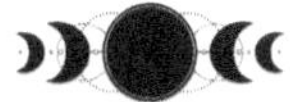

LAYNE WASN'T MOVING. HE lay swathed in light from the streetlamp, and if he was breathing it was at some level that wasn't discernable from where I stood in the darkness. My heart raced inside my chest as I strained to hear a breath. I took a step forward, approaching with careful, mincing paces so I could keep the noise to a minimum. I still wasn't sure what I'd seen—what I was seeing—was real. Furtive, studious glances up and down the street assured me we were alone, that whatever had attacked him was well and truly gone.

All that met my gaze was a lazy street with the warm glow of lights in windows and the flickering of television screens between half-closed curtains. Yes. Alone. With a man who I was certain was not a man just moments earlier. Nothing but a beast could have fought that horror and survived.

Unless he'd not survived. I dropped my gaze to the man at my feet, noting that the entire block had come alive with sound again. Or maybe I was just more aware of sound. I couldn't be sure. Everything had certainly seemed to fade into silence earlier. Now all that had returned, right down to my sense of smell. Even night-blooming flowers in annual pots sent out a myriad of floral scents, all strong enough to make my nose twitch. If this was reality, then what in the name of God was what I'd just lived through?

with my nerves pinging along my spine, I rolled Layne onto his back. Roamed with my hands along the bare skin where his clothes were rent. Wet. Sticky. I knew without looking that it was blood that stained my fingers and palm. Even in darkness, there's a certain feel to blood as it cools against flesh, and enough of it coated my hands to make me very, very worried.

My eyes closed of their own accord, deciding on their own to block out any details they didn't want to register. He'd just fought a beast of some sort. Whatever lay beneath my palm might not even look like a man in the light. And yet, I knew I shouldn't smear any more of his blood over him. The paramedics would have enough to assess through all the blood without me confusing the matter by spreading it everywhere. They needed to find the source of the worst wounds if he was to have a chance of survival. If he was even alive.

But I couldn't think like that. Of course he was alive. Of course he had a chance. My mouth went dry at the thought of what he'd just risked for my sake. It took a supreme effort to shut down the panic rising in my throat. To breathe slowly. To gather my wits.

With a calm I didn't know I could possess, I wiped the blood on my jeans and then sought his neck with my fingertips. Chest aching and heart racing, I brushed away bits of gravel that stuck to his jaw as I tested for a pulse.

A groan of relief slipped from me when I felt it hammering against the pads of my fingers. Strong and rhythmic.

Not dead. Sweet Jesus.

"Lucky son of a bitch," I said as I fell back on my haunches. And then, I realized that lucky might be subjective, considering the amount of blood on him. The realization launched me upward again, sweeping him top to toe for the telltale form of a cellphone with searching hands. My breath caught. There. In his front pocket.

I had to work to shove my hand inside, cursing him beneath my breath for wearing his jeans so damn tight. I had to shimmy back and forth with my fingers to get a good grip and then I pulled it free with a muffled whoop of victory...

Until a grip of iron went round my wrist. Something squeezed. Gently but firmly. I was startled enough to curse, but thankfully not enough to scream. I wasn't sure the beast wasn't still out there somewhere. Lurking. Watching.

"Don't." His voice came out in a rasp. He had to clear his throat to say it again, this time more forcefully. "Don't."

"But I have to call for help," I said, worry coating the words enough to make him squeeze again. "You're hurt."

"I don't need help. I'm perfectly fine."

"You're not fine. You're bleeding. You were passed out."

He used my hold as leverage to pull himself to a half-seated position. A dark, throaty chuckle rumbled from his throat. "About that," he said. "I wasn't exactly unconscious."

I sat back, pulling my hand from his finally.

"What exactly were you, then?" I said, my eyes narrowing. The worry retreated into a dark corner and nasty suspicion started to worm its way out.

"I was watching."

Something went clammy in my chest even as my heart fluttered. The thought that he was watching me, both a thrill and a warning. Shades of stealing peeks at my mother doing unspeakable things crept along the back of my neck, making my voice a little sharper when I spoke.

"Watching what, pray tell? Watching me have a fit because I thought you were dead?"

"Watching you dig into my pocket," he said in a husky voice. "You think any red-blooded man would give up the chance for such a nice pat down from a beautiful witch?"

I knew then he was fine. Yanking my hands back, I brushed them on my thighs. A bit of grit rubbed free. I could feel it in the oily sweat that warmed my legs.

"Bastard," I said. "I was worried about you." I might have choked on the words except I was too angry.

He popped up onto one knee with a dexterity that belied injury and brushed at his trousers. "No offense, Brie," he said, voice still husky and dark. "But I needed a moment to catch my breath, and then when you shoved your hands down my pants—"

"I did not shove my hands down your pants." I recoiled at the insinuation even as warmth crept up my neck to prove otherwise.

"My pants and all things in the vicinity of said pants beg to disagree." There was a smokiness to his voice that made my neck hot. A lot of things went hot, and I retreated to my first line of defense, which was—of course—distraction and deflection.

"You're bleeding," I said.

"I *was* bleeding." He held out his hand and waited, apparently for me to take his hand so he could help me get up.

I brushed it aside. "You need some help old man?" I said, an edge to my voice.

He stood as though his leg muscles were hydraulic pistons while I heaved myself to my feet with all the exhaustion riding my bones. "You're pretty independent for a damsel in distress," he said, and took to inspecting himself with both hands while he watched me sagging beneath the release of the rather large dump of adrenaline.

He cursed when he got to the large gashes in his jacket. "Ah hell. My best jacket."

As if that was all we had to worry about. As though he hadn't just fought off some strange beast that I was sure both of us knew shouldn't be real.

"We're going to just stand here worrying over your wardrobe after what just happened?"

His hands stilled next to his thighs then clenched into fists that he burrowed into his pockets.

I realized I was trembling, and he must have noticed because he stepped closer. I could feel his warmth radiating into my ribs and solar plexus. His breath smelled of mint gum when it swept over me, and that little detail was the one that made the trembling shift into high gear.

I started shaking enough to make my teeth chatter.

"It's gone," he said with a tightness in his voice that worried me because beneath it lurked a rasp that sounded very much like a predator's growl, and I wasn't sure I could even stand the thought of a predator right then. He put his arm around me and pulled me against him, and the shivering eased up. A little.

"I'm sorry I wasn't faster. I should never have left you alone," he said.

But he hadn't left me alone. He'd followed me. Even though I'd asked him to let me go it alone, he'd followed me. I wanted to say something about that, but I didn't know whether I should be angry or relieved. What I said instead was, "You were just right. Not too fast." Somehow that came out sounded decidedly sexual and I clamped my mouth shut before I could make things worse.

He seemed to understand what I meant though. "Last name isn't Garder for nothing." He kissed the top of my head, a soft thing, that was a brief bit of heat one moment and gone the next.

"I'll call an ambulance," he said as he swiped across his cell phone screen. "Have you checked over."

I groaned at the irony of him calling an ambulance for me. "Me?" I said. "You're the one who needs it. I'm just. I just... I'm fine."

But I wasn't fine. I had no idea what was going on, or why he was there at all. Even so, I was so damn grateful that I didn't have the heart to pull away. I wanted the comfort. I needed it, dammit.

"If you hadn't..." I let the words trail off because I didn't want to voice what would come next.

He shoved his phone back into his pocket and cupped my face in his broad hand. He had calluses. They scraped against my skin in a way that made my eyes ease closed as though I were an infant responding to a mother's stroke. Except I felt anything but a motherly love in that touch. I opened my eyes to see him staring down into my face.

"You're alright," he said in a low, throaty voice. "You will BE alright. I won't let anything hurt you."

Most of him was in shadow, but I could swear his eyes had a gleam in them that was yellow and preternatural. I thought of animals in the dark, peering into oncoming cars. Another shiver coursed through me.

"Let's go inside," he said. "We'll get you warmed up and I'll do a cursory check. I was a medic in another life. I'll be able to tell if you're in shock."

"No police," I said with a pitiful laugh.

"Not unless you count me."

I let him walk with me the rest of the way to my apartment. My habitual reluctance to let anyone in, to invite the sort of intimacy that came with admitting a stranger into my home, reared its head as we stepped onto the porch. I pushed it back down. This was no time to be coy about where I lived, and he wasn't a stranger. Not anymore.

If that thing out there had followed me for heaven only knew how long, and now knew where I lived, I might need Layne to know too. I might need an entire squad of policemen.

"It's a bit of a mess," I said, shy as I pushed the key into the lock. I took a bracing breath then shoved open the door with my hip.

"How bad can it be?" he said and then his mouth clicked shut when we entered the foyer.

I looked over the rummage of my apartment with a critical eye. A laundry basket had fallen off the sofa, spilling its contents on the muted tones of the space rug. One of my plants had toppled from the windowsill and left debris sprayed over the back of the sofa. My bathroom door was ajar, showing the piles of laundry and the clutter of empty wine glasses lining the tub.

"I wish I could say I had a cat or dog to blame this on," I said. I sighed wearily and let him brush past me. "Unfortunately, this is my life these days."

I scanned the room with an impersonal gaze as I toed off my shoes and kicked them into the corner of the foyer. I wanted to sag into the nearest chair, but the nearest chair was filled with papers.

When I'd moved in, I'd loved the place. It had a creamy, historical looking yellow on the walls in the kitchen with old whitewashed cupboards. My living room had a stone fireplace with a granite mantel edged in driftwood. The doors were solid oak, painted white-wash to match the cupboards. It had old world charm and gypsy style all in one.

Looking at it now, I saw how uncared for it seemed. I touched the threadbare sofa with a lingering stroke.

"I've been pretty busy."

He picked up a painted mandala beach stone from my foyer table and inspected it. He lifted it toward me in query, as though to ask if I'd painted it, and when I shook my head, he placed it neatly on the mantel so it showed face out.

"Parrish's place is...well, hers is worse. I can take a little disorganization." He tapped the stone.

It was nice of him to call my sloppiness disorganization. It actually put a tentative smile on my face even though, despite his assurances, I had the feeling the mess in Parrish's place bothered him.

I looked at the pants he wore that were torn and the jacket that was now no more than a few scraps with sleeves and remembered there were more awful things to worry about than a bit of laundry. We'd both just faced one of them right outside my door, whatever or whoever it was. I was lucky Layne had been there.

I hugged myself as I thought about what might have happened if he'd not followed me home. It was hard to be angry with him when he had saved my ass.

His gaze darted over my tight shoulders and they eased a bit at his glance. When he stepped closer, almost too close for my nerves, I thought he might take me in his arms until he reached over my head and looped a necklace around my neck. A heavy stone fell over my chest and settled into the crevice of my cleavage. My amulet.

He must have picked it up at some point. Anxious, I retreated further into the living room and cupped my elbows.

I watched him look for a place to sit and gathered up an armful of clothes from the sofa so he could settle down somewhere. He found a nest between a pile of clean towels and an even bigger pile of sheets. Seeing it reminded me I'd not made the bed that morning. The spare set was in the hamper.

"It's too hot for a fire," I said as a sock fell from the edge of the pile and landed on the floor at my feet. "But I think we could both use something warm to drink."

I tried to snag the errant sock with the tip of my toe but all I managed was to push it into a pile.

He lifted his gaze to mine from his spot on the sofa.

"Whiskey would be better," he said.

I grinned at him because I agreed. I knew I had stashed a bottle of Screech (TM) somewhere when I'd come back from Nova Scotia. It would go good right then with a cola and some ice.

"I have some Newfoundland rum," I said and he waved at me like it didn't matter. "I won't even make you kiss a cod to drink it."

I tittered nervously, not even sure he'd understand the Maritime tradition or that he'd care, but it was a relief to yak about something normal. I could fool myself into believing I hadn't just been attacked, that his intervention had created such a whirl of emotions in me that I could barely breathe.

"I have no idea what that means," he said as he pushed the pile of sheets into a tighter wad so he could lean back.

"The Newfies have a screeching in ceremony," I explained. "It involves taking a shot of rum and kissing a codfish."

He gave me a curious look but at least he smiled. My shoulders released.

"And this ceremony," he said, "you know about it how?"

I squared my shoulders beneath the pile of clothes I held onto.

"Been screeched-in myself," I said proudly. "Went to Newfoundland a couple of years back when I lived in Canada. Took my shot of Screech, recited the poem, and kissed the codfish."

"So you don't mind kissing strange things, then," he said.

He met and held my gaze and something shifted in that moment. Whatever crossed his face, some emotion I couldn't name, it played across his expression like a slideshow. The longer I held his gaze, the more I thought his eyes reminded me of rum and not honey.

In fact, I couldn't stop gawking at him. He was a mess, now that I had him in the light and could see him better. A bold streak of blood went from his jaw to his ear. If I was seeing right, that was a long, razor thin scar that ran along his neck. Most of it was silvered already, but some parts near the middle were red and swollen looking as if it was fresh.

I didn't think I'd noticed it before, and I found that strange.

"I'll get a couple of shots," I said, spinning on my heel and breathing a sigh of relief that I'd been able to free myself from his gaze. I headed toward my bedroom's open door to dump the pile of clothes on the bed.

With a near silent mutter to keep it together, I blew out a breath of anxiety. Whatever I thought I needed to keep it together for, I had no idea.

"Should I drop these here too?" he said from behind me, and I startled like a rabbit.

"You scared the bejesus out of me," I said and collapsed onto the pile of clothes with my hand on my chest.

He dropped his armful of sheets and towels onto the bed next to me. I craned to see past him to the sofa. Totally clear of laundry, so he'd brought the whole lot in with him.

"Thanks," I said and he shrugged.

"Didn't mean to scare you."

He stood there, looking so large and so present, that I had to pretend we weren't in my bedroom. It felt too intimate.

I was acutely aware of the bras hanging from my dresser mirror, and the red feather boa I had draped over the other side.

With a sense of mortification, I remembered setting my vibrator on top of my bedside table the night before not three steps away from where he stood. I didn't dare let my gaze travel in its direction to see if I'd thought to put it away afterwards because I didn't want him following my gaze just in case.

In what I thought would be a brilliant move of distraction, I eased off the bed in the hopes I could turn my back to the end table and dump the vibrator inside an open drawer, but in a less than brilliant maneuver, I ended up rebounding off his shoulder.

I ended up dumping myself onto my ass on the mattress.

"Nerves," I said through a throat so tight I was amazed the words came out at all.

I tittered as I tried to tell myself it was anxiety of feeling pinned down in my own home, in a space where I slept and where I was the most vulnerable. The truth was, it was a totally different emotion. One I could deny it if I wanted to, but it was still there. I didn't think I'd sleep that night for all the drenching of sudden lust.

My solar plexus ached all the way to my spine as I imagined him easing me backward onto the bed, pushing aside all the laundry.

We'd make love with the scent of fabric softener swirling around us.

"Brie?" he said and I jerked my gaze to his, realizing I'd zoned out for a bit.

"What's that?" I blinked. "Missed it." My face heated up as I struggled to make my voice sound normal.

"I need to confess something." His words came out in a throaty rasp that made me think that he was being affected too. There was something about nearly dying, about near misses that made the blood sing. Was he about to tell me he was just as hot as I was? Was it even right, for a cop and his charge to abandon everything except skin to skin need?

"I'm no priest," I said in a flippant want that somehow managed to come out in a squeak. "Not even a saint of any sort. But if it floats your boat, go for it."

The chuckle I tried out sounded feigned and forced. He reached for me and snagged my wrist. His grip tightened just briefly and at first, I almost struggled, sensing something dangerous, something beyond seductive that I wasn't ready for.

"Lots of things float my boat," he said in a low tone. "And while I can't deny you're hot as fuck right now with your hair in knots and your panties hanging all over the place like so much litter, you should know I'm not trying to seduce you. I just don't want you to be scared."

I peered up at him, my heartbeat ratcheting up enough to feel it in my throat.

"Why would I be scared?" I said, and even as the words left me, the fear came. Because whatever was in his face was clearly bestial in that moment. He reminded me of the dog that had been trailing me for days. No. More powerful than that. Something predatory.

And even as that thought ran through my mind, those gorgeous eyes of his... They...changed. Right there in front of me. The lovely rum and caramel color swirled to a golden yellow. A dozen thoughts raced each other for precedence in my mind. Had I brought the wrong man into my home after all? But I knew better. Something deep inside me whispered of magic and spells and unearthly things that no matter how much I tried to deny it, was still coiled around the air currents, in my memory, in the shivers that ran over my spine as I watched him.

My mind's eye tripped me right back to the moments outside when whatever predator had attacked me had let me see its eyes.

I'd known it wasn't human then, as impossible as it might have been. I might be able to convince myself of the opposite in the morning, maybe I would manage to forget the feeling that brushed over the recesses of my memory, but right then, the sensation was so acute, I knew the truth right then.

That what I was seeing in Layne's face proved he wasn't human, either.

CHAPTER FIFTEEN

"I DON'T WANT TO scare you," he said again, but this time, the rasp of his voice had deepened to a distinct growl.

Whether or not that was his intention, I was scared.

"Too late," I said, as I pulled my hand from his and bolted to the side as though I expected a swing of fists to come at me. It would take some effort to pretend I wasn't in the confines of my bedroom with a predator.

I rounded the bed with my palm touching down on a pile of clothing and towels. I scooped up whatever met my fist, ready to fling it at him should he decide to lunge for me. Two socks and a hand towel tangled in my grip. Great weapons, I thought.

I almost laughed from pure fear, except my right heel fetched up into the leg of the bedframe.

The sharp jolt of pain tore a yowl from me. I stooped to grab the aching foot. All fear abandoned me then, leaving the rage of hurt in its wake.

"Fuck," I said and glared at him. "What in the hell is wrong with you?"

Because he'd advanced on me, and I didn't like it. And because his hands were out, reaching for me as if he wanted to grab for me. There was no way in Hell I was going to let that happen. Not after what I'd just witnessed. I didn't care if he'd saved me. Whatever had been outside, that he'd chased off and survived was a horrible...unearthly thing. What that said about him, I didn't want to know. I just wanted to know one thing. And if he answered, I'd know the truth. I was sure of it.

"Are you the killer?" I asked, with more of a screech than I intended. Don't scare a chick near to death and expect calm and rational conversation, I suppose.

For a moment, he looked at me as if he couldn't believe his ears. My voice rose another octave. "Well, are you?"

His brow furrowed in consternation. "You think I'm the killer?" he asked softly before his brow deepened to hard lines. "My God, you think I could do that to... Sweet Jesus."

He raked both hands through his hair and turned away, then turned back again to pin me with a disbelieving stare. "What kind of man do you think I am? I just saved your ass, is what I did. I didn't try to slice it open. Fuck."

His hands lay still on the crown of his head as he eyed me. The position showed the broad musculature of his lateral muscles, the thickness of his triceps. The way he held me with his gaze, not quite glaring, just this side of hurt, I felt the shame swim up from my toes.

"I'm sorry," I said in a rush as I stopped dead with handfuls of garments of all sorts hanging from my grip, shaking back and forth as I gestured almost wildly. "I'm so messed up. All this fucking shit has got me in an awful state."

I flung the socks and hand towel across the room. They caught separate air currents and splayed on the carpet several feet from each other. I scowled at them and dropped onto the bed with my legs in front of me. The heels rested on the carpet as I sagged between my thighs. I had to breathe in long drafts just to normalize my heartrate.

"I'm an idiot," I said.

He sighed and moved closer. I knew he was standing over me without having to look up. His presence electrified the air. I thought I felt a hum between us. There was a long sigh before he collapsed onto the mattress beside me.

"I understand. It's been a helluva day," he said. "I should have picked my time better. But I thought... well, I thought you must have seen what I was. I thought it was the right time to show you."

"What do you mean, 'what you are'?" I said, peering sideways at him. All I'd seen was that flash of eyes. It had been something else, something *other*, that had scared me.

"You mean you really don't know?"

I swiveled to look at him. "You're not going to tell me you're a pedophile, are you? Or a married man?"

I openly gawked at his hand, searching for ring or a demarcation of tan lines that would reveal he'd taken one off.

"Interesting that you'd put married last on the list as though it's somehow worse."

He tried to chuckle but cut it short when he caught my eye. I guessed he didn't feel as though his comedic timing was right based on what he saw in my face. His sigh was heavy and exhausted.

"I don't think you can take another shock today," he said. "Maybe not ever. So we'll just postpone the gender reveal of that little confession."

Now he had my attention. After the things I'd seen—what he'd seen—I couldn't imagine what might be worse that he'd need to continue hiding it. I leaned back on my palms, the mattress moving beneath us. As my gaze skidded over his features, I had the horrible thought that it wasn't what he was that was the problem. It was my reaction. Shame slid up my backbone in a cold, greasy slither.

"What could be so bad you would compare it to a gender reveal?" I asked, trying to inflect some casualness to my voice that didn't come out quite right. I leaned forward, my hair spilling over my shoulders as I tried to catch his eye. "I just fought off some ungodly creature out there. I think I can handle whatever it is you need to confess so badly."

His mouth twitched with humor. "I don't think so." He stood up and stretched. I could see his ribcage rise and thrust as he arched backwards. The corded muscles of his neck bunched and let go. My heart rate ticked up annoyingly.

"I'll get Parrish to swing by with a car I can sleep in," he said, pulling his shirt back down over the glimpse of bare, shaved belly. "If you could spare a blanket, we'll take turns watching your house tonight."

"I'm not sure I like the thought of being watched."

He held my gaze, so insufferably calmly that I didn't dare argue when he said. "I told you I wouldn't let anything hurt you. It's not prudent to leave you without protection."

I wasn't sure I liked the way he said it. Like he thought if he wasn't outside, I wouldn't be safe inside. It occurred to me that he had pretty close look at the thing. He'd felt it beneath his hands as he'd fought with it. If he thought he needed to stay and with backup, I wasn't going to argue. So I found myself nodding and trying not to picture the thing hammering away at my door in the early morning.

"You think he'll come back?" I said. "Whoever he is. You think he's the killer?"

"If it does, it won't get a foot on your step."

It. So he'd had enough of a glimpse that he didn't believe the thing was human either.

I was sure of it. While my nerves tweaked at the thought of anyone watching me, I had to admit that I felt safer knowing Layne would be out there. Him and Parrish. I wasn't alone.

He pulled his cell phone from his pocket and busied himself sending out a message as he walked back to my living room. I followed on his heels, my hands running down my arms even though I wasn't cold. He grunted a couple of times then lifted his gaze over the screen to look at me.

"Do you mind me waiting for a while?" he said, distracted, it looked like, by what he saw on his screen. "Apparently, she has some hot date."

He tapped the screen in rapid succession as though doing so could change what was showing on the panel. He growled beneath his breath at it.

"Only if you tell me your secret," I said, pausing to watch him as he leaned his hip against the sofa. "You can't just tease a gal like that and then change the subject. And don't think I didn't notice you doing that."

"And if I don't tell you?" He offered a playful quirk of his eyebrow. "Will you make me sleep in there?"

His suggestive glance toward my bedroom reminded me of the vibrator still sitting on the end table. I sneaked a peek to be sure and inwardly groaned as it loomed up from behind the digital clock.

"I suppose that's one way to keep your guard awake," he said. "If nothing else but to wonder what other interesting devices might be lurking about in that veritable sex shop just beyond the threshold."

So he had seen the vibrator. Well, I would not be ashamed. "Ha-ha," I said. "You think that little thing warrants a sex shop label? Man, you should see my closet."

HIs face blanched, and I took great pleasure in watching his expression run the gamut from shock to interest and then to something more akin to lust. It made my spine tingle. But it might have been a bit more than I should have done under the circumstances because now I was pretty sure he'd never look at me without imagining all sorts of paraphernalia, and a gay friend of mine had once warned me that the male imagination had no limits.

"I'll trade you a blanket for a confession," I said to distract him as much as myself.

When he ran his hand down along his throat, touching down with a feathery softness against the silver scar that looked so much thicker just a few moments earlier, I thought he'd refuse.

"Listen," I said, stepping in front of him as he made to stab at the screen again. "You saw what was after me out there. You touched it. You know it's not human. Not really." Impossible as it was, there was no denying it.

He put his phone back in his pocket and plunged his hands inside too as he faced me. "I did."

"So now you should have a description of the killer. You should be making some sort of arrest, calling for a sketch artist, putting out an APB."

I ticked the things off on my fingers and he watched each time I stabbed at one finger with the other. It infuriated me, the calm way he just stood there. I wanted him to admit it. Admit to me that it wasn't a man, because by the way my skin crawled, feeding me images that came straight from the bowels of dark memory, I could only wish it was a man.

"Well," I said, "what are you going to do about it?"

"I already told you," he said. "I'm staying the night outside your apartment."

I dragged in patience with a long breath, aware I was pinching my nostrils. "Something is going on...and don't say it's a serial killer because hello, I was there, remember?" I forced my hands down against my sides because if I didn't, I was going to use them to punch his chest.

"It's something else. What I saw out there..." I pointed at my door. "What I saw out there wasn't like anything I'd ever seen. It wasn't a man, and you're keeping secrets from me."

It wasn't pleasant admitting that out loud, and it brought to mind the predatory eyes, the arms that looked like they ended in talons not fingers. I closed my fist around my amulet. It was cool to the touch, an inert stone with out of the ordinary patterns engraved in its surface.

He rocked back on his heels and gave one swift, barely perceptible nod that told me he had made a decision.

"Can we get that drink?" he said.

It was an abrupt shift in topic, but he looked like he needed it, so I nodded. He followed me into the kitchen and lurked behind me as I fumbled through the cupboards for a glass. I plucked one from a shelf and pointed at the freezer with my elbow. "The Screech is in there. Get the cola from the fridge."

I waited till he had extracted both and held them in each hand before aiming the rims of two glasses toward him. He lifted one finger alongside the liquor bottle, indicating he wanted me to hold the thought as he opened the freezer. The cold air blasted out at me as I dug into the depths for a few cubes of ice and dropped them into each glass with a clink.

He poured two generous drams of rum over the ice then upended the soda bottle into each glass. The tops of the tumblers fizzled as bubbles danced on the surface and escaped the rims. I watched his face, studying the set look of his brow, and the way he grit his teeth together in thought. Collecting his words, I realized. Figuring out what to tell me and how much. It was an effort to hold my gaze to his eyes and not drop to his throat to watch the powerful play of muscles there as he considered what to say.

The fizz sprayed the tip of my nose as I drank deep. He'd made it a stiff mix, with more rum than soda but I didn't care. I enjoyed the bite of the Screech and the liquid burn it seared into my chest. He downed his in one swallow.

"Hell," I said, impressed.

He nodded and poured another shot. He tilted the bottle toward me with a raised eyebrow but I shook my head.

"I want answers, not a hangover."

He sucked the back of his teeth. "I have a high tolerance," he said. "Couple drinks for me are no worse than a long drink of water. Something about my metabolism." He blew out a long breath that told me he really, really didn't want to have to say more. He muttered something about wishing it could.

I took the bottle from him and set it with a thunk down onto my counter. For as cluttered as my apartment was, the counter was always clear. It drove me batty to have cannisters and toasters and such taking up the valuable real estate when my kitchen was so small. I eyeballed the glass, thinking it looked almost decadent sitting there alone.

I ran my palm along the smooth surface as I studied him, thinking about all those clients, all those desperate but resistant clients, who wanted me to perform some magic that could belie their own senses but who contacted me anyway. They all wanted to believe in something greater no matter how skeptical they were.

They all wore the same, heavy shouldered tension in their upper bodies. It was my job to help them out of that, give them what they needed to heal so they could move on. It wasn't a noble profession like therapist or counsellor, but it had its own kind of goodness.

Layne had the same set to his shoulders right then, like he bore a weight that he really wanted someone to relieve him of or at least make it easier to carry.

So it was time to try another tack. One that might actually get me somewhere.

"I've seen ghosts," I said, thinking of the premonition of the murdered psychics. "I've seen glimpses of demons and been able to move a hard man to love a soft woman. You can't fool me," I lifted my amulet as a means to remind him why he'd sought me out in the first place. "I might not know everything going on, but I'm not a novice at all this."

I leaned my elbow on the counter, using it to support me while I offered a casual, non-judgmental posture that said everything would be okay. I wasn't sure it would be, but he needed to think so. At least long enough to tell me what the hell was going on. Because he knew, damn him. He knew and was playing me.

"Your apartment doesn't have many magical items," he said as he leaned against the refrigerator and crossed one foot over the other. "Odd, don't you think, for a woman of your power?"

"Is this an interrogation?" I said but I shrugged it off like it didn't mean anything to me. "Because if it is, you're barking up the wrong tree. I put all that in my shop."

"For show?" he said. "Because anyone with a penchant for magical energy as you do, doesn't compartmentalize it. It's part of them. It's in what they wear, what they eat, and everything that surrounds them."

Touché. But then, he had no idea what I'd been brought up with. Maybe that would be true for the run-of-the-mill witchy wannabe. Not me. Never me.

Watching him was like watching a big cat. Or a dog. A wolf, maybe. His gaze was so intense. "You're changing the subject," I said.

"Maybe this is the subject."

I rolled onto both elbows and leaned backwards just a bit, letting my weight sag into my forearms and my wrists hang over the counter edge. The wood dug into my back. He dropped his gaze to my chest before dragging it back up to my face, and I smiled to myself.

"I'll answer your question, detective, but you won't like it. It's just so damn simple. I put everything I have, my energy, my desires— all of it—into that shop. I sacrifice my personal environment to make that one everything it needs to be." It was the truth, at least. "My clients need to feel as though anything is possible. If it's even remotely energized, it goes to my shop. I spend the most time there."

That, too, was true. I pushed off the counter and slid the bottle back toward him. "If you think a witch or psychic or medium needs to have objects about her to be powerful, you better take that bottle and drown yourself in it. Because for a detective, you know very little about human nature."

He blinked twice then let a grin slip through the careful facade. "There's more to the killings than a mere man or serial killer." He said it like it was a test of some sort.

I nodded, with a 'you think I'm stupid' kind of expression on my face, and he inhaled sharply as though he was about to take a plunge into icy water.

"Whatever's happening," he began. "It's supernatural. Whatever is killing the women is not human. Parrish and I are probably the only ones who suspect anything other than a deranged lunatic with occult fascinations. We know better. Your shop smelled...real," he said after a thoughtful pause.

I thought it strange that he used the word smell, but I kept quiet, afraid to interrupt him, careful not to show the confusion on my face. Because his true belief in the supernatural made me feel a bit squishy, like I was about to get sucked into a black hole. Despite my efforts, I didn't want him to believe me. Not really. And I wasn't sure why.

He picked up the bottle and twirled it in his grip. I watched the amber liquid slosh around for a few turns before he put it back down and shoved it backward toward the wall.

"What else?" I said because it was obvious he hadn't told me the worst. Something haunted the edges of his eyes.

"What else," he said in a half-mocking echo that was more frustrated repetition than anything else. A way to speak without confessing a damn thing. "Only the thing I'm most afraid to tell you."

I perked up. "What could be that scary?"

He held my gaze for a long moment, those shadows at the edges of his eyes disappearing as he watched me. I had the feeling that confession was coming and I felt even more certain I needed to brace myself.

"Maybe it's best if I show you," he said quietly.

With that, he stepped back and began to peel off his shirt. I expected a scar, or a nasty tattoo. Part of me wanted to avert my eyes to give him some privacy, but the bigger, and admittedly hedonistic, part of me wanted to revel in the skin I was about to see.

But he didn't stop at his shirt.

My gaze was still glued to the muscles twitching beneath his chest as he tossed the shirt aside when those hands went to his belt buckle and then his zipper. I realized he was about to take off every last stitch of clothing.

Chapter Sixteen

IF I THOUGHT I was unprepared for the man to get naked, then I most definitely wasn't ready for what came next. His supple skin and muscled torso started to transform into something that just as definitively was not a man at all. It wasn't even man-like.

A snout formed around his aquiline nose. The whiskers of his jaw thickened. He moaned in pain as a snapping sound cut the air. I started, pushing off the counter and taking a step back as the air sizzled around me. As I realized that what was happening was not some play of the light or the ravings of a terror-soaked imagination. He was transforming right in front of me and that transformation from man to beast was not smooth and seamless. It looked painful. Very painful.

I should have been horrified, but all I could do was stare with what I presumed was a slack-jawed expression. But the rictus didn't last long. Once I realized that the impossible was indeed happening right there in front of me, I had two thoughts.

One: Whatever was taking over Layne's body was breaking his bones and rearranging his spine to do so. And two: even though he'd warned me not to be afraid, I knew I was standing in the burgeoning presence of a predator. And I was indeed terrified.

"Layne," I said, testing the veracity of my eyes just to be sure. I needed to know that the man was still beneath that lupine facade, that I wasn't in the middle of a horror movie where the damsel does nothing and ends up getting killed. And yet, somehow, despite the evidence of my eyes, I still didn't feel as if this was all real. Maybe I just didn't want it to be. And so I said his name again, testing.

"Layne, are we okay here?"

I didn't know what I meant by that except if he wasn't the beast I saw emerging from the skin of the man, then I figured he'd answer. Maybe laugh at me. Maybe whisk me off to an ER somewhere because the shock of the night had finally stolen the last vestiges of my mind.

Instead, he let go a pained moan as something in his back cracked so loudly I thought someone had shot a gun from the hallway.

I jumped, freed finally from the paralysis by that awful sound.

I back-stepped in a hustle I would imagine any horror movie heroine would envy. There wasn't much finesse in the way I scrabbled behind me with hands that sought and found nothing sharp and pointy to use as a weapon.

My fingers did find something cold and solid, and only when I knocked it over with a crash to the floor did I realize it was the vase from my sofa's side table. The book I had been reading went next, a Patricia Briggs new release, and it toppled from the arm with a splat to the floor.

It was the sound of the paper fluttering to a close that gave me the insight.

Werewolf. What was now a nearly changed, half-formed beast in front of me was a werewolf. Or at least it would be if I gave it enough time to change all the way.

"Easy," I said, aware that I was raising my hands as though the policeman beneath was about to arrest me. It was a ridiculous gesture, as ridiculous as letting the man into my apartment in the first place when I knew...dammit I knew he wasn't, couldn't, be only a man. Not after that fight with the beast outside. "Easy, now."

My thumb caught on the chain of my amulet and scooped it up off my shirt. It slipped into my palm with a fit so snug that it surprised me to feel how warm I was when I was so obviously freezing from shock.

I took another step backwards. My heel caught on the leg of the chair, and I toppled into it.

The half-formed creature leapt for me. I flailed sideways as I tried to evade it.

I might have screamed. Someone was screaming, at least. The pitch and noise was hurting my ears.

By the time I got my hands in front of my face to protect myself, thick, callused fingers wrapped around my wrists.

"Brie," Layne said. "It's alright. You're safe."

I wasn't safe. I was hyperventilating like a mother-fucker, and how could that make me okay? Every inch of my body was tingling with fear and adrenaline. My brain was swamped with memories from my child-hood. The terror and awfulness of the things I didn't understand played out again in my mind and in every ounce of marrow in my bones. How dare he dredge all that up? My hands clutched at my throat as I struggled to speak around the tight ache there.

It took several, gasping seconds before I was able, and then I swore at him, yanking my hands away from his grip.

He crouched in front of me, human again, chest bare. I had the ridiculous thought that he must shave his chest hair, he was so smooth. One knee was raised while the other rested against the floor. The gaze that drilled into mine, so intense, so concerned, was yellow and filmy, as though something wrestled with the mind behind those eyes.

"What the fuck?" I found the strength to bolt off the chair and push him aside. I needed space. I needed lots and lots of space. Hours ago, I was drooling over the guy and now I realized 'a guy' wasn't at all what he really was.

"This isn't happening," I said as I pointed at him, all naked and gorgeous six feet crouched still next to my sofa. "This isn't fucking happening and you aren't fucking going to convince me this is happening."

I was shaking again, dammit. "And if this is happening, you have a nerve doing that to me tonight when I already faced God knows what out there." I shifted the jabbing toward the door. "You best tell me this is not what I think it is."

Not magic. Not something from myth. And yet... My breath hitched.

He stood to his full height, not exhibiting one bit of shame at his nudity. "It's happening," he said. "I'm a shifter."

"No shit, Sherlock," I said, clinging to the last vestige of possibility that could explain this away without drawing in the things I didn't want to face. "And I'm tripping on acid or 'shrooms and I have no fucking idea who gave them to me."

I put a finger to my temple and pressed. My fingernail bit into the skin but I didn't feel any weird sensations that might indicate I was high. I shifted my glare to the counter where the glass sat that we'd shot rum out of.

"You dropped something in my drink," I said, and then because he was approaching me, I backed up a step and held my hand out. "Oh, no, you don't. You need to keep your fucking distance."

He sighed but halted. "I didn't drug you. You know I didn't. It's real. My change was real."

My gaze skated down to his hips and then raced back up to his face because the way I felt seeing all that man, all that skin and gorgeous physique did something else to me. And I didn't even want to think about what that made me.

"First things first," I said in as even a voice as I could muster. "You need to get dressed."

Because the last thing I wanted was to be thinking about anything remotely sexual after what I'd just seen him turn into.

He looked down at himself as though he was surprised to find he was naked. He made a sound deep in his throat but it wasn't of embarrassment. I thought it was more that he was intrigued to discover the reaction of his body.

But he did at least stoop to retrieve his pants, and while I tried to avert my gaze, fuck me if I didn't find it difficult not to watch his buttocks flex. He shifted to the side and pushed one leg then the other into his pants, then he zipped up and faced me.

"Better?" he said.

I chose not to answer. I wasn't sure what to think. Instead, I gestured toward the sofa, indicating he should sit down. I elected to stand. That neat psychological trick again. It came handy so often. But this time, I crossed my arms over my chest, hugging myself as I faced him.

He sat, thankfully, but kept his eye on me as he did so.

"I didn't think you'd react so badly," he said, an edge to his voice that I was sure had nothing to do with emotion.

"You told me not to be scared," I said in an accusing tone I knew he'd recognize for what it was. "You must have suspected it."

He canted his head. "Sure, but only because I knew you wouldn't expect it of me. There aren't a lot of packs left. Some witches haven't ever seen a wolf shifter. But I thought at least you'd know about us." He looked honestly confused and even jerked his chin toward the open cover of the Briggs' book to emphasize his point.

I crossed the room to pick up the novel. I closed it after marking the page and used the spine to poke at his chest.

"This," I said. "This is fiction. It's very good fiction, but it's fiction."

"We exist. Just like witches exist." He narrowed his gaze at me as though he was working out a problem. "You believe in ghosts and demons and magic, but you don't believe in shifters. Even after you've seen me. The other me." He coughed.

I blinked at him and when I didn't say anything because I was afraid it would somehow incriminate me, he pushed to a stand.

"Maybe it's something else bothering you," he said in a voice that came out so bitter it made me pause. "Maybe it's not that you don't believe but that you don't want to be associated with it."

He leaned to scoop his shirt from the floor and pulled one sleeve over his arm. "You're all the same, you witches."

He shrugged until the shirt settled down over his chest and belly.

"You see what we're up against," he said, pointing at the door with the arm still free of material. "What that was, what I got cut up and shredded for, that's real too. And it's not a werewolf. I have no idea what in the blazes it is, but it's real and it's killing, and I need to stop it. You can either get over your bigotry and help or you can keep feeling that hatred and get killed."

I sank onto the edge of the sofa. My head went into my hands as I perched there. I had no idea what was happening or how to stop the locomotive from plowing into the damsel on the tracks but it was all too much.

"It's not fucking racism, for fuck's sake," I said, trying to cover my shock and surprise at the same time I tried to smother it. "It's just...it's a lot. I can't process it all. At least not all at once."

He stood there and I sat with my head in my hands, forcing myself to take long breaths. Even though I heard him moving toward me, I was surprised when he knelt at my feet. His warm hand took a place on my knee. I peered through my fingers at him.

His eyes were back to that warm chocolate color that made my belly all tingly. I swallowed nervously, but grateful that at least that one thing was back to normal.

"What the hell is happening?" I asked, my voice so soft and small I barely recognized it as my own.

He laid his other hand on my other knee and spread my legs ever so gently apart, enough for him to fit inside. The intimacy of it felt at both times scary and appropriate. Whichever sensation rode my nerves, I decided I wouldn't resist.

He ran his hand up my leg and the warmth that followed its path made my legs part even more. Sagging open for him, I thought.

"I overreacted," he said in a gentle tone, one that sounded like a lullaby. "It's been a long while since

I've shown myself to someone outside the pack. But I thought you saw me out there...I thought you saw what I was and might think I was the one who killed those women if I didn't prove to you that I was something...else."

"Which I did," I said, angry at myself. "I acted exactly as you feared."

"Oh darlin'," he said. "I don't fear much."

I believed it. Just the memory of him attacking that creature, I imagined fear was something he wouldn't admit to himself even if he did feel it.

"I followed you after you decided to walk home alone," he said and his voice was a mere whisper or it seemed so. Everything seemed so hushed in the moment, I wasn't sure if I was dreaming it all. "I knew you didn't want me to see where you lived, and yet, I couldn't let you just walk alone in the dark.

"I don't know why," he said, answering a question I never asked. "I smelled something in the air. I wanted you to get home safe. It was just a failsafe. I had no idea you'd get attacked."

The mild notion that maybe I should have seen it coming sat in the air, demanding an answer. I wasn't sure how I felt about his suspicion of me, especially since I was already adding up whether or not sex with him would be the worst kind of taboo.

He pulled me from the sofa and stepped me toward the bedroom and my heart raced in anticipation. Was he going to do this now? Was it appropriate? And more than that, did I even care?

I let him take me a few steps before he hoisted me into his arms. I lay against his chest, feeling his heart pound against my ribcage. His voice when he spoke was like fingers smoothing down errant hair. It was filled with careful tiredness.

"I didn't exactly have an idyllic childhood," he said. "Some things follow you, you know?"

I did know. All too well.

We were at the doorway to my bedroom and in seconds, I would be answering my own question about whether or not I had the will to cross the line.

"You need to go to bed," he said as he dropped my legs so that my feet hit the floor. "I'll explain it all tomorrow."

He reached out to the pile of laundry and brushed it aside. Most of it fell silently to the foot of the bed and as I watched those hands making room on the mattress and reassembling the sheets and blankets, I remembered that just a few moments earlier, those fingers had been claws.

Mesmerized, I let him take my hand and hold it against his chest. I almost pulled away out of reflex but for the gentle pressure he exerted, pressing my palm into his chest. I felt his heartbeat there. When I looked up at him, he was gazing at me with half-hooded eyelids.

Heat radiated from him in waves. I might have done something ridiculous, like climbing his torso and wrapping my legs around his waist, straddling him as he stood next to my bed with those half-hooded eyes watching me.

I might have kissed him, if not for the banging on the front door.

He broke away and ran a hand through his hair. In his haste to exit the room, he left me to awkwardly try not to fall backward on the bed. Once I'd gathered my balance, I followed him to the living room and watched him answer my door.

Parrish burst in like she had broken wind in an elevator and needed to exit before someone realized it was her.

"Thank the blistered hands of Satan," she said. "I thought you might be dead."

"Why would I be dead?" he said, leaning past her to check outside.

She tapped her temple as though she thought he had lost his mind.

"Maybe because you're constantly bothering me at all hours of the night with hunches and clues and yet the one time I decide to text you, you can't move yourself to type so much as an emoji?"

She spun on her heel and whipped her phone out to chest height, showing him the screen. "Read it."

"I'll be there in five minutes," he read aloud, leaning in to the phone and straining with narrowed eyes before he peered up from the screen to her face.

She tapped the top of the screen with her fingernail. "And?"

He looked back at the screen. "And make sure I have coffee waiting."

"Coffee," she echoed. "Waiting. For me."

She swept her hands in a gesture that indicated she thought the java should appear from thin air.

"Well, here I am as promised." She arched her black eyebrow at him and glared.

I headed to the kitchen, thinking maybe I should put on a pot, since she'd come here at his behest because of me. Layne held his hand up to me as his other one went into his pocket. He pulled out his phone and industriously thumbed the screen.

A smile pulled at the corner of his mouth when he finished.

Parrish's cell phone rang with a 'Who let the Dawgs out' chime. She flipped it back inward so she could see the screen. She read silently for a second and then made a loud harrumphing sound. When she looked up again, it was to sweep me with a curious glance before she shoved the phone back in her pocket.

"I'll be in the car," she said. "You can bring me a large mug of very creamy coffee out there."

I knew she wasn't talking to me, but her eyes never left my face as she spoke. There seemed to be some silent communication going on between her and Layne, something that went beyond the agreement to share a pot of java or a cold car interior. For the first time in a long time, I felt like the odd man out.

Layne looked like the cat that swallowed the canary.

"I'll be out in a minute," he said and reached down to grab a plush blanket buried beneath the pile of laundry on the sofa. He tossed it to her and she swiped it from the air with such speed it snapped its tail with a crack that made me jump.

She canted her head at my reaction and grinned, showing me it was exactly the reaction she was looking for.

"You know it smells like sex in here, don't you?" she said.

I didn't know if she was trying to make me or him feel uncomfortable, or even if she was doing it as some sort of snarky bid for vengeance, but it was so unexpected, so perfectly untrue that I let go a cackle of laughter that I'd regret later. If there was one thing a gal didn't want, it was for a man to think she' was that kind of witch.

"If you think sex smells like sweat and fear," I told her with all honesty but an equal measure of humor, "then your lovers best strap on their safety belts."

She guffawed. "Won't be the only thing they strap on."

Layne groaned and put his fingers to his nose, pinching the bridge. "Can we not do this? Can we not do the lesbian jokes tonight, Parrish?"

Parrish put an innocent hand to her chest. "You think I'm joking? I'm hurt. And here I came all this way to help you with your girl."

"The last thing I need," he drawled, "is advice from a lesbian who doesn't know the difference between a girl and a woman."

"Okay," she said with her finger in the air. "That's pedophilia and this chick don't roll that way. Besides, I'm more discerning than you think."

He tugged on her arm, dragging her to the door despite her craning to look at me over her shoulder.

"You dated a hooker."

She sucked the back of her teeth. "Like I said, I don't climb into a woman's bed unless I know she can handle the mess."

Layne snorted and barely yanked the door open before he was shoving her through the gap. I could feel the cool air clawing its way in and shivered. It was always cold at night this close to the water despite the buildings creating a nice lee from the mid-summer temperatures.

"Pull that rickety old trap of yours up in front of the apartment building," he told her. "This isn't a stake out. It's a protective detail."

She groaned. "You know, one of these days, you're going to have to pay me for all this bonus help. I might be a lesbian, but I'm not a cheap hooker. Where's my coffee?"

"I'll bring some out," I said. "Decaf or espresso?"

I had a cheap espresso machine and ground my own beans. It was late and would make a ton of noise my nerves couldn't really handle but I was willing to brew it up if she wanted it. I owed her that much.

"Decaf?" She snorted. "Might as well feed me warm milk."

She wrapped her hand against the side of the door as she pushed it back open, moving Layne about a foot backward despite him being as big as she was. She eyed the kitchen counter. "Put some of that in there too."

The rum. I'd forgotten. I was nodding when Layne plucked her fingers from the door frame and shoved her back through the door.

"Booze makes you sleepy," he said. "And you snore."

She was all hands and arms grappling to stay inside and he pushed those out too, then slammed the door on her grumbling.

He turned to me.

"We can talk more about this later?" he said.

I nodded. Whatever it was that needed examining, it could be done in the morning. I was past spent and could feel myself swaying on my feet.

"The gala is tomorrow, remember," he said. "If you don't see me in the morning, I'll pick you up here at seven."

"Sure," I said, even though I couldn't muster an iota of excitement. I must have been worse off than I thought, because he reached out to steady me, laying a palm against my shoulder. I eyed it with a modicum of regret. Ah, but for the interference of lesbians I might have had those hands elsewhere.

"Never mind the coffee," he said. "You should go to bed."

My gaze flicked up to his as he stepped onto the porch.

Unable to manage much more than another nod, I leaned on the door.

I just wanted him gone. I wanted the door closed and I wanted to collapse into my bed, but he kept talking in that buttery voice. I might fall asleep right there.

"Don't worry," he said in a tone that swelled with soothing comfort. "You'll be fine. We'll take turns out there, so nothing can hurt you. We'll make sure of it."

As I looked out into the darkness past his shoulder, I wanted to tell him that some hurtful things didn't come in terrifying shapes and sizes. Not all the bad guys were monsters. But I imagined he already knew that.

My eye trailed to where Parrish had parked the car. I could see her shadow inside, fiddling with what I supposed were the knobs of the heater or the radio.

Standing just to the left of the car, barely out of sight save for the halo of red light that came from no street-lamp anywhere near here, stood my mother. Her hair was long flowing and caught an errant breeze although I felt nothing moving in the air but a bit of odor from the garbage bins.

And while she watched me and I watched her, I knew I wouldn't sleep that night no matter how tired I was.

Because mommy dearest had been dead for years.

CHAPTER SEVENTEEN

APPARENTLY, EVEN SEEING THE ghost of my mother couldn't win out against the kind of exhaustion that took me finally, and despite thinking I'd never find the land of Nod, I slept the sleep of the dead. I figured that beautiful comatose sleep had more to do with the monster lurking outside my door, wrapped in blankets and swilling coffee than exhaustion. There's something about knowing a powerful beast is standing guard that acts as a powerful sedative.

In the morning, that monster and his partner caught sight of me standing on my front step, tumbler of ice water and purse in hand as I contemplated my day and all the changes just a simple thing like going to my shop would entail. The way I would have to conduct business, being ever vigilant, trusting no one, that was the biggest issue that had me staring into my water bottle. Trust had always been an issue, but not one I let my clients see. They needed to feel my confidence in them if they were to see what I needed them to see, hear what I needed them to hear. And I didn't know how I was going to do that without putting myself at risk while that maniac of whatever species and realm it originated from was out there loose.

But the two monsters who watched over me all night and enabled that luxurious sleep nodded at me before they pulled off in the wreck of bright yellow Fiat Parrish drove. The sight of it, and the faces within, I knew, were the reason I would be able to conduct my business in the way I'd always done. Those faces gave me courage and hope.

I stopped at a pop-up cell phone shop and purchased a new phone with the same number and took the time to text Layne a thanks that I sincerely meant. Then I went to my shop. A gal had to work and since I had actually slept without feeling like someone would attack me while I was unconscious, everything seemed much brighter. Even the corner of the street where I'd seen that haunting image of my mom was well lit.

The sun filtered down through the leaves of the decorative oaks and dappled the pavement. Cars that had been nestled into their parking spaces hours before were already gone. My neighbor up the street, who had ignored my calls for help, was letting her cat out again.

I checked my phone for the time. Fifty minutes before I had to open my shop. Layne's comment about me not having any magical paraphernalia about had reminded me I had unpacked none of my mother's belongings. I'd decided before falling to sleep that I would go through the boxes she'd left in the store's attic.

I'd been avoiding even thinking about them since I'd returned home. I'd emancipated my physical self from my mother years ago and after imagining her standing there watching me, I realized I'd not fully liberated my psyche. Those boxes and their contents had to go.

I strolled to the shop with a sense of purpose and excitement. I wasn't foolish enough to just chuck the boxes out onto the street for collection by the city's trash men or the vagrants that might wander by. There might be some pretty good stuff in them, worth selling at the front of the store. I was certain I'd find bottles of powders and warped candles and the like. I'd caught sight of a rather large black onyx mortar and pestle peeking from the peeled back lid of one box on the day I'd moved home.

I wasn't sure who had packed up my mom's things while I'd been away. When I'd been called home at her death, the lawyer had already made arrangements to store whatever had been lying in her apartment. They'd lain blankets and sheets over the furniture and shut off the electric and water. The boxes gathered dust in the living room until I'd arrived and decided to stay. My movers re-located those boxes to the store's attic at my request while I'd renovated the building.

I half expected to see the stray dog hanging around the back door when I turned the corner onto the street that led to my alleyway. I wasn't sure if I could name the feeling as relief when the alley looked no different than it did any other day.

The steel bowls of kibble and water I left out for the stray cats of the quarter were empty and needed refilling. I checked the little milk crate nest I'd left for a pregnant female calico but it was still empty. The wool blanket carefully arranged in inviting rolls hadn't even been touched.

The sun overhead was just rising above the rooftops when I unlocked the back door to the storefront. I stepped in and inhaled a deep draft of essential oils and incense. This was home. No matter that I slept and ate in my mother's house, this shop was mine. I'd built it from my own pure determination to become something better than my mother, to help others where I could.

I'd spent years running from myself. I'd tried walking the straight and narrow and doing the honorable thing of doing an honest day's work. I always ended up failing. When I'd finally accepted that my skills lay in confidence, I decided I'd make those skills at least work for others.

Becoming a charlatan psychic, medium, and modern day witch wasn't that much of a stretch. But I'd discovered something else about myself as I built the business and cultivated a clientele that would trust me. I was good at it, and I loved what I did. The shop became a sort of surrogate mentor, teaching me one sale at a time that absolution could come from magic, even if it was fake.

One day, I planned to sell the brownstone and renovate the upstairs of this building to house an apartment. I'd finally leave all of my mother and her life behind me.

But first, I needed to pull down those boxes I'd stashed and that was going to take a lot of mental preparation. I checked my appointment book just to be sure I was clear for the day and noticed I'd scratched an entire line down the whole page. Strange. I didn't remember doing it at all, and I certainly didn't remember erasing the appointment with the man with the straw-colored hair who had saved me from the nut case.

With a shrug, I turned the lock on the back door and checked my phone. I still had plenty of time to go cart the boxes down from the attic. Fussing over a day's entry in a planner seemed ridiculous, especially when my mind was anywhere the last few days but work.

I mounted the stairs to the second floor located at the back of the shop located between my lovely burled counter and the guest bathroom. By the time I hit the first tread, my amulet dug into my chest, reminding me just how heavy it was to be dangling as I worked over old boxes.

Besides, my chest felt all hot and clammy beneath it. Even when I lifted the pendant from beneath my shirt and draped it against the cloth instead, it felt too uncomfortable. I held it between my finger and thumb and considered just dropping the damn thing in the trash along with the rest of my mother's stuff.

Truth was, as much as I hated the thing, it was part of the uniform I'd decided the shop needed to gain that street cred. The amulet never failed to glean a comment or two.

So I'd keep it. But I wouldn't wear it upstairs. No one would be coming in after all.

I made my way back through to the main shop and dropped it onto the counter and followed it up with the large garnet ring I'd bought in Nova Scotia. That one was just because I didn't want to lose it through the floor boards as I worked. I'd lost a few pounds recently and it swiveled on my finger more than I liked.

I headed back to the stairwell and tapped the bathroom door as I went by, thinking about Layne in there washing up from cleaning the graffiti. It would be a pleasant enough image to carry with me upstairs as I worked in the dusty space above the shop.

The building was an old one, and the door at the top was very much like I might have seen in a horror flick where an old aunt might be lurking to look out the circular window. But when the door swung wide, the fullness of the attic space spread out in broad oak floor boards that still shone from century's old polish even if it was lurking beneath a layer of dust. Put some beams up, some gypsum board and paint, and I'd have a gorgeous open concept apartment. The chimney that climbed the far wall took up several feet and would make a nice backdrop for a wide screen television. I could put a plush leather sofa in the middle, several shelves, and a comfy love seat.

I didn't need much space since it was just me, and the smells of the shop leaked up through the floor boards to create a heady mix with the wood polish and brick dust adding to the mix.

But for now, all the space held were three big cardboard boxes and an old traveler's trunk. I could smell the musty paper from the top of the stairs.

I heaved a bracing breath. I could do this. I had to do it.

I crossed the room toward the box stuffed so full, that the seams were bulging. Poking through the material at the top, I spied the pestle handle that went along with the mortar set I'd remembered. It would bring in a pretty penny if marketed just right. The set was larger than I remembered and as I dug around in the box, I found the mortar itself, a gigantic thing that took both hands to lift.

I sniffed at it and recoiled. Whatever she'd been grinding into the bottom, it still lingered in a miasma of funk and cloying juniper. A residue clung to the sides, thick and grimy as though some oils had solidified and collected dust from the air. It would take a good deal of cleaning, but the symbols on the handle of the pestle matched the ones at the bottom of the mortar.

They even looked a lot like my amulet. Great. The branding was intact.

I smiled to myself as I held it up to the light with both hands. Sun streamed in through the eastern window, casting dust motes into a beam reminiscent of divine glow. I felt like an old world goddess lifting a sacred vessel to the sun and I didn't bother to smother the urge to laugh out loud. It was liberating, to be honest, and the thing really was gorgeous.

Tourists would pay big for the thing.

I set it down with a thunk on the wooden floor and leaned over to dig further into the box. As I did, the hair raised on the back of my neck.

Something was watching me.

Just the thought of it made my shoulders tighten. A knot of fear tied itself into my intestines. I didn't dare swallow for fear the sound would drown out the noise of something moving in the shadows. Because there were shadows now that I paid attention. The corners of the attic were out of reach of that glorious sun streaming in from the east window, and the dappled light leaking through the other, smaller windows built in to offer the attic some breath.

I tried to look sideways at the gloom, using my peripheral vision to tease out what couldn't be seen by looking straight on. As I did, I stood up. Slowly at first, then with more determination.

I swung on the corner. The smell of sulfur and lavender rose to my nostrils, seeming to lift from the box and from all around me.

"Sweet Jesus," I said, but there was nothing there. Just a deep corner with a clumps of dust and several mouse nests.

I could hear my own breath in my ears. Obviously, I was still too strung out from the previous night to be doing this sort of work up here alone. I decided to cart everything back downstairs for now and empty it all out in the full brightness of the shop.

The first box wasn't heavy, really. I lifted it with a grunt and balanced it by using my belly as a sort of shelf as I maneuvered back down the stairs.

I made several trips back and forth for the rest of it, trying not to dally too long over the esoteric items I found in both boxes and in the trunk that tempted me to pause for a longer inspection.

The mortar and pestle went first, and then the armfuls of books inside one of the cardboard boxes. The others, the ones in the trunk would also have to be lugged down armful by armful because they were much bulkier. Some of them were leather bound, some filled with vellum. A few of them were bound in a pinkish sort of coating and waxed over. I decided to put that tedious job off until last.

The second to last trip was for the small wooden box I'd found at the bottom of the trunk, the one filled with cork stoppered vials of fluids and powders. It was settled into a nest of flowers that still smelled strongly of fragrance. If it was an apothecary's chest, then it would fetch a pretty penny once I cleaned the vials of the contents.

I had it in my arms and was scanning the space one last time when I felt it again. That hair-raising sense that someone was watching me. This time when I gave the corner my attention, I saw something.

Or someone rather.

My mother. Again. Watching me. Like the evening before, her free-flowing black hair moved ever so slightly as though caught by a breeze.

Except this time, when I moved, she did too.

Chapter Eighteen

In an instant, I was six again and my mother knelt with her back to me over a small stone she'd set in a dug out hole in the basement floor. If I concentrated, I could just make out the monotonous cadence of her voice as she sang words beneath her breath. I smelled something burning, skin or fat or hair, I wasn't sure. Maybe it was all those things, but as a kid, I didn't know the complexity of the odor. Couldn't have individualized or cataloged the intricacies of it. I just knew that whatever it was, it mixed with the sweet smell of flowers and the rotten mudflat stink of boiled eggs.

The result was so noxious that I gagged as I tread on the last step. A small flame licked up over my mother's shoulder, and I realized she was burning something on that little altar. Whatever it was, it was the source of the odor. My stomach heaved as it tried to expel the full glass of milk and peanut butter toast I'd eaten.

I paused, my bare foot scraping the edge of the tread as my stomach lurched again. This time, it rejected the sandwich, and it came up in a flood over my feet and onto the dirt of the basement floor. The sour reek lifted to my nostrils, and I cried out in fear because I didn't know what was happening and I was terrified I'd make her angry.

It had been two months since my father's death, in what I would learn later was a motorcycle accident. He'd hit a deer on a rural road just as the sun set on the summer solstice. I had no way of knowing it then, as a kid. I just knew my dad was gone. I slept poorly. I had nightmares.

My mother cried a lot.

But right then, she wasn't crying. She was singing to that flame. She stopped when she heard me, and she twisted around to face me.

Her face was lit on one side by the firelight as it burned the remains of what looked like the neighbor's pit bull. Her black hair was tied back so it wouldn't catch alight, and it was topped with something that looked like my dress up tiara. It glittered in wavering prisms of red and orange, and it was so beautiful I might have sobbed in envy because my little crown didn't look nearly as pretty.

But that was where the beauty ended. Below that gleaming crown peered two equally gleaming red eyes. And in the moment, I was sure I saw three faces instead of one. That illusion disappeared when I realized that my mother's usually beautiful face was creased with grief and anger and something else I couldn't name.

Right then, I had the terrible, awful, certain feeling I'd done something really bad. I'd caught her in something I should never have seen and the guilt and shame washed over me like the swell of an ocean wave.

I staggered backward, slipping in my own sick, and fell onto my bottom on the dirt. I wanted so badly to run away that I could feel my heart racing in place of the feet that wouldn't move. I curled into a ball, making myself a tight little fist that she couldn't penetrate as she rushed at me.

I cried loud and hard and I couldn't—wouldn't—look at her and no matter how much she shushed me and crooned to me and tried to wrap me in her arms, I wouldn't relent. She was unholy. And whatever she was doing, it was unclean.

I felt exactly the same way when I spied her standing in the corner of the attic as I cleared it of her junk.

I dropped the box of apothecary bottles with a thud to the floor as I staggered backward. The bottles clinked against each other with a sound that told me I was still entrenched in reality and not memory.

"Oh fuck no," I said to the shade. "You're dead. You can't torment me anymore. You should be gone. Really gone."

The shade wavered. When it appeared again, more solid than before, it was a good foot closer. Her eyes blazed a bright red. I could swear I saw a crown nestled in tangles of her black locks.

"Back off," I said, inching back another step. "I don't know what the hell you want, but you're gone. I don't need you. I don't want you. You're dead."

I had the feeling I'd heard the words before and thought of poor Sherry, who I'd conned into thinking I'd conjured her dead father. I waved at the shadow and when I spoke again, it was in a harsh rasp that made me want to sob. "You're not real."

My mother's lips moved without making a sound. She took a step toward me and I shrieked. Loud.

It was enough to snap off the vision as though I'd flicked a switch.

I stood there gaping at the empty corner before I found the courage to move, let alone to make my way back down the stairs. And when I went, it was backwards so she couldn't creep up on me from behind.

My heart was racing hard enough to hurt. I realized by the time I got to the bottom of the stairs that I was hyperventilating. I panned left and right in a numb shock, looking for something that could help. Water. I needed a drink. My throat felt like it had been scraped raw by a firebrand.

I fumbled for the bathroom and ran the faucet. It took several moments before I realized my hand was getting cold in the water.

When I looked at myself in the mirror, I flinched. No wonder I felt so drained. All the color was gone from my face. My gaze lingered on the black circles that stood out against the pallor.

"Best find some rouge, old girl," I said, more to test my voice than anything else. When it didn't come out shaky, I felt a bit more rational, but not any better. I turned off the faucet and gave myself a hard study.

I didn't spook that easy. Not usually. I'd seen enough awful things in my day to be fairly desensitized to most things. But the events of the week were too much. For my psyche to throw me back into a very realistic memory of my childhood, the one a dozen therapists had tried to coax from me to no success, was an indicator of just how badly I was taking all this new experience.

I patted my cheeks to get some color back. I had never told any therapist what I'd seen that night or the things I'd seen afterwards, in the nights that followed when she thought I was in bed and she was free to cast her impotent but terrifying spells.

My poor, deluded mother. A woman who claimed to be a witch. A woman so grief-stricken over her husband's death that she fancied she could bring him back to her somehow with spells and magic and sacrifice. I hated her every living moment after that because she stole something from my childhood I could never get back, and that was what I told those therapists. She'd hurt me. Badly. And they took me from her, the government did. Many times.

And I reveled in that freedom.

I felt like Sherry as I stood there in front of the mirror. It wasn't a great feeling. I pitied her and the trauma she came to me to aid her with, and I felt ashamed of the con I'd done on her.

I resolved to make it right as soon as I could, and I'd use whatever influence I had with her to suggest that whatever we'd done already had the desired effect. If she believed I could help, then I needed to let her know he was gone.

She could finally be free. No more spells or magic needed.

I couldn't help with the trauma she'd experienced with her father, but I wasn't going to exploit it any longer for my own benefit.

I clutched at the edge of the sink as I stared at the boxes I'd lugged down and left at the bottom of the steps. My breaths came in slow, measured inhalations until I found some oasis of calm within. All the junk inside would be my own peeling away of trauma. I was doing the right thing by getting rid of it.

Deciding a thing and doing it are two different concepts, however. It took me longer than I wanted to make my way over to the box with the mortar and pestle and by the time I was kneeling in front and had everything laid out on the floor around me it was already past lunch, but I was too deep in the middle of sorting to stop.

I leaned back on my haunches and surveyed the items, trying to decide which things could be sold immediately and which ones would need work.

The mortar needed cleaning and there were a few sheaves of parchment and old vials of powders that needed a brush of a duster to spruce them up. The labels on those were still clear.

A few bottles were relatively new and empty with pristine cork stoppers and were big enough to make a few witch bottles out of them. Those I could either sell the spell craft items or sell a spell to the person willing to buy but who didn't have a magical bone in their body.

I noted a neatly folded cloth fringed in gold threads with one small circle of scorch in the center. I could market it as a vintage witch's altar cloth. A smaller box held a slew of black and red candles that were smooth and mark free. Those could all go to the front of the shop.

I was planning a display to showcase them all as one unit when someone rapped on the door.

"Not open today," I started to shout over my shoulder and realized it was Layne who stood there.

My heart would have sped up even if he wasn't holding out two large disposable cups. A fat paper bag rested under his elbow, nestled against his ribs. I closed the distance across the shop in record time.

"I hope that's java," I said as I twisted the lock on the door.

"Better," he said. "Lattes and meatball subs."

"God, I'd kill for a donair right now," I said, extracting the cup from his grip and eying the paper bag. I was famished now that I thought about it. A donair was a savory wrap made with ground meat and spices and a sweet sauce that was a specialty sold in Halifax and the surrounding areas.

He frowned at me and snatched the bag back when I reached for it.

"I'm already busy with a magical serial killer," he said. "I don't have time to arrest and jail you for murder for ... what was that again? A Donner?"

I rolled my eyes at him and laid the back of my hand along my forehead to swipe off the beads of sweat that had collected. "You wouldn't say that if you'd ever tasted one. Totally worth killing for."

"I'll stick to good old fashioned Italian heroes, thanks."

We settled behind my counter to eat while I tried to explain to Layne the virtues of souvlaki's cousin, but he just gave me strange looks until he finally shoved the edge of my sub between my lips. Suitably chastened and silenced, I took the sandwich from him and squished it flatter to fit in my mouth. It was pretty large and messy.

He watched me with a grin, and I had to nudge him to ask what he was smiling about. Not that he answered me. He shook his head and ran an imaginary zipper across his lips. I shrugged and pinched the bread tighter together, which brought on another snort from my companion.

"Seriously?" I said. "You're an adult."

He wasn't exactly confessing but I could figure out what he was thinking behind that hooded gaze, one that lit with sudden innocence at my comment.

I put my sandwich down, watching the bread rebound into its original shape.

"You bought me a hero sandwich so you could imply phallic jokes?" I said. "And bad jokes at that?"

His coffee bean colored eyebrow lifted. "Never."

He looked at me with such earnest dishonesty that the corner of my mouth twitched.

"Don't con a con," I said and picked up my sandwich. I was chewing a delicious mouthful when he canted his head at me.

"Is that what you are, Brie?" he said. "A con?"

The question was unexpected, and I regretted right away the offhand joke. I had a hard time holding his gaze because the question hit too close to home.

The truth was, I was getting uncomfortable with lying to him about what I was. He deserved better. I considered coming clean with him, and even started to form my answer, but he brushed at his jacket, tossing crumbs onto the floor as he stood up.

The moment when I might be able to give him my honesty disappeared. I ended up stabbing at my sandwich with a sullen finger. He noticed and made a thoughtful, even apologetic sound.

"The detective switch doesn't have an off button," he said.

I propped my elbow on the counter and waved away the explanation.

"I know a guy who can fix that for you," I said and wrapped up the rest of my sandwich. If he was done, I would be too.

He must have been feeling the tension because he jerked his thumb toward the pile of junk I'd assembled in the middle of the floor.

"Looking for shoes for tonight's ball?" he said.

I'd forgot the gala dinner. I'd wanted to get all that stuff cleaned up in one day because I didn't think I had the resolve to let it bleed into two. Talk about having a preserver tossed into the murky waters. Mention of my mother was the one thing that could throw ice water on my nerves in a heartbeat.

"Cleaning out some of my mother's stuff," I said. "Gonna sell it."

I licked my fingers clean and examined him as he stood there, leaning against a built in shelf filled with all sorts of chalices. He really was a gorgeous man. A gal could drown in that pheromone if she didn't find some sort of life raft.

"Actually, if I'm going to make it to that ball, I might need a bit of help carrying a few things." I cocked my hip at him, this time in mocking echo of a melodramatic sex siren and said in my best kittenish purr, "You look like a strong young man."

"I'm no man, young lady, nor am I young," he said as he puffed out his chest. "But I think you'll find me plenty strong. Show me to your wares."

I wasn't about to go back up those steps until all of my mother's old things were completely removed from my shop and the threat of her ghost haunting me again was gone. I gestured toward the stairs.

"There's a trunk up there," I said. "I can't lift it, and I'd love to have it down here."

I pointed at the space on the floor where I'd arranged the other items.

He narrowed his gaze at me. "It better not be filled with dismembered bodies."

"If you want to count a few desiccated beetle carcasses and legless daddy long legs, then yes, it is." I grinned and held my hand up in a boy scout salute. "But that's it. Honest."

I waved him up the stairs, standing back as he ascended to watch the view, and when he opened the door at the top, I could hear him tread across the floor. I wasn't aware I was chewing on my fingernail until I bit down on the tip.

He lugged the trunk down the stairs with a minimal amount of cursing and only once did he ding up the wall with a corner. When he grunted it into place at my feet, I was already mentally sorting through the vials of powders and bags of crystals.

"The damn thing is awful heavy for a box filled with spiders," he said and made to lift the cover until I swatted his hand away.

"One takes precautions raising the lid of an old trunk," I said. "Germs. Micro-toxins, et cetera."

I yanked the lid open with a flourish.

"Good thing you're not lifting the lid of a sarcophagus," he said. "Or we'd both be cursed right now."

He leaned over the top as I peeled the lid back. He whistled as he strained to see over the lid. I peered up at him.

"That's some collection," he said, catching my eye.

I didn't so much disagree as make a disagreeable sound in my throat.

"She fancied herself a witch or something," I explained when his eyebrows rose in query.

"Or something?" he said and came around to kneel at the side. I noted he chose to ask about the 'or something' rather than the 'fancied' part. He lifted one book after the other as he dug around to the bottom.

I sighed. "Long story," I said but he seemed to have already lost interest in favor of spying a large black book with frayed leather binding. The wear on the edges indicated a tome that might be a first edition.

I wasn't sure what it was, but I was already calculating what it might bring in.

"Careful with that," I said and reached for it.

He pulled it out of reach. "Have you seen this before?"

I shrugged. "How can I know with you hogging it?"

He spun it around to face me, holding it with both hands because it was so big, cover facing me, so I could get a good look at it.

I'd never seen a grimoire before, but I knew without ever having held one, that was what I was looking at. Except it wasn't the symbol embossed into the cover—the same one as on my amulet—that made me gasp without meaning to. It was the stains on the gilt edging. Stains that I knew Layne recognized as well as I did.

Blood.

CHAPTER NINETEEN

THAT AMOUNT OF BLOOD wasn't an accident. It coated the edges of the paper and stained the leather on the front and binding. Whatever she was into, my mother committed to it wholeheartedly.

I fell backward onto my haunches, the black wash of nausea creeping over me. While Layne prodded me verbally to tell him what was wrong, I tried in vain to push myself to my feet. I gathered I looked distressed because I felt his warm hands steadying me and helping me to stand.

"I'm fine," I said, shoving him off me and making my way to the counter.

"I don't think you are," he said.

He carried the book to where I stood and dropped it on the counter. He flipped through it absently, probably giving me time to collect myself, and I inhaled one breath at a time, purposefully and with methodical slowness.

I hated that every time I was with him, I ended up feeling weak and powerless. It made me look like a coward. I didn't want him to see me that way. But at least, the deep breathing was working. I started to feel better.

"This is pretty weird stuff," he said, with a darting glance my way. He fanned the pages and stopped here and there when something caught his eye.

I glanced at the book with a sigh. "Yeah, well, like I said—"

"Look at this." He laid his hand flat on a page of the open book and then slid it toward me. "Have you read this stuff?"

"I've been gone most of my life. Someone else packed up this junk," I said. "I couldn't care less what's in there."

He narrowed his eyes at me. "I take it that means no."

He tapped his finger on the page.

I shrugged. "Take what you want from the comment, but sure. I've never looked through her things before."

"Then you might find this interesting." He pushed the book even closer and finally, I dropped my gaze to the page he kept tapping.

"My amulet," I said without planning to say anything at all.

He nodded. "Sure looks like it."

There on the page was a hand drawn necklace. It was surrounded by symbols in a careful, precise order. I was also pretty damn sure it was my mother's handwriting, even though the book looked like it was generations old.

I scanned the pages, searching for things I might recognize. She had drawn pictures of flowers and dogs along with the strange symbols.

"You know, that dog doesn't look like any breed I've seen," he said, pointing at one of the larger canine drawings that crouched over half the right-hand side of the page. "I wonder what it is."

There were several drawings of the dog, and they all looked very much like the stray that kept coming around. But what really caught my eyes was the Latin word *invisibilia*. It was written in the middle of a list of words that were in both script and symbols and I guessed that perhaps the list was the same word translated multiple times in different languages. Kind of like a Rosetta Stone.

And because I dealt in things that other would-be witches wanted to buy, I recognized the list on the opposite page to be a list of ingredients. Many of them looked familiar.

"Looks like a recipe," he said as he came to stand next to me. He smelled of mint gum and aftershave and something more subtle that was the innate smell of him.

"It's a spell," I said. "This must be her grimoire."

"Can you read it?"

I wavered my hand over the pages of the book in a seesaw motion. "Maybe some of it. Grimoires are notorious for being unique and esoteric. Every witch has her own where she writes her own spells or instructions on how to make magical objects or..."

I paused as the thought struck me of what the other thing a grimoire traditionally was used for.

"Or what?" he said.

I lifted my gaze from the drawing of dogs and flowers to catch his eye. "Or amulets."

I tapped the page with my finger.

"You know what this is," I said. The drawing and my mother's amulet were the same. They both had the same circle of Hecate on it.

"You're saying she must have used this book to create that amulet?" he said.

"I'm *saying* if she didn't make it herself, she must have thought she was imbuing it with some power with this spell. I mean, this..." I ran my finger over the drawing.

"This is the symbol for the goddess of witchcraft. Every witch knows it."

My finger lingered over the circle and then moved sideways to the ingredient list.

"This can be very much like a recipe," I mused aloud. "But sometimes spells are indecipherable and look nothing like directions and more like a puzzle."

I ran my finger down along the ingredients, thinking all the while that my mother did a whole lot worse in the name of her delusion than just write down a few notes. But at least, her conviction was real. That or she was deeply dedicated to her conviction of pretending she was something she wasn't.

I recognized the use of sulfur and the multiple sigils of protection.

"I think she thought she was putting some sort of protection power on the amulet," I said. "But I can't figure out why she's using the ones for invisibility too."

"Where is your amulet?" he said. "Let's compare.

I ran my hand along my shirt out of habit even though I'd taken it off earlier. "It was bugging me," I said and nodded toward the counter. "I put it there somewhere."

There meant just a few feet from where we stood, and yet the counter was empty of anything but the book.

I frowned at the space I thought I'd put it. "It must have fallen on the floor."

He stooped, scouring the area in back of the counter and in front but came up empty.

"Maybe that's not where I put it," I said, trying to think back to the moment I'd taken it off. "I wasn't really paying attention."

I returned to the book while he toed around the base of the counter, more bothered by the mystery of what my mother was trying to do than with the amulet itself. After all, where could it have gone, really? The shop was small. I'd been alone inside all day. It would turn up eventually. It would have to.

I traced my finger over the drawings in the grimoire. I hadn't realized my mother had any artistic talents, but the ink sketch of the amulet was colorful and filled with lovely perspective. Even the chain she'd drawn to clutch the amulet in a claw like grip looked ornate.

The chain was the only discernible difference between my amulet and the one drawn in the book. I guessed that at some point, my mother had decided on a leather cord instead of a chain.

Regardless of the material that would loop the amulet around the wearer's neck, the spell showed indications of its intent everywhere.

"Maybe it was like in Harry Potter," I said. "Maybe it was her invisibility cloak."

He popped up from where he'd stooped to do a check of the inside of the display case and I knew just by looking at his face what he was thinking.

"Oh, my God," I said as the knowledge took me by surprise. "You read it. You're a Harry Potter fan."

He shrugged. "Someone told me there was a werewolf in it."

"That was in book three," I said. "You had to read a lot of it to get that far."

He grinned. "What can I say, I'm a sucker for fiction where a wolf shifter doesn't fawn over or share some kickass, but somehow vulnerable, chick." He screwed his expression into one of distaste. "Most wolves I know don't share their mates."

He held my gaze a little too long to be comfortable and I found I had to drop my gaze back to the grimoire. I tried not to think about the way he'd said mates, or that he'd mentioned more than one shifter. I didn't think I was ready for any of that info yet.

"You know, the more I look at the spell, I more I think it was a cloaking sort of amulet." I tapped the page where the word for *invisible* was written out in beautiful script. "There's too many ingredients and items that would refer to enemies and protections to be anything else. This really looks like a protection spell."

"Interesting," he murmured and came around from behind the counter to look at the pages with me as I examined all the items that bespoke of cloaking from magic. He drew so close to me I could feel the heat coming off him in waves and smell the mint on him. My throat ached all the way to my sternum.

As though he knew the effect he had on me, he edged even closer. We were hip to hip and in order to lean into the book for a better view, he had to put his arm around my waist. I thought I heard him drawing in a deep breath.

"So you think maybe she thought she was creating an amulet that could hide the wearer from her enemies?"

The moment he said it, I knew he'd just articulated what was running through my mind.

I sent him a sharp look. "I think that's it," I said. "Although I can't imagine what sort of enemies she would have unless it was the SPCA."

I tried to chuckle at the jest but the laugh caught in my throat. I didn't want to have to bring that bit of past up.

Thankfully, he didn't ask.

"Let's hope it isn't something meant to cloak you from your enemies," he said. "Because if you can't find the damn thing with that serial killer still lose, there might not be anything to protect you."

CHAPTER TWENTY

I SUDDENLY FELT PRETTY sick. The comment was a stark reminder of all the things going on around me. Even his look of concern wasn't enough to make me feel better.

He slapped the book closed.

"Maybe we should call off the date," he said.

"Oh, hell no," I said. "Let's just call off the day."

I looked askance at the pile of inheritance and knew I'd not have the heart to do any more. It would have to wait until tomorrow, but at least I wouldn't have to close up my shop tomorrow and pick at the job between customers. Unless the work went on into Monday, God help me. Maybe in that case, I'd cord off the area like a crime scene. I tittered at the thought and I waved off his look of concern that I was laughing to myself for no reason.

"Just go home and get yourself all dandied up. I'm fine." I pulled out my phone to check the time. "There's still plenty of time for me to shower and meet you at the hotel."

At first I didn't think he'd give in, but when I agreed to let him hire me a cab to the party, he did. He came with me back to my apartment and walked me up to the stoop like an old-world gentleman. I found myself wondering all sorts of things about him as he dropped me off and I went in to clean up.

I watched him walk away through the sidelight window of my door. I couldn't wait to get the grime of memories off my skin, and although it took a steaming shower to rid myself of the residue of distaste, eventually I pushed aside the image of that grimoire.

I put all my focus into looking ravishing, then back pedaled on my choice of descriptors. Ravishing might not be the best adjective to describe myself for a date with a wolf.

I pulled on a dress that made me look about as good as I was ever going to get. It was blood red, form-fitting material with ruching around the midsection to disguise any hint of belly fat. The neckline was square and had a little diagonal cut-away that showed a decent amount of cleavage.

I pushed my feet into gold high-heeled sandals and stuck golden hoop earrings in my lobes. I spent a ridiculous amount of time giving myself smokey eyes, but looking in the mirror afterward proved it was worth it.

I added a pink tinge to my hair from a cosmetician's bottle and swept the whole lot back with hair putty, leaving a few spikes at the ears for added framing. Some women don't have the jawline for a razored cut, but one thing I did get from my mother was a delicate profile and well-placed features. I may have hated my mother, but I loved the excellent genes she'd passed on.

I was grateful for the cab when it arrived because, at an inch, my heels were made for standing and sitting, not trekking across town.

When I slid from the seat out of the cab at the end of the ride, Layne was waiting for me outside the hotel lobby. He looked so amazing in his suit and tie that I must have said what I was thinking out loud because the cab driver said, "I'd fuck him too, and I don't swing that way."

I gave him a nice tip.

Even though I was dressed appropriately, I still got nervous when I saw the spread of servers milling about, guiding the guests toward a vine trellised garden party. I hadn't really expected the gala to be so posh.

I realized I might be a little out of my element when I noticed several more servers holding aloft silver trays laden with colorful drinks and flutes of champagne. Each guest plucked a cocktail of choice from the tray before disappearing through the archway.

At least a hundred people strolled the grounds beyond the hedge ways of the garden and a dozen more servers catered to them. I was pretty sure I caught sight of a raven haired beauty wearing a tiara.

"Sweet Jesus," I said to Layne as he approached. "You said fancy, but you didn't say it was going to be *this* fancy."

My gaze trailed from the spectacle beyond the hedge to his face and then of course, to his mouth, which was full and luscious and very much moving in speech.

"What was that?" I said, realizing I'd completely zoned out at the sight of him.

"I said you look good enough to eat."

It could have been sexual, and I might have taken it that way but the grin that lifted his mouth and crinkled his eyes buffered the innuendo and tilted it more slightly toward the reminder of what he was beneath all the civility.

"You're a bastard," I said but took the elbow he was wobbling in my direction.

He chuckled. "That's pretty much exactly what Parrish called me when I told her I already had a date. She wanted to come."

I smiled nicely for the server who approached with a clipboard and pen, but she didn't look at me at all. If I'd ever seen a hungrier look, it would be on a caged lioness. Feeling territorial, I angled myself so that I was blocking Layne, but the server neatly sidestepped me and gave him a coquettish look, tilting her head so that her throat was slanted toward him.

If he noticed the very submissive way she was presenting herself, he didn't show it. Instead, he looked past her and cursed out loud, which the woman took to indicate he was displeased with her. Her lash extensions swept her eyebrows as her gaze widened in surprise.

I felt bad for her then. I'd been that woman a few times and it always hurt.

"I think we're on the list," I said to her, allowing her to get back to business where she was the one in control. "Garder."

I nodded toward her clipboard.

"Yes," she said and scanned the paper with her pen, dragging the back end of the tip along the list till she found his name and then flipped it over and made a noisy check.

Her eyes lifted to mine.

"Guest of Honor, it seems," she said and gave him another longing scan until he turned back from whatever had caught his eye past the archway and smiled at me. Then she was all business again.

"You can go in, Mr. Garder," she said, gesturing toward the arch where a fresh batch of servers stood with renewed trays of champagne. "Cocktails and hors d'oeuvres are in the garden for the next hour. Dinner is in the dining room half an hour before the presentation."

He nodded his thank you and this time rewarded her with a broad smile that allowed her to reclaim her dignity. Perhaps he'd understood what his reaction had cost her and was trying to make up for it.

"You didn't tell me you were the guest of honor," I said to him as he guided us toward the closest server and plucked a flute from the tray.

"What?" he said as his gaze traveled to my throat and pinned there before it lifted to my face again. "Oh, not really. There are several of us, actually. Some silly plaque or some such. Doesn't matter to me but folks like to give those sorts of things out. Just a reason to party, I think."

I stored that information away for the time being as I considered what his reaction was telling me that his words were not. For all he dressed like a men's store mannequin, he didn't like to be fawned over.

"This from the guy who wears Hugo Boss," I said, lifting the flute to my mouth and letting the bubbles pop against my nose as they escaped the glass.

"Whose boss?" he said.

"Hugo Boss. Your suits." I angled the flute toward his shoulder.

"My suits?" He laughed and reached for my free hand so he could aim the backs of my fingers against the fabric of his sleeve. "This is Brioni."

I shrugged. "Never heard of him."

I thought he was going to make a remark about my ignorance but a tall, heavily made up Parrish came up behind him and tapped him on the shoulder with the butt end of an empty cocktail glass. Somehow, she managed to look gayer with all the mascara than she did without.

Layne didn't turn around at her insistent prodding. Instead, he pulled my hand to his chest and said, "Please, tell me it's not her."

She laughed from behind him and I realized by the slightly off-kilter tenor of it that she had emptied at least three of those glasses already.

"I shouldn't lie," I said as she draped an arm over his shoulder. "It might offend the gods and I need all the help I can get at the moment."

He let go an indulgent and patient sigh as Parrish leaned on him heavily enough to make him buckle at the waist.

"You thought you could keep me out," she said as she craned her neck to look at him. "But I got me a date."

She spoke with such a sense of victory I knew they'd been arguing about her attendance for a long time.

He closed his eyes and sighed, and I couldn't help laughing.

"Lord have mercy, you're drunk and it's only..." He looked down at a gold watch on his wrist. "Eighteen hundred."

"Of course I'm drunk," she said. "How else will I endure the poor sod's pawing at me?"

He shifted subtly to the left, which left her staggering to regain her footing when her arm fell off his shoulder.

"So who's the unfortunate fellow who thought pawing at a lesbian your size was a good idea?" Layne asked.

She swayed a bit as she blinked slowly at him. Then she spied a server on his way past with a tray of filled glasses. She homed in on a flute stem the way a sharpshooter took aim at a target and snagged it so expertly, I doubted she was as drunk as she pretended to be.

"I bribed one of the waitstaff," she said with an air that it should have been obvious how she'd got an invitation. "He gave me the names and numbers of three men who listed without a plus one."

"One of those was me," he said and swung to her and took in her full regalia of black dress, clunky shoes, and fake pearls that showed off a pretty decent figure but that also looked just slightly uncomfortable on her frame.

I guessed she didn't enjoy dressing up, based on the way she kept tugging at the décolletage. I hadn't expected her bosom to be so full. It nearly spilled over the top.

"You're all frilly," he said, not without a hint of wonder in his voice.

"I'm gay," she said. "Not a feminist. Sometimes we like to wear sexy dresses and go without panties."

She caught me staring and elbowed me.

"Pretty good for a dyke, huh?" she said. "Found it at a thrift shop. Nothing trolls in the muffin munchers like a tight little black dress."

I didn't know what to say to that but Layne apparently did.

"That's exactly why I wouldn't bring you," he said.

"Why?" she demanded. "Are you saying you wouldn't bring me because I'm gay or because I'm a gay gal without panties? You stupid bigot. How else am I going to get laid?"

He ran a hand over his buzz cut. "I couldn't care less if you fuck a sheep. It's your insistence on shocking people that's the problem." He sighed. "My father is here, for Pete's sake."

She made a thoughtful sound deep in her throat, then chose what she must have figured was the high road.

"So you brought a witch because you need a normal woman on your arm for dear old dad, huh?" She chortled. "Good luck with that."

He made a show of turning his back on her again.

"It's not like that and you know it," he growled under his breath.

"It is so like that," she said. "And we both know it. You've been trying to live up to your old man for a hundred—"

He laid his finger along her mouth, effectively stopping her from speaking.

"What?" I said. "Don't stop the argument on my account. I do look forward to hearing about how our prickly Pete here can't please dear old dad."

I grinned at him. It was somehow refreshing to see I wasn't the only one with parenting problems.

"Don't encourage her," he said and tugged me along with him toward one of the circular tables laden with what looked like different cheeses. In the center sat an entire wheel of Parmesan. My mouth started to water. He passed me a small plate with a miniature silver fork.

"There's prosciutto and a table of meats to the left," he said, piling several hunks of cheese onto his own plate. "Someone will replace your champagne with a glass of red or white if you finish it now. I'm guessing they'll offer the Teanum. It goes great with the parm."

It was a little overwhelming to see all the tables heavily laden with so many meats, cheeses, and if it my reckoning was right, asparagus wedges wrapped in delicate frays of smoked meat.

"I'm not sure how hungry you are, but the main course will be a sort of handmade ravioli and truffle sauce, and there will be a few courses before that."

I was nibbling of the best piece of Parmesan cheese I'd ever tasted when I discovered he was completely right about someone swapping out my champagne with red. I was barely finished the flute when a server politely pressed a small wine glass in my hand. And he was right again when I sipped at the edge of the glass with the residue of that cheese in my cheeks. I might have moaned a little at the decadence.

"I'm not sure I can eat after hearing that," he said.

I caught his eye and realized he was staring at my mouth. Flustered, I took another sip of wine.

To break the tension, I asked, "So you never said why you were the guest of honor. Are you getting a medal or something?" I skewered another piece of cheese from my plate. "And why would Parrish need a date to get in if it's a police sort of thing?"

He lifted his finger, indicating he'd answer when he finished the large hunk of prosciutto wrapped lobster he'd bitten into.

"First," he said around the last of the mouthful, "she's assistant ME, not a detective. Second, it's not a police thing. It's a family thing."

Small clusters of guests eddied toward the dining room entrance.

"So family, meaning this is some sort of wedding or something?" I asked. "Should I have bought a present?"

He chuckled and took my elbow, leading me along with the others toward the entrance. "Not quite. My family is sort of old and reputable. Once a year, we donate a large sum to a worthy cause here in the city. Last year, we built a wing of the hospital. This year, we paid for the construction of a library wing."

"Oh, my fuck," I said, unable to keep the reverence or the crassness from my response. "You're rich."

He shrugged. "My father is rich. My uncle is rich. I merely have some money."

"You're *the* Garders," I said. "Good Lord, no wonder you wear Hugo Boss all the time. You guys are like the Pinkertons."

"Brioni," he said, correcting me with a broad grin. "But the business has been around for longer than the Pinkertons and far more secretive. The company made all its money during the roaring 20s and prohibition. Now, the business isn't security so much as it's training. I'm not sure you'd find it interesting, really. Lots of boring details about special ops and secret this and that. I preferred to help the huddled masses instead of politicians and celebrities. I don't think dear old dad will ever forgive me for that. No money in it."

He laughed as though it didn't matter, but there was an edge to it that said differently.

I wondered where Parrish fit into all of it. She obviously knew the family but didn't get an invite. I wanted to ask but caught sight of her trailing along behind a woman in a slinky dress. Layne might have been entirely correct in his assessment of her behavior.

Inside, the entire room was swathed in candlelight and flickering tapers set in candelabras. The linens weren't paper or plastic, and the round tables held silver chargers and several wine glasses. Even before I sat down, I knew I'd have to check the Internet for help on which utensil to use first. It was overwhelming and anxiety-inducing because I knew I'd be thinking about this night for months, maybe years.

But first I had to get through the opening course.

That was going to be impossible, as it turned out, because in the next moment, someone screamed from the other side of the room.

CHAPTER TWENTY-ONE

LAYNE WAS ON HIS feet in a heartbeat and was threading his way through the crowds to the source of the yelling, because by then, that was exactly what it had devolved to. Pained, frightened, and hysterical shouting.

I followed him because I couldn't just sit there at a linen-covered table with my hands beneath my ass. Not when my date had taken off like a streak of white noise. Not when the assistant medical examiner was hot on his heels, as though she hadn't drunk several glasses of wine and wore no underwear beneath her skimpy dress.

If a woman ran without regard for who would see her ass, then the problem was mighty big indeed.

Several people tried to cut me off as I pushed through and I had to shove back with equal fervor and then some. One primly dressed matriarch even stuck her foot out to trip me as I jostled by.

"Careful, dear," she said. "You might get trampled."

I shot her a rude gesture and continued on all the way to the hotel lobby where a cluster of servers huddled together as though they were a herd of gazelles on the Savannah.

"I'm with the police," I said to the nearest wait staff, a female server with her strawberry hair in a top bun.

She was wringing her hands and whispering to one of her companions about dead guys and crime scenes. She looked about nineteen and by the way she kept trying to see over the heads of her fellow workers, I guessed she was too young to really know what death meant.

Too many hours of video games had desensitized so many millennial already. I hated to think she'd have to see a dead body to regain her healthy fear of violence.

She extricated herself from the herd and pointed toward the automatic doors that turned the whole front of the hotel lobby into a great atrium.

"Is it true there's a dead guy out there?" she said.

I jerked my chin toward the crowd that kept me from pushing past. "I'll only know if I can get through. Think you can help?"

She grinned, realizing she might be able to get a close-up peek at the rumored body.

"Sure." She yanked on the sleeve of a uniformed security guard. "Help us get through," she said to him.

Luckily, he didn't ask questions, just demanded the crowd part so he could let the police through. I kept my head down so as not to attract too much attention of the wrong sort. I just wanted to get to Layne and Parrish, where I could feel somewhat less abandoned and less isolated.

I was already getting the creeps.

Layne had put together a makeshift barricade from chairs and luggage racks, effectively shutting out much of the area from those who considered a crime scene a free peep show. The fact that he'd set up a perimeter so quickly indicated whatever it was, it was bad.

I hoped no one was dead and he was doing it out of regular procedure, but all my instincts told me I hoped in vain.

Someone was probably hurt, and badly.

The security guard and the little server pushed back the last of the crowd of hotel guests who had gathered around to rubberneck. She whistled a high pitched, ear-splitting whistle and lifted her hand to indicate she was trying to help.

"We have another officer here," she shouted. "Make room."

The far-away sound of a siren sliced through the fog of distance and grew louder by the heartbeat. Layne was outside the hotel lobby, just past the automatic doors. He'd thrown his jacket—his very expensive Brioni jacket— over the top half of what looked like a man's body. It covered his head and most of his torso, but left his legs freely splayed open on the curb.

"Are you alright, officer?" the security guard said to me. "You're looking pretty pale."

I turned to him in a daze. "Yes, yes, I'm fine."

The female server gagged and bent over double. My gaze darted over her shoulder to a gap in the barricade where a pool of blood and something glistening and brackish funneled into a low spot on the grading.

A moan escaped me that took the guard's attention. He grabbed my elbow and exerted enough pressure on it that I realized I might have been getting ready to faint.

"Afghanistan," he said when I looked up into his face. "Two tours. You don't get over death but you get used to it."

He nodded to where Layne and Parrish were busily scoping the scene.

"Take your time," he said. "Looks like your partners have it under control anyway."

I dragged in a bracing breath and nodded. I didn't have to go out there. I was perfectly safe where I was out of sight, out of mind and with a man who had no doubt done some awful violence to an unseen enemy to keep me company. I couldn't see myself getting much more safe, to be honest.

That safety lasted about three minutes. While Layne hadn't caught sight of me yet, Parrish had and she waved me over with a frantic gesture.

She said something to Layne, which made him look in my direction with a grim line transforming his sensual mouth into a seam of barely controlled anger. Even from the distance I stood from him, I could tell his eyes had shifted color to what I now recognized as the more bestial part of him.

Not good. Not good at all.

"Looks like they spotted you," the guard said. He ran his hand over his short cropped hair and then inhaled sharply. Seemed the bracing breath wasn't just for the uninitiated.

He gave the last final shove through the crowd and past the luggage racks toward Parrish. She swayed on her feet and looked like she was going to be sick. The robust complexion and dancing eyes were decidedly dull.

I wasn't sure why, but that made me feel much better.

"Thanks," I said to the guard. "I'll be fine."

He nodded and used his departure to press back the crowd even further. Layne sent him an encouraging nod and then the guard took point, managing the scene like a pro. Maybe he was.

I picked my way over to Parrish, aiming for the legs of the downed man instead of the head where the pool of blood was the largest.

"You should look at this before the rest of the unit gets here," she said. "I'm not sure you'll be allowed to see it then."

Confused because I'd been allowed on scene before, I asked her what I should be looking for and why.

She just shook her head. Whatever it was, it was obvious she wanted my untainted reaction.

Layne waved me over and Parrish backed up so I could get by. Without a word, he knelt next to the man's body. I crouched next to him, feeling the heat radiate off him like a furnace. I wondered if the wolf inside was burning to get out. I didn't dare touch him to find out. I had the feeling he was tightly wound and working hard to keep the wolf contained.

Everything, from the way the muscles in his jaw clenched so hard that his earlobes turned white, to the way his fist tightened on the hem of the jacket he'd lain on the body, bespoke of a man on the threshold of his control.

I wished I knew more about wolf shifters because I wasn't sure I was safe next to him, let alone the crowd of rubberneckers. And to think his father was here somewhere.

He looked at me sideways and that was when it hit me. Whatever he was struggling with inside, he wouldn't show it to the rest of the world. It was his battle and no one else's.

I touched his arm with a bit of hesitation until he sagged beneath my touch. Then I felt better.

"What is it?" I asked him.

He didn't speak, just lifted the edge of his jacket from the body. He didn't fling it back, but held it aloft in such a way that it veiled the body from the crowd's viewpoint. Whoever stood on the opposite side of the street from the hotel would only see two crouched figures next to a man lying down.

What I saw, however, was enough to put a knot in my throat. I barely got one word past it.

"Jesus," I said and not just because the man looked like he was shredded from his neck to his belly button.

"It's yours, then?" Layne said and his voice was a rumble and a growl all at once.

I nodded before realizing he couldn't hear the answer. He wasn't looking at me but at the amulet that had been looped around the dead man's neck.

"Yes."

He grunted as though he didn't really need the affirmation. I swallowed hard.

"What does this mean?" I asked. "I don't understand what's going on?"

"Well, the first thing it means, is that spell your mother cast didn't take. If it was meant to cloak or protect the wearer, then it failed."

"This isn't the time to joke," I said.

He shook his head. "I'm not. Not really. But it's better than telling you the real meaning."

"I look like a suspect," I guessed.

"Yes," he said. "And that means they'll want to question you."

He was curt but not unkind when he said it, indicating he was unhappy about the whole affair.

"And this will have to go into evidence." He started to drop the jacket back down over the man's torso, but I stopped him before I realized what I was doing.

"Wait," I said, and leaned against him for support. "Can you show me his face?"

I had the feeling I might need the solid weight of him holding me up if he looked anything like Iris had. I didn't think I could stand looking at his eyes but I needed to see. "His face...it's okay, isn't it? I can look at it?"

Layne regarded me thoughtfully and I was afraid he'd refuse, but then the ambulance siren pealed all the louder and I knew it was close. Maybe too close because he lifted the jacket higher so I could take in the man's face.

"You know him," he said when I made a small sound in the back of my throat.

"It's the guy who attacked me in my shop." I fell onto my knees so I could hold myself up by my palms. The whole parking lot felt like it was spinning.

"You're sure?" he said and I knew he was thinking what I was. This man lying dead with his belly cut open could not possibly be the killer. And if he wasn't, then we were right back at square one with no suspects and no end to the killings in sight.

I nodded. "He was yelling about frauds and charlatans. Tried to yank the necklace right off my neck." I swung my gaze to Layne's. "If that other customer hadn't been there, I don't know what he would have done."

He touched my hand, slipping it into his broad, warm one, and only then did I realize how cold I'd grown.

"That's actually a positive thing," he murmured as the ambulance careened into the parking space just behind us. "Having his statement will at least raise good questions that will cast doubt on your involvement."

"My involvement?"

"Your amulet at this scene. His attack at your store. A suspicious detective would presume you were involved somehow."

"But I'm not."

He dropped the jacket onto the man's body, effectively covering the worst of his injuries. I hadn't looked hard, but I did notice his belly was torn open. It was hard not to smell the viscera.

"We really need to find the other man," he said. "I've spent too much time looking for this guy." He dropped the jacket back down over the vandal's face. "And this guy was a dead end no matter which direction I came at it." The sound of defeat in his voice didn't bolster me any. I'd hoped he'd have found something by now.

"Wasted time," he said and it almost sounded as though he blamed me. "If I'd not wasted it on investigating him as a killer, I might have saved his life."

I looked at the fabric as it sopped up blood in the center and wondered how anyone was able to dump a body in that state right out in the open and not get noticed.

Parrish's big clunky shoes came into view of my peripheral vision, and I peered up at her. She leaned over with her hand out. I took it and let her help me to my feet. Layne remained where he was, jotting down things onto his phone screen. More police were arriving and wrestling the hotel guests back inside, widening the perimeter.

I caught sight of a man who looked to be about fifty-five standing off from the crowd but very much interested in what Layne was doing. He was well-muscled for a man who looked to be in his early fifties. Dangerously handsome in all the right ways.

"Layne's dad?" I said to Parrish without so much as turning in his direction.

She nodded. "At least you won't have to worry about meeting the old man. And Layne won't have to introduce you. For now." She might have been trying to joke but it came out flat and she sighed. "You need to get home, Brie. We both have a lot of work ahead of us."

I nodded mutely, noting that this time I hadn't been asked for insight. I couldn't miss the connection Layne had made earlier about my possible involvement. They probably didn't want me around contaminating the scene. Even if they saw it as a separate crime to the psychic killer, they would see me as one more suspect to clear.

But I wasn't worried about that. I was innocent and they'd figure that out quickly enough. The real issue was that I knew both were connected. Even if this man wasn't a psychic or a woman of power and thus fit the modus operandi of the psychic killer, in time they would realize the connection too. They would have to. Because on examination, they would see the thing I'd noticed written in blood on the man's hand. A number thirteen.

I hadn't said anything to Layne about it because that number terrified me. The first had been a three, the next a seven, and now a thirteen.

I wasn't sure if it was the amount of murders or the victims to come.

Chapter Twenty-Two

I KEPT SEEING THE man's shredded and bloody body every time I blinked. I rode in the back seat of an old taxi that smelled of vomit and air freshener, staring out at the darkening evening with a sense of trepidation because I knew I'd be seeing the horror again in my nightmares for months to come.

Despite the sense of evil that permeated every inch of the surrounding air, I knew it was only my own sense of dread and shame that would keep me awake at night.

While I hadn't killed the man, I bore some responsibility. He'd been in my shop. He'd attacked me and tried to pull the necklace right off my throat. His determination to reveal me as a charlatan was almost too desperate. It was as good a motive to kill psychics as any if you were psychotic enough.

But he wasn't the killer, which left me questioning why he would want to attack me at all. Or even why he wanted the amulet badly enough to break into my shop later while I'd been upstairs, and found the stone on the counter.

While I'd been rummaging in my mother's things, he'd pocketed it and let himself back out without bothering to attack me again.

So what was different from the first time he'd visited the store?

The amulet itself had no intrinsic value since it wasn't made of precious stone or gold. Even if he knew of its power, he'd have had to be able to track it to me, and that wasn't possible since I didn't know him.

I could think he might have been a client's partner. Maybe even Sherry's. She was the last person I'd worked with, so that might make sense. Perhaps she'd realized I was a fraud, and he'd come to revenge her and seeing the amulet on my neck, seized on the opportunity to take it.

And if that was the case, then at some point, he had encountered the amulet before either he or Sherry saw it on me. Since it was something my mother drew in her grimoire, something she wore every day, I concluded he must have known her. And if he knew her, maybe he too believed it to be a shield of some kind. In the right circles, it would be worth money.

That might explain his rage at me being a fraud. Maybe he'd tried to fence it to the wrong person and caught the eye of the killer when it had turned out to be nothing but a bauble. And then enraged, the killer—murdering psychics because of fraudulent magic—dumped the offensive vandal's body under the nose of the detective investigating the crime with the amulet on his chest as a way of thumbing his nose at it all.

In the end, whatever the man had wanted the necklace for, the amulet was no better than a decorative bit of jewelry with an esoteric, otherworldly appeal. It lent the wearer a sort of mystique and that was it. And the killer just got even more furious.

It was a mixed bag of suppositions and I knew it. The frustration of gathering even the thinnest threads was a task that made me feel like I had six thumbs and a lizard brain.

All I knew was that I wore the thing despite it being a visual reminder of the woman who had abused and neglected me because it added an element of mystique. And I would be damned if I'd let my mother's memory get the best of me. My childhood and her abuse was a badge of honor that I'd survived.

That amulet and her grimoire were no doubt just a means to sell herself as something she wasn't. Much like every other psychic or medium or witch I'd ever met.

I considered telling Layne I was a fraud. That all the women were too. Maybe whatever was killing us had a vendetta against mediums and witches or maybe it was just plain fury at being duped. It seemed like as good a motivation as anything else.

The guilt I felt, the nagging sense that I should come clean, cloaked me in the darkness of the cab, and it was as heavy as wet wool. It stank about as much.

I was a charlatan. We preyed on people's desires and hopes. Sometimes we exploited their fears.

It was how we made our living. Read the body language. Tap out the truth from the nuances of expression and questions they asked. Use it all to secure our livelihood and to sell ephemera and spell work and anything else we could foist upon the unsuspecting.

Sometimes it was a long con, and sometimes it was a short one, but it was always a con.

When I'd first begun my business, I'd thought I could actually go ahead with the ruse, but I'd quickly learned I didn't have the stomach for outright conning. Instead, I'd tried to use the opportunity to help my clients when I could. Create a symbiotic relationship of the exchange to assuage my guilt and heal from my past.

So no, that my mother might be a con as well didn't surprise me. What really surprised me was how devastated I felt to discover that after all I knew, after all I had done and seen, that I'd actually hoped the magic was real.

That moment in my shop when I'd found her grimoire and examined her spell work, I'd thought for an instant that maybe there was something to her claims. A self-proclaimed witch who spent month after month trying to raise the man she loved from the dead in the basement of our house by burning alive puppies she brought home from animal shelters all over the city.

That had to have some sort of higher calling.

And all I could think was that I wanted it so badly because it might absolve her from all that evil. I might be able to finally reconcile her deeds in some way, rationalize the inhumanity if she'd had the power to do something with all the cruelty.

But just like all the rest of my mother's life, it was a facade. A hoax. Just like she was, and I'd learned the art of the great con from her in those early days when I believed those things she did in our basement were frightening enough to be real magic.

All that was left was pain and horror and trauma. And a man left dead, shredded like pulled pork despite wearing an amulet presumably bespelled by strong protection magic and enveloped in a power to cause the wearer to wander about all but invisible and invincible.

I stared out at the streetlights that passed by as the cab turned street after street. There was so much about my mother and my childhood I'd purposely buried. Moments my therapist tried to pull from me with hypnosis and guided meditation. He'd always said my memories lurked behind a cement wall that would come down on me one day if I didn't admit them one by one in a safe environment.

But as I cocooned myself in the warmth of the cab and let myself drown in the lights that spilled out over the streets and the people strolling along the sidewalks, a flash of memory came to me. One that tried to peer out from the depths when I'd peeked under Layne's jacket and seen my amulet lying there. One I'd thought I'd tamped down mercilessly but that returned to me when I least expected it.

I'd had a flash of my mother shouting into the phone at someone. She clutched her amulet with a white-knuckle grip as she rasped into her end. The power she owned couldn't be taken. Not unless they burned her bones and drank her blood. They could try if they wanted, but there was no power on earth that could steal it.

Terrifying things to hear coming from your mother's mouth when you're six years old.

I shivered and hugged myself as I pressed deeper into the back seat. My mother was crazy. She was mad, and she was delusional. Her amulet was as dead as she was and now someone else had died for it as well.

I caught the cabbie's eye watching me in the mirror and realized I was muttering beneath my breath.

"I'm sure I'm not the first fare you've had that talks to themselves," I said, angry for no reason at a man who couldn't do anything to make me feel better.

His eyes flicked back to the windshield, but not before he informed me that I was the first to complain about witches and werewolves.

I tried to pretend his comment didn't bother me. I wasn't sure it worked, but he left me alone after that, and I went back to looking out the window and seeing nothing. I thought of Layne and Parrish scouring the crime scene and was jealous for a moment that they might gain insights while I stewed and brooded.

Layne had been right about the questioning. I got the call early in the morning. I'd lain awake most of the night, mulling over everything I might get asked and preparing answers.

I rose and got up at six am with a bit of a headache that didn't fade until I'd sat in front of a dough-faced detective and gave a few cursory answers to questions that seemed pretty soft-ball all things considered.

They let me go after twenty minutes, telling me to stick close to home. No problem there.

With half a day left, I determined to be productive. My shop wasn't open on Sundays and that would give me the whole afternoon to sort through all the stuff I'd abandoned on the floor.

I hadn't heard a word from Layne or Parrish, so I headed to my shop with a bagged snack and lots of water.

I wanted answers and if I could find anything to help, it was time to dig in despite my aversion to my mother's things. I sat on the floor with my water bottle beside me and a deep breath to brace myself.

Just in case, I made a little pact with the shade of my mother that if she stayed away, I'd be respectful of her things. Because by then, I was pretty sure her ghost was real.

I worked through several boxes that had items that did nothing to enlighten me about my mother's past or her amulet, but that I could resell or display. I didn't bother with those.

The real gem was the trunk. With my mother's shade appearing right around the time I was digging through her trunk of books—real or not—I was willing to bet that was the best place to begin.

At first, I found nothing but dusty old tomes and while I enjoyed a good read as well as any fiction fan, I didn't find worn down and beaten up copies of the *Iliad* and several hand written journals interesting enough for a second glance.

So the going was slow until I'd emptied out the trunk and found nothing useful. I threw the closest book in a rage across the floor. It skittered along the laminate until it struck the counter and flipped open.

That was when I found the real gold.

Pages of newspaper clippings flew out and landed on the floor. I crawled the few feet to pluck them from the scattered places they'd landed. Some of them seemed random, with pictures of groups of people posing in front of various buildings.

I put those aside in favor of the one that showed a sober looking woman and a tag line that read: Cult Baked a Member to Death in Homemade Brick Oven. A quick scan yielded enough savory details that I dug through the remaining moldy books.

In several of them, I found similar clippings of a cult led by a woman claiming to be a messenger for the angels. All added even more gruesome and salacious detail to the one story.

My mother had kept these clippings. For whatever reason, she found them important enough to hide away in her trunk.

Reading them was like hopping into a rabbit hole head first. They all followed the story of the Blackburn Cult, centered around one woman who claimed, among many things, that she could raise the dead.

It didn't take too much imagination to read what the reports didn't say: the leader who conned dozens of people out of their life savings in the name of Christ was a witch.

But the most interesting fact, that the papers didn't make too much fuss over compared to the stories of naked dances in the woods, was that a young girl who had been killed with the intent of resurrecting her was also interred with flowers, spices, and the remains of seven dogs.

I gasped, finding a direct correlation with what my mother was doing in the basement of my childhood. Was my mother a member of this coven?

It seemed likely. A quick Google search indicated the cult, as it was termed, had disbanded when the leader died.

I was still mulling over whether my mother was involved, with four clippings spread across my legs as they splayed out in front of me, when someone rattled the door to the shop.

I didn't think anyone could see me from the closed door window, but I leaned sideways to catch sight of who might be out there.

No one. And yet the rattling continued, punctuated by several loud and impatient knocks.

I heaved myself to my feet and dropped the clippings on the counter on my way by.

"I'm not open," I shouted to the door. When I closed my hand over the knob, it twisted. Someone was turning it from the other side. I leaned to see if I could catch sight of who it was, assuming it was Layne, but ready to sideline a customer if it wasn't.

"I don't open on Sundays," I said.

"But it's an emergency," a masculine voice said, and I recognized the man who had rescued me from the intruder in the shop. The nice one with the straw-colored hair and the walking stick.

I chewed my lip. I did owe him. And what harm would it do to open for ten minutes? He'd said it was important.

I unlocked the door and swung it wide. He looked much the same as he had the first time. I briefly wondered if it was his daily uniform. I back stepped a few feet to give him room to enter.

"I can give you a few minutes," I said. "If it's important. But not much more. I'm in the middle of sorting through things..." I let the sentence trail off as he came inside.

My eyes darted to the arm at his side, the one clenching the handle of a walking stick the way a hand might heft an axe.

As I watched, that walking stick started to transform. One second it was a cane, the next, an axe, and finally, it changed into the same scythe I'd thought he'd carried into my shop during his first visit.

I didn't have time to run. My gaze stuck on the blade of the weapon as horror filled my mind.

This time, the scythe was dripping blood.

CHAPTER TWENTY-THREE

I WOULD HAVE BEEN uneasy at the best of times, but when the man reached to lock the door behind him, I felt my legs turn to sacks of cornmeal.

"What do you want?" I said, doing my best not to sound terrified and yet my mind was already slide-showing through all the murder scenes I'd examined the last few days. It didn't take long to put myself into a tableau. For some reason, the reel stuck there and that last slide was all I could see. "Did I miss our appointment?"

I kept an eye on him as my hand searched my pocket for my cell phone. The relief that washed over me as I felt the telltale edge of it was enough to put some calm in my voice as I slid the phone out.

"Would you like to reschedule?" I asked, more to distract him than anything else. Maybe if he saw me with my phone out and very capable of phoning emergency, he'd think twice before attacking.

When he shook his head but didn't answer, I knew things weren't going to be easy. And to think he'd been so talkative before. I took a step backward. His other hand went to the handle of his scythe, and he lifted it with the kind of motion you knew was going to result in a hefty, powerful swing.

It came down in a swipe that would have struck me in the shoulder if I'd been any closer.

He took one step toward me, and then mercifully, my brain made contact with my legs. I twisted my entire torso around before my feet caught up. I was able to get three full, leaping steps in before I staggered and started to lose my balance.

I pinwheeled for the counter with no thought other than that I needed some sort of barrier.

I skidded and slid, leaning in as though I was riding a motorcycle. My palm on the counter helped traction the turn.

I thought it would be enough to gain some space. I thought if I could at least put something between us, it would freeze frame things long enough for me to think.

I was wrong.

The scythe came down in a swipe that dug into the counter. I heard the whoosh of movement, heard the dull thunk of metal meeting wood.

My beautiful Nova Scotian burled wood counter.

"Bastard," I said, and I might have felt a momentary relief if the tip of the weapon had stayed stuck in the wood like an axe.

He pulled it out after it bit into the varnished wood and heaved it upward again.

I sobbed without meaning to, my gaze trapped on his face the way my feet were rooted to the floor.

His expression was as bland and unemotional as a sink full of dirty dishwater. I caught sight of those eyes and my stomach turned to stone. I'd never seen eyes like that before. They were black. No iris. No whites. Just one big pupil with a tiny glowing red spot in the middle.

"Please," I begged even as I found a way to move one more inch toward the other edge of the counter without him advancing.

It was open on both ends, which made it easy for me to maneuver behind from anywhere in the shop if someone wanted to buy something. Quick sales. It was always about the quick money. Get them in, get them convinced, get their money. Leaving the counter open on both ends allowed for speedy processing. It had been intentional.

Now I wasn't sure if it was a blessing I'd done that or a curse.

I could get out of his way in seconds and head for the stairwell and lock myself in, or he could come at me from either direction.

He lunged for me again, this time with his scythe raised so far over his head that it was angled behind it. Once the weapon came down again, the blade would take my head off.

I darted for the opening at the end of the counter in the opposite direction. He was already arching his back to give weight to the swing he was aiming at me. He grunted with the effort of bringing it down with force.

I leaped, pushing off with all my weight from my toes and reaching with arms extended in case I could grab something, anything, that I could throw at him.

The scythe came down with a breeze behind me.

Pain sliced through the sole of my right foot. I gasped, then staggered. The stairs were so far away even though they were a mere five feet from the counter. Despite the flood of adrenaline making my heart pump in a crazy rhythm, I wasn't going to make it.

The pain in my foot had already begun to burn. I slipped on something greasy and I went down on my knee. My palms slapped the laminate flooring with an echoing crack.

My phone skidded a foot away, face up. The glow of the screen light told me I'd at least managed to activate it. I might not be able to touch the screen, but I knew if it was turned on, I could voice call whomever I wanted.

I shouted at the phone in both relief and excitement. "Call Garder," I yelled at it.

The voice activated engine repeated back what it thought I said: Call Gardening? I whimpered and dragged myself another few inches, noting that my foot was warm and wet. I was bleeding.

"Call Garder," I said, this time with a shaky, but more controlled timbre. I just hoped it was enough because if it hadn't heard me correctly, I wasn't going to get another chance.

A sound from behind me indicated my attacker had closed the distance between us with an almost deadly aim.

I propped myself up onto my knees, facing him.

The scythe was over his head again, and this time his other hand was nothing but a large set of claws. I thought of that thing that had attacked me in the street outside my house and I knew instinctively that this was the same creature.

He might have entered the shop as a man, but the humanity was gone. What stalked me now wasn't a man at all. And now, despite him seeming blind before, he held my gaze with a focus that was as deadly as it was terrifying.

I screamed. I couldn't help it. My hands flailed behind me to pull myself out of harm's way, and my fingers touched down on something hard.

The grimoire. I knew it by the leathery feel. It was hefty enough to make a good weapon and light enough that I could hurl it. If I could lift it from the awkward position of lying flat on my back, at least.

Instead of hefting the thing straight up, my palm spread over the pages, unable to get good purchase. A warmth or an electric buzz, or maybe both, spread across my palm. It was almost enough to make me yank my hand back in surprise but before I could even react, a vicious growl sounded from beyond me.

A blur of black leaped over my head and sailed over my supine form to collide with the creature. The sound they made together when they met was one of howling pain and anger.

This time, when the stray dog met the attacker, it went berserk. This was no tentative attack meant to test the opponent or scare it away.

This time, the dog knew what it was up against, and it didn't hold back. As if it knew the subtleties of its opponent's weaknesses and strengths, the movements it would make to defend or attack, the dog turned into a roiling mass of shadow, one moment solid, the next a blur of motion that kept the creature on the defense.

The growling, the snapping of teeth, the guttural, awful sound of it tearing into flesh and shaking limbs was enough to make my stomach roll.

This time, I wasn't foolish enough to stick around to help. Didn't matter if the dog had come to my rescue and ended up dying in my defense; I was getting to somewhere safe.

I couldn't let myself pity the stray. I couldn't let myself think beyond moving.

I rolled onto my knees and pushed myself to my feet. I had one thought: get to the attic. My foot burned when I touched down, but I told myself to ignore the pain.

I made the stairs in a heartbeat. The sounds of fighting behind me had grown more vicious. The yelping didn't sound remotely canine anymore. They sounded human.

Whether the noise came from the dog or the man with the scythe, I bolted up the stairs, taking them two at a time when my good foot lead, and one at a time when I had to use my bad one for push off.

I tore open the door when I reached the top and flung it shut behind me. I twisted the lock in a frantic movement that made me jam my finger into the metal before I realized I was too close.

My chest heaved as I put my weight against it. I splayed my arms out wide against the wood. It was thick, solid oak. It shouldn't break easily. I was safe for the moment.

With the respite I'd gained from getting upstairs and locking the door, I had the time to realize I'd left my phone downstairs.

"Of course I did," I muttered, scanning the room for anything I could use that would practically get me out of the attic if that thing downstairs managed to get past the dog and cut through the door.

But the attic was empty. I'd made sure of it the day before with Layne. Not that any of my mother's things could have helped.

Except they had, hadn't they? As impossible as it might be, it was too much of a coincidence that I'd felt the book respond to my touch and the stray somehow found its way into the store when all the doors were closed and locked.

Impossible. But Occam's razor couldn't be ignored.

It took a few moments of me mulling over the possibility that some sort of magic had taken place before I realized there was no sound coming from below.

My heart pounded at the thought of investigating but I couldn't just stay up there all day. I had to go down.

I winced as I pried open the door an inch to listen. Nothing. No growling, no sounds of things being trashed.

Complete silence met my ears. I strained to hear more, pressing my ear against the small gap in the door.

I did hear something. Like someone pounding on wood. I opened the door a bit wider. This time, the shouting was clearer. Someone, a male, pounded on the window of the shop.

But there were no responsive sounds from within to meet the noise from without.

I had to be alone.

Before I could decide it was prudent to leave the attic, the pounding stopped. A door slammed toward the back room. Layne's voice drifted up the stairs to meet me as he called out my name.

"Intruder," I yelled down as I descended the stairs, terrified he'd just think of the time I'd called on him for a cat, and prayed he'd believe me.

I hoped the one word would at least warn Layne until I could get down the stairs.

"That thing is back," I yelled. "It attacked me."

I was on the middle tread by the time he rounded the corner and started up the stairs. He had his weapon drawn and while he walked on two feet, he looked far more lupine than man. I paused, the residual terror still controlling my reactions.

"Nothing down here," he said with a growl in his voice. Gold swirled in the depths of his eyes.

"Nothing up there, either," I said, clutching the banister.

His shoulders relaxed. The jawline that had been clenched so tightly eased and let color move back into his chin.

"I heard you scream."

I nodded, not trusting my voice now that my stomach trembled. If I opened my mouth one more time, it would be to cry and I did not want to cry.

"I heard..." He raked his hand over his head and I could see that his hand, too, shook. "I got here as fast as I could."

He didn't make a move toward me. I thought he realized I was fighting for control of my emotions. We stood there for a long moment, holding each other in our gazes, both of us probably seeing fear in the other. It took a supreme amount of will for me to force myself to move one more step. I wasn't thinking about my sore foot until it was the one I led with and the pain lanced up into my calf.

He was up the remaining stairs and catching me before I fell, so when I collapsed from adrenaline and pain, I just sagged into his arms.

"I think I know who the killer is," I said.

CHAPTER TWENTY-FOUR

I DIDN'T EXPECT A wolf-man to be tender, but Layne helped me down the rest of the stairs and into a chair so gently I didn't feel any pain. He collected several of the novelty throw pillows from the front of the shop and tucked me into the hard-backed chair. He moved around my store silently, glancing at me now and then, maybe expecting me to speak but giving me room to gather myself.

After he'd found a first aid kit in my bathroom and bandaged up my foot, I felt better. Less raw. I left him to go burrow through my kitchenette and put water on to boil. When he pulled down my Buddha urn, I had to stop him.

"Not that one," I said with a shake of my head. "The tea is in the basket."

He took Buddha's head off the top and peered inside while my stomach knotted up.

"Looks like tea," he said, but then he canted his head and caught my eye over the urn. "But it isn't."

He replaced the lid and set it back on its shelf.

His gaze went steely, but he said nothing as he turned away in time to catch the kettle popping. He lifted it and poured a good dose of water into the mug. It was obvious he wasn't a tea drinker. Any good tea addict would add the bag first.

"Don't judge me," I said to his back. "I don't think I could take it right now."

He twisted to pull the tea basket down and opened a packet. "What you do in your spare time is none of my business."

I could smell the orange ginger from where I sat, and I knew he believed I used the mushroom mixture for my own purposes. But things had changed in the last few days. I wasn't the same woman I was before we'd met. He deserved to know my truth.

I sighed. "It's not for me," I said, and when he quirked one eyebrow with just a hint of skepticism, I rushed on before I could lose my nerve. "Some clients are suffering. Psychedelics are known to help ease trauma. There's research to indicate it helps with post-traumatic stress."

He gave his full attention to squeezing the bag of its last oils and liquid. "So you drug them."

"I offer it to them," I corrected. "They have full control."

I didn't say more. I might be evolving, but not to the point I'd want to incriminate myself.

"You didn't answer my question," he said. "And mark me, we'll discuss it at some point, but right now, I'm worried about you."

"That's how you show concern?" I asked. "By interrogating the victim."

He faced me with the mug in one hand and raised the other. "Truce, alright?"

When I nodded, he crossed the room and pressed the mug into my hands. The aromatics rose to create a comforting steam around my face. I closed my eyes and took a moment to send signals to my body that the worst was over. I could relax.

"Tell me what happened," he said, and I opened my eyes to see him crouching in front of me. "I may not look like it, but I'm on the edge. I need to hear what went on so my wolf will settle."

I told him, even though the trauma of the experience still shivered through my bones. When I was done, he collected all the clippings from the floor and scattered around where the air currents had shoved them when I'd taken to running. He quietly sifted through them as I sipped the tea that was beginning to grow cool. We both needed time to process it all.

He made small musing sounds as he read, and I curled my legs up beneath me. He was giving it all much more study than I had. Probably the detective in him looking for things I couldn't consider. At one point, he backed up toward me and leaned against my chair. I let my legs down to straddle his shoulders, tucking him in and he didn't resist or move to extricate himself. Occasionally, he'd lift a clipping up over his head with a comment and I'd study it and answer his questions.

It went on like that before he laid a handful of paper onto his lap and leaned his head back on the chair. The top of his head was right there between my legs and I could run my hand over the top of his hair if I wanted.

I might have come very close to doing just that, but he broke the spell with a strange comment.

"For centuries, every male in my family has been turned," he said. "Like the Spartans, we are put to the test. Can we survive being made into a werewolf? Can we learn to control our beast? The transformation happens on our eighteenth birthday and those who could not or would not survive as a dual entity are euthanized."

"That's...shocking."

"It hasn't happened that way for more than fifty years," he said. "The mothers of the 60s wouldn't have it. We lost control of them right about the same time they realized they didn't have to wear a bra."

The way he admitted it all sounded very much like he had firsthand knowledge.

"That's horrible," I said. "Not just the killing of innocents, but that you all thought women were a thing to be owned. Thank God for women's lib."

He twisted and looked up at me. "The new wolves were not innocent," he said. "When I say wouldn't or couldn't live as a dual entity, I mean it. They became more animal than man. They were a danger to everyone and every beast. As for the women, I totally agree. But hasn't man always sought to control women? The wolves were no different."

"Why are you telling me this?"

He sighed. "To be honest, it's because of these clippings. I had no plans to reveal my nasty past or that of my family."

"But...?"

"But I think there's a connection, and not just for your family. My pack were the muscle for a coven of powerful witches generations ago. Family legend says we emancipated ourselves when they turned to very black magic."

"You think your family might be connected to this Blackburn cult?"

"The Blackburn cult is a modern day incarnation of the types of things my family abandoned their witches over. Our coven disappeared right around the time of our emancipation. Either that or they went underground."

"You're thinking they went underground."

"Yes, and they emerged as this cult led by this woman." He tapped the paper in his hand with the back of his fingers. "I think maybe your mother was one of them."

It was what I thought too. "So what do they want, I wonder. Do you think they're behind the killings? That they are killing other psychics out of some sense of warped supernatural eugenics?"

"Witches," he said, correcting my terminology. "Maybe the women are witches."

I blinked at him.

"I'm not a witch," I said.

"You've told me that." He grinned.

"No, I mean, I'm not anything. I'm a cheat and a con." I twirled the teacup in my hands.

He began laying the papers back down on the floor, one on top of the other.

"You called to a familiar," he said, jerking his chin in the direction of the grimoire. "You used your mother's book and you called for help. Help came."

"That's not my magic," I said and he twisted right around then and laid his hands on my knees as he looked up at me.

"Then it's your mother's magic."

That wasn't something I was prepared to hear, not out loud. I struggled with the hope that my mother had some power so that at least the things she did had some higher purpose. But hearing she was involved with black magic, didn't sit well.

All this time hoping she was real but believing she was a charlatan like me, made something inside ache. I pushed out of the chair, shoving him aside, and stooped to pick up the papers. None of this was getting us any closer to finding the killer and stopping him.

"What's that?" I said, noticing the last thing he'd lain on top of the pile. A faded photograph of a group of people stood in front of a hotel. The man in the middle looked familiar. I held it close to the salt lamp that sat on a corner table.

"Sweet Jesus," I said. "Did you look at this?"

He came over to look over my shoulder. He sucked in a sharp inhale.

"It's him," he said. "It's the man who was dumped in front of the hotel gala."

"But this picture is dated," I said. "Thirty years ago. He looks exactly the same."

"Did you notice the sign on the hotel?"

A symbol of Hecate just like my own branding.

"Tell me again about the night you were attacked," he said. "Tell me how you felt, what he did. What the creature's reactions were until I got there. And then tell me about your graffiti intruder."

I went through it all again. He stopped me every now and then to ask questions. Did the creature seem aware of its surroundings? Did it notice the woman putting her cat out? I told him it did, both times. It just hadn't seemed to be able to pinpoint where I was.

"Your amulet," he said. "You were wearing it?"

"Yes. And it felt odd," I said.

He thought about that but didn't ask me what odd meant. His mind had already moved to the stray dog.

"I think you're the only one who can see that stray," he said. "It's your familiar, maybe."

"But I'm not a witch."

He made a thoughtful murmur but didn't argue.

"Fighting the creature was like fighting smoke at times," he said. "But at others, it was like fighting a dozen wildcats all at once. You say the man carrying a scythe had come into your shop a few days ago?"

I nodded. "But he was a man," I said. "A real man. The guy in the picture, the dead guy, he could see him too."

"Magic can be strange and unpredictable," he said. "Take wolf shifters for example. How do you think this body is able to remake itself over and over, how it's able to heal? How I can communicate with my pack even over distances?"

"Your pack?" I gave him a curious glance.

He looked sheepish. "Yes. We're a pack species. There are several of us in the area, although I'm the only one on the police force."

I narrowed my gaze.

"Parrish," I said. It was obvious his father was a shifter since he'd already told me the males of his family got turned on their birthday in some barbaric rite of passage. But Parrish was a woman.

"Parrish is a wolf shifter, yes," he said. "She's not from my family, though. She was a lone wolf, turned by a rogue in the 60s. Other packs have no qualms about turning a woman. Some do it for sport, some want their mates in their packs.

"Parrish was different. Because she had no pack and desperately needed one, we took her in. Hers is our only female wolf. While some packs will turn a woman, they don't always make it through the change. It has nothing to do with the physical change. Women actually get through that part pretty easily...better than men most times. But when they discover they can't bear children, something just snaps inside. Survival as a wolf shifter is less about the physical for a woman and more about the will."

I didn't think I wanted to know more right then, and I could tell by his expression that he didn't want to continue. But I'd asked about Parrish and so now I knew. She was part of his pack.

Pack. I was still getting used to the idea of him being a shifter let alone there being a whole pack of them.

"So do you think the scythe guy is a sort of shifter?" I said.

He shrugged. "I don't know what he is. But I do now think that amulet has power. I think since it didn't keep your graffiti attacker from getting shredded, that the power is specific to you. I think your mother did manage to charm that amulet. Whether or not it was made by her or just charmed by her, she succeeded."

I thought about that, recalling the spell work and all the symbols.

"It was meant to protect her," I said, working out the ingredient list and what they might mean. "Maybe even make her invisible to her enemies."

I thought of how the street had sort of phased out and that my neighbor couldn't see me.

"Maybe it didn't just make the owner invisible. Maybe it phased them just out of sync with things."

Again, he shrugged. "However it works, it's a powerful bit of magic, and one that seems to work only with you and that means one thing more. We need to get it back. Even if we have to steal it."

Chapter Twenty-Five

BREAKING INTO A POLICE station was going to be one more thing I went to hell for. Of course, it helped the conscience to be marched into the precinct with one of its detectives at three am. The physical break-in? That was much easier. Looking like a victim who barely survived an attack made folks turn their gazes away.

Layne marshaled me past the dispatch clerk with barely a howdy do, mentioning that he had a witness to the serial psychic killings and wanted her/me to get a good look at a few suspect pictures to see if I could ID the killer.

The clerk seemed interested in the psychic killings part right up to the time he asked me if I got a good look at the bastard and I told him I wasn't sure. He went back to his Internet searching with a grunt of disappointment, and I took that to mean he was hoping I'd actually seen enough gore to regale him with gossip.

I had seen gore, but it wasn't an interesting bit of gossip. It was a nightmare-inducing consequence.

The evidence room clerk must have spent far too many nights alone with dusty boxes because he just flipped a sign in clipboard in our direction without asking any of the questions the dispatch clerk did.

Layne told him I was sure I'd seen the killer leaving something at the crime scene. A ring of some sort, maybe, or a piece of paper, he wasn't sure, but it bore checking out. It was a good cover because we both knew there was nothing in evidence about a ring, so we couldn't get asked about it later if my amulet went missing.

"There's nothing in the log about any rings for the case," the clerk said, leaning over to look at his logbook.

"You know how those logs are," Layne said. "They're bare lists. I want to know if there's anything in any of the boxes that might trigger her memory."

"She can't go in."

Layne drilled him with an icy glare until the clerk sighed and said, "You can take the stuff upstairs to your desk if you want and she can look at it there, but she can't go in. You know this."

Layne swiveled to me with an overbearing look of concern, far too worried a look for a stranger he'd just met.

"Do you think you'll be alright waiting here with Avi?" he said. "He's an okay sort. Doesn't bite."

I took that cue to mean I should look scared. Scared enough that Avi wouldn't be interested in caring for me should I begin to panic in the vestibule while Layne was in the depths of the evidence locker.

I started to shake. Just enough to make the clerk run me over with a nervous eye. I hugged myself, tightening the grip on my elbows until I could feel how white my knuckles were.

"Are you sure he's safe?" I said in a shrill tone that made even my own ears hurt. "He looks an awful lot like the man I saw slicing into that poor woman's belly."

I gave him a squint-eyed stare, as though I was trying to overlay his image with a memory. I made a show of hyperventilating.

His eyes never left mine, but he said to Layne, "Take her with you. Last thing I need is to get picked out of a lineup because she thinks I look like whoever that bastard is."

He dragged his eyes from me to take in Layne, who was doing his damnedest not to smile. It ended up making him look terrifying.

"You know how witnesses are," the clerk said. "Sees me down here and says stupid shit like I look like him and next thing you know I'm pointed out in a court of law because she altered her own damn memory. Fuck that. Take her in but don't stay long."

"We'll be out in two shakes," Layne said. "I know just the box I'm going for."

The clerk heaved a long-suffering sigh. "If she freaks out in there, it's on your head. I never saw you. In fact, I was out taking a piss when you let yourself in."

He dropped the keys on the counter and came out from behind it. He gave me a long look then went out through the door to the hallway. I knew the restroom was halfway down the basement hallway.

"Are there cameras?" I said to Layne as I followed him into the evidence room.

"If they worked, do you think he'd have let you in?"

"Good point."

As if Layne had already been in here, rummaging through all the items, he made a beeline for a table on the left wall. Three large boxes rested there with writing in black marker. I recognized the date from the first murder. Next to it was the second, a smaller box with a date on it. The third was neatly labeled as John Doe. He lifted the lid from the box.

"Stand back. Some things you don't need to see," he said.

"I could have waited outside if you didn't need me to do anything but stand here and look pretty."

He gave me the once over. "To be fair, you look a little too damaged at the moment to be considered pretty."

He leaned over the box and surveyed it.

A thought occurred to me. "You didn't need me in here with you at all."

"Nope."

I clenched my jaw. "You figured if I was here you could blame me if someone noticed the amulet missing."

He grinned as he plucked it out. It was sealed in a plastic bag big enough to store a pizza in.

"I can't afford to lose this job," he said and folded the bag in half.

"You're rich," I said through gritted teeth.

He tucked the bag and the amulet beneath his jacket. "I told you. My father is rich. I'm well-off. But I wasn't speaking monetarily. My father needs me here where I can monitor any unnatural activity."

I was going to ask why but I caught sight of the clerk's head through the window in the door and stepped in front to block his view. Not that it mattered. Layne already had the top back on the box.

"It's illegal to tamper with evidence," he said. "And while I can change at will, there are certain peculiarities about being caged, i.e., imprisoned, that would make my condition a danger to anyone in a cell with me.

"Besides, I couldn't live with myself if you ended up hurt because you didn't have this when you needed it."

"Not to mention the hunch that you have something in mind for it?" I suggested.

He tapped his nose as he brushed past me, snagging me with his free hand as he went by. He was pushing the door open when I realized what it was he had planned, but I said nothing until we'd signed out and walked to the elevator. I started to speak when he put his finger to his lips.

"Not here."

Not here meant we had to wait until we stood at the site of the first crime scene. It looked much different than it had that morning, and in the night than during the day. The bustling activity of the docks had petered to a few local lobster fishermen prepping their boats for an early morning disembark. They liked to be at their grounds before daylight so they could begin hauling at dawn.

Layne headed straight to the hoist where the first three woman had been hung. The lights strung over the pier illuminated most of the wharf but there were still shadows here and there. He stopped just shy of a darker spot on the asphalt where the women's viscera had lay coiled in one large mess.

"Are you ready?" he said.

"Ready for what?"

In answer, he pulled the plastic bag from beneath his jacket and tore it open. He dangled the amulet in front of me. "Put it on."

Obediently, I looped it over my neck.

"Good," he said and pointed to that blackish spot beneath the hoist. "Now go over there."

I might have rolled my eyes at the naive hope in his, but before I even stepped toward the hoist, the amulet began to grow hot. I felt it through my shirt and jacket. I thought I heard him say something but I was already moving, reaching for it so I could yank it off my chest.

Too late, I realized touching it was not a good idea. A crack of sound split the air around me. Blue light in one swirling, twisting line that ended at the hoist coiled about my hand. I yanked my fingers away, not sure if the searing heat had burned my skin.

A heartbeat later, I felt that same sort of vacuous sensation. Layne spun around in a circle, his mouth working in what looked like my name. I felt electric, as though someone had touched me after scuffing across an old carpet.

I realized as I stood there that he couldn't see me. I also noticed a trail of black smoke emitting from the stone and coiling around me. It hadn't done that before, but if I looked long enough, I could just make out a long black tail and a snout with very canine looking teeth. If I stared at it straight, the shape disappeared, but if I looked at it askance, the resemblance to the stray dog, however smoky, was uncanny.

Both frightened and exhilarated, I backed away from the crime scene. I made it several yards before the night air went back to normal. I hollered to Layne and, surprised, he lifted his hand in the air.

He started to trot toward me, so I guessed he could see me again. Relief made me blow out a breath of air. I hadn't realized just how nervous I'd been until he responded.

He stopped short to check his phone several yards away from me, and I waited impatiently till he finished and trotted to my side.

"That was freaking weird," he said. "You just disappeared." He jerked his gaze back to the crime scene.

"You won't believe what I saw," I said, feeling as though I had to one-up him. I gave him the details, all the while feeling as though he was getting more antsy as I continued. By the time I got to the stray dog, he looked outright pained.

"What's wrong?" I said because I knew something was off. He was giving me those kinds of vibes you get when someone is trying to tip toe around you.

If I tell you, you have to agree to do what I say."

"That's pretty cryptic."

He nodded. "Promise."

I held my hand up, first two fingers glued together in a traditional salute. "I swear. I'll do exactly what you tell me."

"You need to stay in a hotel tonight," he said.

"A hotel? Why?"

"That was Parrish." He took my elbow and hastened me along with him as we left the pier.

I felt my heart sink. We were getting somewhere. I knew we were. I wanted to talk about what had happened with the amulet. I wanted to know what he'd seen.

"Don't you want to know—"

"You disappeared," he said curtly. "We were right. The amulet has the power to cloak you."

He took the wind out of my sails, sure enough.

"But why didn't it do that the first time I was on site? Why now?"

He shrugged. "I have no idea, but it's working now." The gentle guiding he was doing using my elbow turned more insistent. "I need you to be compliant. Don't argue."

He all but dragged me to his car where I fought when he tried to push me into the passenger side.

"You promised," he said.

"And you're lying." I resisted his shove into the open car door.

He sighed. "There's been another murder. Another woman."

"Fuck," I said. "Don't you need me to help?"

"I don't think it's a good idea. What I think is a good idea is for you to take that amulet with you and book a hotel room for tonight."

My hackles went up at the tone in his voice. He didn't just sound serious. He sounded worried.

"You're not telling me something," I said. "Something I should know because unless you tell me, I'm not honoring our bargain."

He stared ahead over my shoulder to the crime scene behind us so determinedly that I knew what he planned to tell me was not pleasant. I prodded his leg with my index finger and he inhaled sharply.

"All right," he said. "Do you know a psychic who has a shop around the corner from you? A little palm reading cubbyhole?"

"I do," I said. She was a nice lady. A decade or so older than me, and the first one to welcome me to the community. She wasn't a threat to my business nor was I to hers. We did different things, but she did send me customers now and then. We even lived on the same block.

"Adele," I said. "She's pretty good at her craft."

I didn't say 'craft' meant the art of conning.

"She might have been good at her craft before today," he said. "She's the one who was killed."

I felt like someone had kicked my knees from behind and the only reason they didn't buckle was because he was holding me up. I let go an aggrieved *oh*, and he squeezed me tighter against his side.

"So you don't want me to go home because you think the killer might find me there? I have the amulet," I said, touching the once again inert stone. "Surely, it will cloak me."

"That's not it," he said. "I'm pretty sure you're safe with it for now."

"Then what?"

"I don't want you to go home because her body was found right outside your apartment."

CHAPTER TWENTY-SIX

THE KILLER HAD LEFT me a gift. A promise, is what Layne said. He probably lurked outside my apartment waiting for me and when I didn't return on a timeline that made him happy, he'd designed a little tableau of death outside my front door. Just like a favorite pet brings its beloved owner a mouse or a bird.

No one saw it happen. No one saw him dump Adele's body. She was found by the neighbor with the cat when she'd had to leave her apartment to collect her pet after it made a beeline for the crime scene. She'd got there just in time to keep her precious cat from running off with one of Adele's eyeballs.

So the killings were getting worse. I didn't ask Layne what it meant that the cat was able to pick up one of the poor woman's organs and try to run off with it. I didn't want to know. But it was clear the scene was bad enough I couldn't return home. At least, not till everything was examined and cleared up.

I didn't even ask if they'd found a number at the scene. I didn't want to know. Not right then.

I knew Layne would be there for several hours. I was exhausted just thinking about it. He drove me to a nice enough hotel closest to the original crime scene, a posh-looking thing perfectly located to take on all the tourist traffic.

When he tried to park and walk me to the lobby, I lifted a hand in protest.

"I'm a big girl," I said. "I know how to check into a hotel."

I hadn't meant to sound blunt and curt, but I was exhausted. I knew he was exhausted. There was a pinched look around his eyes that was evident in the golden pool of light that struck him from the car's overhead.

Good conscience wouldn't let me force him to escort me into the building, not when I knew how much work he'd have ahead of him for the night.

If he felt anything like I did, it was akin to the sensation of hanging from a wire by my fingernails.

"Go," I said, trying to soften the tone. "I'll be fine."

"When I saw the blood on the floor of your shop, I nearly lost myself to my wolf," he said in a raw voice.

"I'm sure later on I'll feel like Red Riding Hood being threatened by a wolf," I said, "but right now the thought of being eaten by you doesn't scare me in the least."

I had my fingers on the handle of his Mercedes when I felt his palm on my leg, stalling me. I turned to look into that face and my throat clogged up with all the things I wanted to say.

He waited the barest of moments before he leaned across the cabin and brushed his lips against mine. Nothing sexual, nothing demanding, just a warm touch of lips that could have been a chaste gesture of comfort, except it made my stomach burn with unexpected desire.

He pulled away with the ghost of a smile playing across his mouth.

"I would never want you to be afraid I might eat you," he said. "I'd much rather you beg me for it."

I wasn't sure if he could smell my desire or read my mind, but I fled the car with my cheeks flaming and closed the door behind me without daring to look back. I imagined him chuckling to himself as he revved the engine and pulled out of the parking lot.

I knew the hotel gave out warm cookies on check in and that the rooms were massive and the beds comfortable, but as he was driving off, I realized I couldn't afford the lovely hotel he'd thought to bring me to.

I guessed with his kind of money, he didn't think about the costs. He probably never had to. I stood on the sidewalk, working my heel back and forth as I thought about my bank account and the three maxed out credit cards in my purse.

I pulled my sweater tighter around my shoulders, pinning it together at the throat with closed fists. The sea breeze had come up over the last hour and a hint of fog tainted the air with seaweed and brine. I shivered beneath the fabric as the cold seeped in between the gaps my hands made of the material from bunching it so tightly in one spot.

I had a cot in the back of my shop from the days I'd done long hours of decorating and clean up when I'd decided to open the business. It was still in the closet with a set of sheets, a pillow, and a wool blanket. It was big enough to lay out flat on my back or curl up sideways.

Just thinking about being in a familiar space instead of a cookie cutter hotel room made me spin on my heel. I was within walking distance of my shop anyway. A few blocks.

I stepped up the pace, being careful to stay lit by the street lamps and not wander too far into the shadows.

Every noise made my heart rate tick up. I wasn't the least bit relaxed until I found myself in front of my back door. I rattled the key into the lock and twisted the knob. I flung the door shut behind me and laid against it while I caught my breath.

I hadn't realized how amped up I was until I heard my own rasping breaths. But I was safe. And it was free.

Exhaustion began to overtake the adrenaline. I needed sleep. With heavy steps, I headed to the storage closet and pulled out the foldaway cot. It was right where I'd left it, and to my delight, I'd thought to put the pillows and linens in a plastic bag with a sachet of lavender blossoms. The faint whiff of orange and patchouli came out too, and the sheets were that fuzzy kind that felt so soft against your skin.

"Boss," I said to the past self who had thought to prepare for this possibility long in advance. I'd have patted myself on the shoulder if I could, but I satisfied myself with running the sheets over my nose before snapping them open in a shake as good as any strong wind might do if they were on the line.

When my phone made a noise, I realized it was my online calendar, reminding me of an upcoming appointment.

I was busy making the bed up in the back room when another noise caught my ear. At first, I thought it was my phone and checked to see a message from Layne. They'd found a number at the scene, cut into the victim's cheek. A number seven. Definitely not in order at all. I was musing that over when the sound came again, and I cocked my head to listen more intently.

It didn't sound like anything I recognized. Sometimes, birds got caught in the old chimney, or mice scuttled across the floor every now and then but it didn't sound like that either.

I paused, hand in the middle of smoothing out the wool blanket, when the noise came again, and this time, I strained my ear toward where I'd thought it had come from. Beyond the beaded curtain and hallway that separated the back room where I conducted séances and had my office, the shop was wide open.

I waited for what seemed an eternity before another noise came. This time, I was ready, and I knew, just knew, it had come from the storefront. Something was out there. It had all the hallmarks of a dog shoving its muzzle into something overly fragrant. A snuffling sort of noise.

So not a bird or a mouse. The stray dog, maybe? The beast Layne was sure was the familiar of the amulet? I ran my hand along my jeans to feel for the necklace. After I'd literally disappeared from view the last time I'd worn it, I was nervous to put it around my neck.

Now, I pulled it from my pocket, along with my phone. I draped it over my head and swiped my phone screen to ON. Because a bit of invisibility might be a good thing under the circumstances.

Better to be safe than sorry. I texted Layne, telling him there was something in my shop. I felt too guilty to admit I hadn't stayed at the hotel he'd brought me to, but I did confess I was in my back shop and heard the noise.

I waited, heart in my throat, for an answer.

Nothing came. It was as I was staring at the screen, waiting for a text to come back that I realized I'd left the phone sound on. If something dangerous was on the other side of the beaded curtain, a text notification would alert it. Bad enough I'd been humming to myself as I made up my cot.

I hurriedly turned off the sound, then I crept to the doorway, staying far enough away from the curtain that

I couldn't accidentally touch any of the beads and make them clack together.

It was dark in the storefront. I usually left a few mood lights going to discourage any would-be thieves but from my vantage point, which was deep in the back of the building, and past a long hallway I'd converted into an apothecary space that I called the gallery, I couldn't quite see the entirety of the storefront. Just that unending shadow right down the middle.

I took a deep, bracing breath, deciding I couldn't wait for Layne to come to rescue me. Hadn't he said he wasn't partial to damsels in distress? And what if it was the dog? It hadn't hurt me so far.

I felt very much like the foolish horror movie heroine as I crept through the curtain and tiptoed down the hallway toward the shop.

The noises stopped by the time I got to the end of the gallery. I halted, leaning against the brief bit of space along the wall that wasn't covered in bottles and ointments and tubes. My mouth had gone dry and my pulse was so rapid I could feel it in my throat.

But it was the dog out there. It had to be. It had made a habit of showing itself even when I wasn't in danger and it had risked itself for me over and over. My door was locked, but the dog had shown an ability to move like smoke into the shop when it attacked the scythe man.

If it was out there and needed me, I had to do what I could.

I swallowed. I'd never be able to sleep unless I saw with my own two eyes that the store was empty or that it was indeed the stray. And whatever it was, if anything, I wanted to see it before it saw me.

Plus, I knew if I left the store without making sure it was empty, I'd never be able to come back inside no matter how much money I needed to earn.

I didn't count on my shoulder hitting the light switch and flooding the storefront with incandescent illumination. Something crashed into my shelf of candles. They rolled across the floor, those that were pillars and tapers. The ones in glass shattered in a cacophony of noise.

It wasn't my stray dog that stood in the midst of my shop. It was a man, and I recognized that face. I knew the scythe he held in one hand.

"You," I said, like some vapid horror movie casualty. But that one word said everything my mind was already tripping over in its haste to make sense of what was happening.

His face jerked toward where I stood as though something had yanked on his neck.

"I'm here for my appointment," he growled in a voice more beast than man, and then he snarled with lips drawn back exactly the way a rabid dog might. Wrapped around the form of a humanoid shape, was the black and wispy visage of something more bestial. Not a panther, not a wolf. But... something.

The entire person-shaped being beneath it disappeared, and any resemblance to a man was gone. The straw-colored hair transformed into a thick mat of fur like on the back of a bison and it took several seconds before I realized it was some sort of cloak.

More than that, I didn't care to work out. I turned heel and bolted for the back room even as I heard the thunder of its steps on the floorboards. It was silent other than that and I wasn't sure as I fled if it was a dozen feet behind me or an inch. I only guessed it was out of range because I didn't feel the slicing pain of that scythe in my back.

I got tangled in the beads when I hit the threshold of the door to my back shop. One of the strings caught on my amulet's leather thong. It yanked me back as I forged through and part of the leather chaffed into my neck.

I clamped down on a moan of frustration and pain.

The beast was already there. I had no time to extricate myself. I was dead if I didn't do something. The beast came at me, barreling behind me with feet that sounded more like hooves pounding the floor instead of shod feet. It drew in a long, questioning breath as it drew near. It swung its big head back and forth, panning the area around it as it came.

When it struck out with the scythe, the blade came within an inch of slicing into my belly. I screamed involuntarily and its head snapped up. It canted its ear to the side.

Listening.

It jabbed at open air with the weapon again, and this time I managed to bite down on the scream that tried to slip past my lips. Listening, I told myself. The amulet. I'd dropped it around my neck and it was cloaking me.

I might have felt elated if I wasn't so damn terrified.

With my breath hitching and my heart hammering, I carefully untangled the string of beads from the necklace. I didn't take my time, but I did work as silently as I could.

The last of the beads dropped out of my grasp right around the same moment Layne's voice called to me from the front the shop. The beast turned, raising its chin to the air. Its nostrils expanded.

Then it turned in a movement so graceful it reminded me of a panther moving from a tree limb to climb back down a tree. It shivered in the light. The thick, viscous looking black shadow moved silently back down the hallway.

Toward Layne.

Because of course, the detective did not have a cloaking amulet with magic designed to protect him.

The beast disappeared as it rounded the corner and went into the shop proper. A mental image assaulted my memory, of Layne and that creature in the shadows of night, wrestling to be the one who lived. I couldn't chance it again. Last time I had run away. This time I was going to run ahead.

I was going to make a difference.

I rushed headlong down the few feet of the apothecary gallery and stopped in my tracks.

The door to my shop was split in two. The beast had no doubt cut through it with his scythe. Layne stood there with his gun drawn, the creature a thick, awful shadow in front of him.

Layne spied me right about the time the beast roared. He couldn't shoot, not with me standing right there behind the intruder.

I reacted out of instinct, but only because the amulet grew warm against my shirt. The smell of scorched material lifted to my nose. The stone was powering up.

I grabbed the amulet, ignoring the heat it produced, expecting it to burn my hand and yet it didn't. I felt a charge go through me. My back arched as some connection was made. An electric sort of pain burst through my spine and spiraled down to one spot in my solar plexus.

I felt as though whatever connected me to the amulet was as tenuous a thread as a black widow's gossamer. I didn't dare move as that spot of connection burned badly enough it stole my air.

The beast lunged for Layne. A sound of wood splitting rent the air as a burst of light shot out from the amulet.

It netted the beast in a web of power so bright I had to squint. The beast roared in pain and anguish. It twisted as though being manhandled by a hundred hands. His feet lifted off the floor. Tar dripped from his feet and melted away from his form like a puddle of water sluicing off a rock face.

Layne was still standing there, watching me, aiming for the beast as he waited for me to step out of the way.

But I couldn't. I was frozen, held tight in the power that jolted through me and the amulet. That gossamer thread joined me to the beast writhing in the air.

Except slowly as it hung there, suspended, it looked less like a beast and more like the man who had come into my shop and gave me help when I needed it.

I almost went to him, so strong was the look of agony on his face, but then he caught my eye and what I saw there in the depths of his was terrifying. Nothing but blind rage and hatred.

Then the amulet let him go and he collapsed to the floor with a loud thud that shook the crystals on the shelf closest to him. Layne rushed to him, ordering him to remain on the floor.

"Doesn't matter," I said as Layne pulled his hands behind his back and cuffed him. "He can't move anyway."

He looked up at me.

"Passed out?" he said, and I nodded. I didn't need for him to check to know it. I felt his consciousness leave him. I wasn't sure how, but I had.

I peeled the amulet from around my neck and dropped it on the counter. I had no idea how I found the steam to walk across the room at all but I lost that ability by the time the necklace met the burled wood. I slid down along the counter wall to my haunches.

Distant sirens cut through the darkness of the streets outside. The coolness of the fog crept in and chilled the shop. I smiled as I thought about how nice it was that it was all over.

I watched with a strange sense of detachment as Parrish barreled into the storefront through my splintered door. Several cops came with her, swarming my space with such efficiency I worried they'd find all my little secrets. But it was hard to fret about them too long. I was alive, after all.

I vaguely heard Layne asking me if I was okay and looked up to see him hunched in front of me, his face close to mine. He smelled of mint gum and ashes. His lapel was scorched.

Some of the magic must have got him.

"Brie," he said. "Are you going to be alright?"

I let my fingers roam his lapel, where the burn marks marred the gorgeous material. He waited for me to answer, the tension in his shoulders revealing his worry but he gave me the space and time to answer.

Except I didn't know the answer. I wasn't sure I was okay. I wasn't sure I'd ever be okay again.

Chapter Twenty-Seven

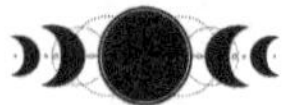

THE AMULET PULSED FOR a long time as it sat on my counter, casting faint flickers of light onto the dull, aged wood beneath it. Shadows danced along the walls of my cluttered shop, a blend of dim twilight from outside and the dimming bulbs above creating an eerie half-light.

The scent of dried herbs and incense lingered in the air, a heavy contrast to the sharp, metallic tang of blood. I watched the amulet from across the room, nestled between shelves of old tomes and trinkets, because I was afraid to touch it again. The cool chill from the open door swept across the floor, making the air inside feel cold and thin, as if the magic in the space had somehow drained it of warmth.

The officers at the crime scene had already begun cordoning off my shop. Their voices were muffled, their heavy boots thudding over the worn hardwood. They cataloged the items nearest the body, snapping pictures of the mess—a mess that spread far beyond the pool of dark blood staining my favorite rug. I winced as one of them trampled over a delicate vase, its sharp crack like a gunshot in the heavy silence. The destruction was chaotic, each toppled shelf and shattered object a reminder of the violence that had stormed through this place just moments ago.

Layne, in contrast, moved quietly and surreptitiously, bagging up the necklace to return it to the evidence locker. The edges of his face were hidden in the dim light, his expression a mix of concentration and something I couldn't quite place. Since it was part of another crime scene, they wouldn't notice it was at mine, I supposed.

If I hadn't been watching the stone pulse so keenly, I wouldn't have seen him slide it off the counter into a bag. He caught my eye as he tucked it beneath his jacket, the weight of unspoken words hovering between us. Outside, the evening sky darkened further, a sliver of moon just barely visible through the dust-smeared window.

As for the killer, I had no idea what he'd confess to in custody. If he decided to detail the entire episode in my shop and spoke of the amulet, would the officers believe him or just think he was crazy? I guessed the latter, but it wasn't my problem. It seemed pretty cut and dried to me, regardless of how he explained it. Layne had found him in my store after he'd hacked through the door with what now merely looked like a hunter's axe as it lay on the floor, waiting to be cataloged. The floor beneath it was splintered, the marks from his assault creating jagged scars in the wood.

Pretty hard to find an innocent explanation for that one, especially if I made a statement to corroborate Layne's that the intruder had attacked me with an axe.

Except he hadn't. Not really. I was still in shock at the thought that magic had cloaked me from a killer's detection by an amulet my mother charmed. I was even more shocked that what had been so recently a long, powerful scythe was now just a squat axe lying on my floor. The dim shop lights glinted off its metal surface, a dull gleam in the otherwise shadow-filled room.

I knew as I stared at it that beneath some magical façade, lurked the same weapon I'd seen the first time the intruder entered my shop.

I gave the weapon a wary eye as I curled into one of the chairs I left everywhere for tired shoppers. The cushions were still soft, but the fabric was damp with sweat and dust, and I could feel the weight of my exhaustion sink into my bones. A customer who dawdled in a magic shop tended to buy more. I made sure they were good and comfy while they were inside.

Now, that comfort felt mocking. The peaceful sanctuary I had built for others was shattered. The chair groaned softly as I shifted, eyes still locked on the axe.

I had a good view of the axe and was more than a little nervous it would somehow transform back into the thing I knew it to be. The killer himself remained unconscious until the paramedics arrived and even then, he didn't come to. The scent of antiseptic filled the air as they hovered over him, the flashing red and blue lights from the ambulance outside painting the room in eerie, pulsing colors.

"Self-defense," Layne said as he crossed the room behind the paramedics.

They continued out the door with the killer on a stretcher, tied down nice and tight, while Layne stood in front of me. I didn't want to look up into his eyes. I wasn't sure how I'd keep from crying if I did. My reflection in the glass cabinet across from me looked pale and drawn, the shadows beneath my eyes more pronounced in the half-light.

He crouched next to the chair where I sat like a statue. His knees popped in resistance and he let go a soft groan. The faint sounds of the officers rummaging in my shop still grated against my nerves, but they were distant compared to the thudding in my chest.

"That felt good," he whispered. "They were so close to shifting they needed a good snapping."

I lifted my eyes to his then. A lopsided grin played on his mouth but it didn't make it to his eyes. His eyes looked worried.

"I didn't want my unit to see me like that," he murmured. "Bad for morale."

It was a joke obviously, but I didn't see anything remotely funny in the situation.

"You wouldn't have had time," I said, admitting the thing that bothered me most. "You wouldn't have shifted in time to defend yourself. He would have killed you."

Layne rolled his shoulders in his suit jacket.

"That's something about us you don't know." He looked around to be sure no one was listening. It was a wasted gesture because they weren't. They were all too busy rummaging through the debris, touching my things. "We're pretty strong even when we're not...you know...changed."

I lifted an eyebrow in surprise. "You could have taken him as a human?"

His jaw seesawed back and forth. "Probably not," he said with a rueful glance at the axe that we both knew wasn't an axe at all. Or at least, it hadn't been. I was still confused about all the details.

His palm touched down on my knee, banishing the cold that had started to creep in.

"I'd have given it a good fight, though," he said. "A hell of a fight."

I knew it was true. I caught sight of Parrish over his shoulder and noted she was watching us even though she was pretending to take notes in a little notepad with a marker.

"Will they charge his ass? Not just for here." I gestured to indicate my entire shop. "But for all of it?"

"There's nothing specific to tie him to the murders," he said. "Not yet anyway. But I know he was the killer and I'll keep digging till I find the proof. At least we have him in custody."

"Spoken like a man who believes in the guilty till proven innocent concept."

He made a grim line with his mouth. "His stink was all over the crime scenes. Even Parrish agrees. She has the best nose in the pack."

"What will you do if you can't?" I said. "Find the evidence, I mean."

"The murders will stop. It will become a cold case in my load. No one else will get hurt." He said it as if that was all that mattered.

"But those families. The women all had families somewhere. They need closure."

I thought of poor Sherry, and of myself. I felt panic rise at the idea they would be stuck in limbo for years. Decades.

He shrugged. "Do you think they'll believe the truth?"

"They don't need the truth," I said, remembering how I felt discovering my mother was a real witch. I'd spent decades telling myself the opposite when all the evidence had been right there in front of me. "They have a suspect. They have a man in custody. Just convict him."

"You don't need to convince me," he said then gave me a long, secretive look because one of the officers was wandering too close. "I told you it would end up a cold case in my load. If that happens, I have the whole of the pack to investigate. Why do you think I'm on the force? What do you think we do? Now, I have to take the amulet back to the locker."

I nodded. "Perfectly fine by me." I was still buzzing with the effects of the magic. "I never liked the thing anyway."

"There's no way to tie it to what happened tonight, but it will need to get cleared from the last crime scene before you can have it back."

He sounded apologetic, and he had no need to be. I didn't care what happened to the thing. As far as I was concerned, I never wanted to put it around my neck again.

"I'm sure it'll clear quickly," he said. "Because it was stolen from here and you did leave a statement to that effect."

I hadn't, but it was a moot point anyway.

"Doesn't matter," I said. "I don't want it."

He must have looked me over and found something he didn't like because he swore and pushed up off his knees with clenched fists to stand over me. I felt how imposing his height was as he loomed over me. If he was crossing his arms over his chest and glaring at me, I wouldn't be the least bit surprised.

"You should have stayed in the hotel," he said.

There it was. The blame. I'd expected it eventually. It got me to my feet. I faced him with a bristle in my spine.

"Sure, because staying in a hotel at those rates is a no brainer for someone like you." I stabbed him in the chest with my finger, ignoring how hard and immovable it was beneath each jab. "You have all the money in the world. Your wallet doesn't cough out dust when you open it."

The fear, the anger, and the sense of impotence all got delivered in that first jab and by the time I was stabbing at him for the fourth time, my finger just hurt.

He leaned back and grabbed my hand, pulling it down to my thigh. He leaned in so close I could see the gum he shifted to the inside of his left cheek.

"I gave them my credit card," he said. "It was already paid."

I blinked at him and a slow smile moved across his face.

"You fucking idiot," he said as he realized why I hadn't checked in, but the tone was indulgent, not mean. "Did you think I'd just drop you at the most expensive hotel in the city on a whim? I called ahead and had the bill already taken care of. You just had to pick up the key."

His hand wrestled with mine against my leg until he had it clasped firmly in his grip.

I squared my shoulders.

"I'm not some prostitute who needs to be bought," I said, stubborn.

His dark chuckle drew my gaze to his. "Hell no, hookers would have stayed there and had a party."

"You could have just told me you paid for the room," I said. "How was I supposed to know?"

He raked his hand through his hair and sighed, but he didn't concede defeat. Instead, he angled me toward the door and gave me a gentle shove.

"I've called you a cab," he said. "And it's paid for in advance. I'll make sure the mess is cleaned up. You won't think a thing out of place happened here when I'm done."

I noted he said when he was done and not the unit. I had the feeling he'd be staying to clean up personally. I'd have protested, but I just didn't have it in me.

It was right about then that Parrish blustered over in her usual manner and shoved him sideways with her hip. That she could move him said a lot about her strength. I looked her over as she whispered in his ear, knowing she was one of the rare female wolf shifters, and I wondered what that might mean to her, to be alone in a pack of males.

My musing was cut short when Layne jerked his shoulders and swore out loud. He swung his gaze to me. Parrish followed suit.

"What?" I said. "What happened?"

"Fucker's dead," Parrish said and Layne elbowed her. "What?" She directed the word at him. "You want me to be delicate about a bastard who tore the insides out of half a dozen women? Dying's too good for him if you ask me."

I might have said something to that, but I discovered I'd collapsed into the chair again and was looking at both their knees. While there was an acute relief that whatever or whoever he was, was gone, I didn't need to be told the implications of his death.

"We'll never figure out what he wanted."

"Who the hell cares? He didn't get it." Parrish gestured toward the door. "You want me to scare off that dog?"

I looked past her to where the door hung on its hinges. The big stray sat beside my planter of herbs, looking in. When it saw me, its jaw dropped and its tongue hung out. It barked and several police officers jumped. One of them shooed it away by tossing a sandwich out onto the sidewalk.

Parrish made a thoughtful sound and shrugged.

"Guess I don't need to scare it off now," she said and then turned to me. "You okay?"

I waved at her as though I was swatting flies. "Just dandy."

I heaved a sigh I felt all the way down to my toes. I wanted to go home. I wanted it all to be over. Knowing I'd be kicked out soon anyway so they could work without me contaminating the scene, I pushed myself out of the chair. My knees didn't buckle. I wasn't bleeding. I didn't want to pass out.

Not unscathed but not a casualty either. I could live with that.

I heaved myself to my feet and crossed the room to collect my Buddha urn. Tucking it under my arm under Layne's watchful eye was a bit of a rebellion, but I did it anyway. I knew he knew what was in there, but I also suspected he understood what I was going to do with the contents.

There was no way I was leaving it here in the shop. I was done with it. There was already too much magic in the building what with an amulet and grimoire and a stray dog whose connections to me I still hadn't worked out.

I had no idea what triggered the amulet to activate or how to stop it if it did accidentally. My last experience with the urn and Sherry's reaction was bad enough. I didn't need to add any more uncertainty to the mix. I was going to contact her. I had the spell I was supposed to give her and she'd be coming in the next few days to pick it up. When she did, I was going to tell her it wasn't necessary. She was in the clear. For real. And anything else I did for her or anyone else was going to be done the old fashioned way.

However, I *was* going to pull out the drugs when I got home. Not hardcore ones like crack or heroine, just some good old-fashioned caffeine and chocolate. I'd soak in my tub with a mug of true mocha coffee and pop a bubble or two that floated away from the pillows of foam I ran into the bath. And I would have myself a good old-fashioned cry. Because I was not a powerful werewolf with lots of magic and power. I was just a regular woman with a traumatic past, and I'd barely survived the attack on my life.

Maybe it was the fatigue settling into my bones, but something in the air seemed to shift as I headed for the door. A chill ran through me, raising goosebumps. The kind that doesn't come from a waft of cold air.

Nerves firing, I glanced back over my shoulder, taking in the whole of my shop from the countertop to the gallery and beyond to the back room. The subtle aroma of sulfur caught my attention. A tang of ozone, like the way the air smells when you've lit a birthday sparkler.

There, lingering in the gallery between the shop and the back, where the shadows pooled the darkest, that big stray sat on its haunches, watching me as though it hadn't just somehow slipped past a dozen officers without being seen. Its jowls turned up. A smile, I thought. And I shivered.

Because no matter what anyone thought. I knew this was far from over.

About Author

Thea is a NEW YORK TIMES and USA TODAY Bestselling Author. She used to have a black lab at her feet when she wrote, warming up the calves. It can be cold in rural Nova Scotia. Now it's just a cuppa tea keeping her warm.

Whether she's finding ways to lure Isabella Hush into the Shadow Bazaar or throwing the switch on a new monster, her urban fantasy pulses with dark themes and action-packed intrigue. Her characters are always deeply wounded creatures struggling for redemption. The romance is slow-burn but worth it, and the humor just might have a touch of Canadiana.

As a fan of Dannika Dark and Patricia Briggs, she hopes you enjoy slipping into the skin of her characters as much as she enjoy theirs.

Hang out with her on the socials:

Pick up bonuses by joining her email reading group. For more information visit theaatkinson. com

9 780099 214 8928